Maggie Co...

And if there wa... it
was trouble—es...

Everything about her, from her expensive,
inappropriate clothing to her fine-boned face and
soft, elegant voice, was wrong. She didn't belong on
the Whispering Wind dude ranch, and he didn't want
her there.

Still, he had to hand it to her—she had guts. Not
many men stood up to him the way she did. And her
reckless challenge stirred something inside him,
something too close to interest, too close to
anticipation, for his liking....

Dear Reader,

From a most traditional marriage of convenience to a futuristic matchmaking robot, from a dusty dude ranch to glistening Pearl Harbor, from international adventure to an inner struggle with disturbing memories, this month's sensational Silhouette **Special Edition** authors pull out all the stops to honor your quest for a range of deeply satisfying novels of living and loving in today's world.

Those of you who've written in requesting that Ginna Gray tell dashing David Blaine's story, and those of you who waved the flag for Debbie Macomber's "Navy" novels, please take note that your patience is finally being rewarded with *Once in a Lifetime* and *Navy Brat*. For the rest of you, now's the time to discover what all the excitement is about! Naturally, each novel stands solidly alone as, you might say, an extra special Silhouette **Special Edition**.

Don't miss the other special offerings in store for you: four more wonderful novels by talented, talked about writers Nikki Benjamin, Arlene James, Bevlyn Marshall and Christina Dair. Each author brings you a memorable novel packed with stirring emotions and the riches of love: in the tradition of Silhouette **Special Edition**, romance to believe in . . . and to remember.

From all the authors and editors of Silhouette **Special Edition**,

Warmest wishes.

NIKKI BENJAMIN
On the Whispering Wind

Silhouette Special Edition

Published by Silhouette Books New York

America's Publisher of Contemporary Romance

For Cathy Loyacano—
thanks for understanding when
I have to work, for knowing when I need to play,
for making me laugh and letting me cry,
for sharing the good times and the bad.
Thank you for being my friend!

SILHOUETTE BOOKS
300 East 42nd St., New York, N.Y. 10017

ON THE WHISPERING WIND

ISBN: 0-373-09663-1

First Silhouette Books printing April 1991

Printed in the U.S.A.

Books by Nikki Benjamin

Silhouette Intimate Moments

A Man To Believe In #359

Silhouette Special Edition

Emily's House #539
On the Whispering Wind #663

NIKKI BENJAMIN

was born and raised in the Midwest, but after years in the Houston area, she considers herself a true Texan.

Nikki says she's always been an avid reader. (Her earliest literary heroines were Nancy Drew, Trixie Belden and Beany Malone.) Her writing experience was limited, however, until a friend started penning a novel and encouraged Nikki to do the same. One scene led to another, and soon she was hooked.

When not reading or writing, the author enjoys spending time with her husband and son, needlepoint, hiking, biking, horseback riding and sailing.

NEW MEXICO

OKLAHOMA

ARKANSAS

LOUISIANA

Lubbock

Dallas

Fort Worth

TEXAS

Austin

Fredericksburg

Houston

San Antonio

Bandera

The Whispering Wind

MEXICO

Gulf of Mexico

Underlined places are fictitious.

Prologue

"You can't do it, Daddy. You can't sell the Whispering Wind. You *can't*. It's our home. And you love it as much as I do."

"It's not the same anymore, Elizabeth. Not since your mother died."

Mackenzie Harrow stood before the massive stone fireplace that filled one corner of the long, narrow living room, his right arm braced against the wide oak mantelpiece, his left hand stuffed in the back pocket of his worn, faded jeans. His back to his eleven-year-old daughter, he stared at the flickering flames, haunted by thoughts of what might have been, thoughts that left him aching with emptiness and uncertainty.

If only they hadn't been so busy the summer Jo first mentioned feeling tired all the time. They might have realized that more than hard work was dragging her down. But she had been so determined to increase the number of guests they could accommodate on the ranch. And he had been equally determined to expand his growing herd of prize quarter horses, as well as enhance his reputation as a talented trainer.

They had put in twelve- and fourteen-hour days, concentrating on their personal goals instead of each other. And they hadn't realized that she was sick, very, very sick, until it was too late. If they had, then maybe, just maybe, despite what the doctors had said, she'd still be alive today.

She had been his wife, his lover, his business partner and his best friend. She had been tall and strong, bright and funny, kind and sensitive. She had been...everything...he'd ever wanted or needed. Now, almost a year after her death, Mac wasn't sure that the work and worry of running a dude ranch and raising and training quarter horses were worth it anymore.

"Dale Sherman is willing to pay more than a fair price for the property, and Steve Elliott has offered top dollar for Windstorm and the brood mares. I can pay off the loan we needed to build the cabins and put in the swimming pool Then we can buy a nice house in a Dallas suburb with good schools, and put the rest away for your college education. With my CPA certification and my professional contacts, I shouldn't have any problem finding a job. And we can spend our summer vacations like normal people. We can...travel...."

He was rambling and he knew it. But he wanted Elizabeth to understand. And he wanted her to agree that his decision to give up the ranch was the right one for them, even though he hadn't quite convinced himself yet.

When she said nothing, he turned to face her. The amusement dancing in her dark eyes, Jo's eyes, surprised him. He had expected to see anger or tears rather than a teasing hint of laughter.

"I don't want to live in a Dallas suburb. I want to live *here*. I want to go to Canyon Pass Middle School with my friends. And I'd rather spend summer vacations on the ranch than travel. I get carsick on long drives, and you hate to fly." She held his gaze, her wide brown eyes sure and steady. "Please, Daddy, don't sell the ranch. Don't sell Windstorm and the mares. We can make it. I know we can."

She looked so much like her mother, tall and slender in jeans and a bulky red sweater, her long brown hair bound in a single braid that hung over one shoulder. And he'd never been able to refuse her mother anything.

But Elizabeth was all he had left, and she deserved so much more than he could give her if he kept the ranch. Eventually, when the changes had been made, and they were settled in their new lives, she would realize that he'd done the right thing.

"I've made up my mind, Elizabeth. Try to understand. It's something I have to do." He turned away from her, focusing on the firelight once again.

"What about Juan and Rosa? I don't think Mr. Sherman will let them stay on the ranch, even though they've lived here for years and years."

"I gave them the deed to their cabin and thirty acres of land after your mother died. Whether I sell the rest of the property or not, they'll always have a home here."

"I wish we could always have a home here, too," Elizabeth murmured. When her father didn't respond, she hesitated only a moment, then pressed on. "Do you have to sell the ranch right away? Could you, *would* you wait until August? If we could have one more summer here, just one more summer to remember always and forever...."

"Ah, Lizzie Beth," he muttered, shaking his head. "I don't think I could handle another summer like last summer, trying to juggle guests and horses on my own."

Because he was a solitary man by nature, coping with twenty or thirty people at a time had tried his patience to the limit under the best of circumstances. It had been even worse when he screwed up reservations or room assignments. And it had been downright chaotic the few days Rosa had gone to El Paso to help her daughter with her new baby.

Worst of all, he hadn't been able to devote enough time to the horses. He'd lost two foals and one of his best brood mares. And he'd had to refuse several requests to train cutting horses for neighboring ranchers he'd done business with regularly in the past.

Unfortunately, in order to make a reasonable profit, to make the loan payments and live through the winter, they needed the income from guests, as well as horses. However, he simply couldn't handle both on his own, and he couldn't afford to hire the kind of full-time help he needed, either.

But staying a while longer on the ranch seemed to mean so much to Elizabeth. They'd be able to live on the money he'd set aside from last summer's guests through the end of May, just as they'd always done. To stay through the coming summer without guests, however, he'd have to tap into their savings.

Or he could sell the trail horses, a couple of foals and stand Windstorm at stud. Though Steve Elliott's ultimate goal was to own Windstorm, he'd be satisfied with the yearlings, at least for the time being. And he'd be willing to pay a sizable fee for the stallion to cover his mares.

"If we cut our expenses to a minimum, I guess we could manage to stay through the summer." He rubbed a hand over his face, then raked his fingers through his thick, shaggy dark hair, pushing it off his forehead. "But I don't want any strangers here. I'm going to write to the people with reservations, tell them I'm closing the ranch and refund their money."

"That would be fun...just the two of us," Elizabeth said. "Is it a deal, then? We can stay until the end of the summer? Then, if you still want to sell the ranch, I'll...I'll understand."

"All right, sweetheart, it's a deal." He moved away from the fireplace, grabbed the heavy denim jacket lying on the sofa, and headed for the door.

Neither Sherman nor Elliott would be happy about the delay, but that was their problem. If Mac Harrow was anything, he was honest. And being honest, he had to admit that he really wouldn't mind spending the next six months on the Whispering Wind, especially if it made Elizabeth happy.

But toward the end of August he was going to sell the ranch. He'd buy a house in a quiet Dallas suburb, get a job, a normal nine-to-five job, and give his daughter everything he'd never had time to give her mother.

"Where're you going, Daddy?"

"Out to the barn. The wind's picking up, and the temperature's dropping. I want to check on the horses before it gets dark."

"I'll get my jacket and go with you."

"Thanks, sweetheart. I appreciate the offer, but it won't take me long. You stay in the house and stay warm."

As her father closed the door behind him, Elizabeth Harrow crossed the living room and stopped in front of the old, rolltop desk. Sliding onto the wooden desk chair, she pulled out a drawer marked *Reservation Receipts* and removed the contents. Shoving piles of papers and stacks of ledgers to one side, she laid the slips out one at a time, reading the names and addresses of the people planning to stay at the ranch during the summer, searching for...what? She wasn't quite sure.

Halfway through the receipts a name caught her attention, a familiar name that jogged her memory. *Maggie*

Connor. According to the slip, Maggie Connor and her son, Christopher, 1500 Rio Verde, San Antonio, Texas, had paid in full, in advance, for two weeks on the Whispering Wind. And they were scheduled to arrive on the first of June. Closing her eyes, Elizabeth murmured a simple, heartfelt thank you. Then, a soft smile tipping up the corners of her mouth, she opened her eyes and gazed at the receipt in her hand, recalling her first and only meeting with Maggie Connor.

The previous August, Elizabeth and her grandparents had spent a day at the Six Flags amusement park near Dallas. It had been a wonderful day, but when they'd returned to the car late in the afternoon, they'd found the doors locked and the keys in the ignition. Maggie Connor had just unlocked her car, which had been parked nearby, when she'd noticed their distress. She had opened her trunk, pulled out a coat hanger and come to their rescue.

While her son had stood silently, she'd talked and laughed, teasing Elizabeth's grandfather and reassuring her grandmother. When her grandfather had complimented her skill at breaking into a car, she'd mentioned that she was a widow and that she'd learned to do a lot of things on her own over the past few years. When the door lock had finally popped up, she had accepted their thanks with a gracious smile. And she'd also accepted a Whispering Wind brochure from Elizabeth. As she'd watched her drive away, a twinge of longing had tugged at her heart, and Elizabeth had hoped that one day they'd meet again.

Now, by some strange and wonderful twist of fate, Maggie Connor and her son, Christopher, were supposed to stay at the Whispering Wind for two weeks in June. And Elizabeth had no intention of allowing her father to cancel their reservation. He had said that he didn't want any strangers on the ranch, but Maggie Connor and her son weren't really strangers. Were they?

Still smiling slightly, Elizabeth tucked the slip of paper into the side pocket of her jeans, then gathered up the remaining receipts and stuffed them in the drawer. She might be making a terrible mistake. And she had no doubt she'd be in a lot of trouble if her father discovered her deception. Yet she was willing to take the risk because she had a feeling that once Maggie arrived at the Whispering Wind, somehow, some way, just as it had been at the amusement park, everything would be all right.

Chapter One

"'It was a dark and stormy night....'" Maggie Connor quoted, drawing out the *dark* and *stormy,* her voice barely audible above the rain pounding on the roof of her car. A bolt of lightning split the sky, followed closely by a rumbling roll of thunder.

"Mom, it's not funny," her son chided. "We shoulda stopped at a motel in Bandera. Or we shoulda just stayed home. But, no, we have to spend two weeks at some stupid—*look out!*"

She saw the sign at the same instant her son did. Pavement Ends 100 ft. "What in the world..."

She eased her foot off the gas and onto the brake, attempting to slow the small, brand new ultraexpensive foreign car that had been a birthday present from her parents. She didn't dare dent it, not on this particularly unpopular outing. Her father, her mother and her son would never let her hear the end of it.

Obviously not quite as intelligent as advertised, the car ignored her efforts and continued to slide forward as if determined to find out what awaited them at the end of the pavement. Peering through the steamy windshield into pitch-black night and pouring rain, Maggie fully expected that what awaited was a drop off the face of the earth.

"Mom, do something. Stop!"

"Christopher, I can't."

With a slight bump, then a downward dip, the car bounced off the pavement onto a wide dirt-and-gravel track. Actually, mud and gravel was a better description, she thought, as the car finally slewed to a stop. Mud, as in mired in mud, she reminded herself, pressing down on the accelerator again. The back tires spun for a moment, then caught in the gravel and pushed the car forward.

"Mom, what are you doing? We have to turn back. I think we're lost—again—and I don't want to be lost on *this* road. We could get stuck."

"Not if we keep going. And I'm sure this is the right way. I remember the instructions in the brochure included a warning that the road changed just before the entrance to the ranch. That certainly was a road change. Watch for a sign, okay?"

"I can't see anything but rain. No, wait ... slow down. Is that it?"

A narrower gravel track veered off to the right. Just within range of the car's headlights a wooden sign had been nailed to a tree. The words *Whispering Wind* were printed on it, along with an arrow pointing toward the narrower road.

"Yes, this is it, Christopher. This is the Whispering Wind. We found it," Maggie crowed, unable to conceal her childish delight and her relief at having arrived at their destination at last.

If everything had gone as planned, and if she hadn't forgotten the brochure with its detailed map, they would have been here hours earlier. They would have found the ranch easily in daylight, and they would have arrived well ahead of the storm. But, of course, nothing had gone as planned.

It had taken Maggie much longer than she'd anticipated to complete the end-of-the-school-year paperwork generated by twenty-five third-graders. Then she had tried, unsuccessfully, to bribe Christopher into a better mood with a meal at his favorite Mexican restaurant. By the time they'd finished eating and were on their way out of San Antonio, it had begun to rain. The rain had slowed her down just enough so that it was nearly dark by the time they'd reached Bandera. And Maggie hadn't been able to find the Whispering Wind brochure among the papers in her purse.

Unsure of the way and hampered by pouring rain, as well as darkness, she'd taken at least two wrong turns, once ending up halfway to Fredricksburg, once ending up halfway back to San Antonio before realizing her mistake. But now, finally, they'd made it. They had arrived at the Whispering Wind Dude Ranch, and they were going to have a wonderful vacation.

They *were*, despite the bad start, and despite her son's near refusal to go with her. Two weeks at a dude ranch hadn't been his idea of fun. He had wanted to spend half the summer with her parents at their River Oaks mansion in Houston and half the summer at computer camp in Dallas. He was her son, and she loved him dearly, and she did appreciate his quiet, studious behavior. She knew that at least in part it was his way of coping with Mitch's death and the changes in their lives.

But he was only eleven years old. Deep down inside he was still a little boy. And what a little boy needed, really *needed*, was to cut loose, to get down and dirty, to be *bad*. Maggie hadn't been able to think of a better place for a young boy to cut loose than on a dude ranch, especially after reading the brochure Elizabeth Harrow had given her last August after she'd helped the girl's grandparents break into their car. Christopher could hike, ride a horse, swim in the pool, fish in the lake, float down a portion of the Medina River that cut through the property in an inner tube. She couldn't wait.

"Oh, no," Maggie muttered, her spirits sagging as suddenly as they'd soared, when she turned onto the narrow track. Barring it was a wide, metal gate.

"Well, I guess they're closed. Guess we'll have to go back home. Right, Mom?"

"Wrong, son. We are *not* going home."

Slamming the gearshift into park with one hand, Maggie reached for the door handle with the other. Taking a deep breath, she swung the door open, slid out and ran for the gate. She ignored the icy rain that washed over her, plastering her curly auburn hair to her head and her pale blue silk shirt to her body. She ignored the mud and grit that oozed into her brand new, white-on-white Italian leather sandals and spattered the backs of her legs and the hem of her narrow white linen skirt. They had arrived at the Whispering Wind Dude Ranch and they were going to stay, gate or no gate, even if she had to chew through a padlock with her bare teeth.

Thank heavens there was no padlock, just a wide, heavy metal chain looped over a fence post. Maggie pulled it free, shoved the gate out of the way, squished back to the car, drove through, then reversed her steps to close the gate. Back in the car at last, she sat, panting and pushing her wet hair away from her wet face as a shiver stole up her spine. Beside her the silence was ominous.

"Don't say it, Christopher. Just...don't...say...it."

"Say what, Mom?" he asked, his voice just a shade too innocent.

"Don't say anything like we should have stayed in Bandera, or we should have stayed at home, or you hate horses, or…or anything like that. All right?" Maggie turned to face her son, just barely controlling an urge to cry. Or was it an urge to laugh? Sometimes, where Christopher was concerned, she wasn't always sure.

"All right," he agreed. Then, with a sudden hint of his old mischief, he pushed her just a little. "What about Grandma and Grandpa and computer camp? Can I say anything about them?"

"Not a word. Not tonight, not tomorrow, maybe not even the next day. Just keep your mouth shut and pretend we're having a good time," Maggie commanded, easing the gearshift into drive and pressing down on the gas pedal.

Surely the main house was somewhere up ahead, somewhere at the end of this climbing, twisting, muddy mess of a road, somewhere…somewhere over the rainbow….

"Look, Mom, it's all dark. It's closed. I *told* you."

"It's *not* closed. It's dark because it's late, and almost everyone is probably asleep. But a dude ranch is like a hotel. People arrive at all hours, and someone is always available to check in latecomers. See, there's a light on in the main house."

Maggie slowed the car to a stop for what she hoped would be the last time that night, parking as close as possible to the side porch of the three-story stone house at the end of the road. She switched off the engine and headlights with a gentle sigh of relief, not to mention a strong sense of pride. Despite the harrowing drive, her thorough soaking and her sulking son, once again she'd accomplished what she'd set out to do. And although the cabins lining the right side of the road leading to the house were dark, and none of the outside lights were lit, a pale, welcoming glow filtered through the downstairs windows of the main house.

"We made it, kiddo. And now that we're here, we're going to have fun, aren't we?" Tucking a dripping curl behind her ear, she glanced at her son, a smile tipping up the corners of her mouth.

"Sure, Mom, lots of fun," he muttered, as a gust of wind rocked the car, and the rain pounded down with renewed intensity.

"Come on, we'd better go inside before it gets any worse out here. Grab the overnight bag from the back seat. We can get the suitcases out of the trunk in the morning."

"Mom, it's pouring. I'm going to get all wet."

Her smile, her patience and her good humor fading fast, Maggie shifted in her seat to face her son.

"Christopher, there are times, and this is one of them, when I wonder, when I *truly* wonder, if they gave me the wrong baby at the hospital."

She held his gaze for several seconds to emphasize her point. Then leaning over the back of her seat, she grasped the handle of their overnight bag and pulled it into her lap. Without another word, she picked up her purse, opened the car door and slid out. A few moments later she pushed through the heavy wooden door that opened into what appeared to be the main dining room of the ranch house, followed closely by her silent, scowling son.

As the door swung shut on a gust of wind, Maggie dropped the overnight bag and her purse onto the floor. Using both hands, she smoothed lank tendrils of sopping wet hair away from her face as she searched the dimly lit room for signs of life.

Several rows of long, wooden dining tables and tall, ladder-back chairs filled its length. At the far end, a light glowed above a narrow staircase leading up to the second floor. The wall to the right was broken by a set of swinging doors, inset with squares of glass at eye level, doors Maggie assumed opened into the kitchen. To the left, a pair of wide archways led into what must be the living room.

Lured by the warm, bright light that spilled through the archways, as well as the faint strains of a symphony that drifted toward her from that direction, she put an arm around her son's shoulders and began to weave her way through the maze of tables and chairs.

She saw him the moment they walked into the living room. He was sprawled on a long, deep sofa, his arms resting on the back cushions, his denim work shirt unbuttoned to the waist of his faded jeans, his bare feet propped atop a scarred wooden coffee table next to a half full glass and a bottle of bourbon. He was a big man, a dark, handsome man, his five-o'clock-shadowed face lean and hard beneath a shaggy mass of thick, straight brown hair.

As he turned his head to look at her, a welcoming smile curving the corners of his mouth and gleaming in his pale gray eyes, Maggie allowed herself another small sigh of relief. Unfortunately, her relief lasted all of ten seconds. That was how long it took for her to realize his smile had disappeared behind a cold, hard, steady stare that went so far beyond mere disapproval that it stopped her dead in her tracks.

She tightened her hold on her son, a shiver racing down her spine as the man's gaze flicked over her, his lips drawn together in a thin line of silent warning. As if she'd crossed some invisible boundary, as if she'd violated his territory in some unknown yet unforgivable way.

She had never felt quite so unwelcomed, so unwanted in her life. What had she done to earn such sudden, overwhelming animosity from a total stranger? She wasn't sure she wanted to know, but she didn't seem to have any alternative. He was obviously the person in charge, even though he was half undressed.

"Uh, hi. I'm . . . I'm Maggie Connor. And this is . . . this is Christopher . . . my son." Mentally cursing her slight stammer, she lifted her chin. Trying to ignore her dripping hair and her damp, clinging clothing, she pasted a reasonable imitation of her mother's lady-of-the-manor smile on her face.

Who was he, anyway? Probably just some lazy cowboy who, considering the bad weather, had assumed he'd have nothing better to do than drink himself into a stupor, she thought, arching a brow as she eyed the liquor bottle and glass on the table. She had every intention of reporting him to his employer in the morning. But for now she'd content herself with staring him down while she waited for him to make some sort of reply to her introduction.

Mac groaned inwardly as he held the woman's gaze. He had been so deeply asleep that he hadn't heard her car pull up outside, but the sound of the side door slamming shut had brought him instantly and completely awake. He hadn't bothered to get up because he hadn't expected anyone to be out on a night like this except Juan or maybe a neighboring rancher stopping by to report a power outage or a downed telephone line. He certainly hadn't been expecting Maggie Connor and her son, Christopher.

Trouble, nothing but trouble, he thought, allowing his eyes to rove over her. And if there was one thing he didn't want or need now, it was trouble, especially the kind she could be.

Everything about her, from her expensive, inappropriate clothing to the holier-than-thou expression on her fine-boned face, to the soft, low tone of her elegant voice, grated on his nerves. She didn't belong on the Whispering Wind and he didn't want her there. He wanted her out of his house and off his property. He wanted her gone, and he wanted her gone *now*. He wasn't sure why, but he did.

Like a wolf cornered in his lair, he felt threatened. *Threatened?* Now *that* was crazy. What could he possibly have to fear from Maggie Connor? If anyone had anything to fear, it was she, simply because she had invaded his space. And he had never taken kindly to strangers invading his space.

Leaning forward, he wrapped a hand around the glass of bourbon. He lifted it to his lips, his eyes holding hers over the rim as he swallowed the last of the single drink he'd been nursing for almost two hours. "Maggie Connor, huh? Name doesn't ring a bell."

Shifting on the sofa, he sat up and poured two fingers of the smooth, dark liquor. He didn't want another drink, but something about the look on her face told him he might need it. Settling back slowly, he allowed himself another long look at her, a subtle, unmistakable suggestion in his eyes.

"So, whadaya want, Maggie Connor? Maybe I can give it to you. Then, again, maybe I can't." He lifted the glass and drank again.

His voice was deep, rich, rough, and if she was any judge of slurred syllables, more than slightly whiskey-soaked. But even if he was three sheets to the wind, that didn't give him the right to be so rude, so...so...crude, so socially unacceptable. Especially in front of her son, although she was sure Christopher hadn't understood the man's sarcastic insinuation.

Drawing on every ounce of training she'd received during twelve years of convent schooling, she lifted her chin another notch. Narrowing her eyes, she held his gaze, ignoring the hot flush that traveled up her neck and across her cheeks.

"Listen, mister...mister whoever-you-are, believe me when I say that if you were the last man on earth, you wouldn't have anything...*anything* I'd want. However, since you seem to be the only one available, perhaps you could just grunt or mumble the proper procedure for checking in, and I'll take it from there.''

"The proper procedure for checking in?" In one smooth motion, he swung his legs down, thunked his glass on the table and stood up. He towered over her, his bare feet planted wide apart, his hands on his hips, his pale eyes glittering dangerously in the lamplight. "What do you mean by checking in?" His tone of voice was even more dangerous than the glitter in his eyes.

"I mean *checking in*. This *is* the Whispering Wind Dude Ranch, isn't it?" she demanded, bracing her hands on her hips, imitating his stance.

She had assumed that he was a big man, but she'd had no idea how big until now. She had to tip her head back to meet his pale silvery gray eyes. And he wasn't exactly dressed. His shirt hung open, revealing a broad expanse of bare chest covered by curling black hair, and his worn jeans, unsnapped at the waist, hung low on his hips.

She had also assumed that he was drunk, but he wasn't. The slurred words had been an act, she realized, her eyes narrowing even more as she gazed up at him. He was as sober as a judge, a hanging judge who'd like to slip a noose over her head. But he didn't frighten her, not one tiny bit. Three years ago maybe, but not tonight. He wasn't scary. He was just…just… Why was *dangerous* the only word that came to mind? How silly.…

Yet when he took a step toward her, then another, it was all she could do to stand her ground. The urge to back away from him was almost overwhelming, but she fought it with all the courage she could muster. If she gave way to him, she might as well turn and run, and she refused to run from the likes of him. Unfortunately she had no control over the tremor that shook her, a tremor she wanted to blame on her cold, wet clothing, but couldn't.

"Mom, let's go, okay? We must have made a mistake."
Christopher tugged at her elbow, his high, clear voice cutting through the silence of two adults facing off over a battered coffee table.

"Christopher, please, be quiet. I'll handle this."

"But, Mom—"

"Christopher!" She whirled around, glared at her son for an instant, then turned back to the man standing in front of her.

For just a moment, Mac shifted his attention to the frightened boy beside the woman, and cursed himself for being so rude. He had never used his size and strength to intimidate a woman, much less a child. Why was he doing it now? Because he didn't dare encourage their uninvited intrusion, he told himself, gazing at the woman again. But there were better ways, kinder ways to discourage her.

"This is the Whispering Wind Ranch," he ground out between clenched teeth, trying to regain control of his temper. "But, lady, we don't do dudes anymore."

"What do you mean *we?*" she demanded, refusing to give an inch.

He had to hand it to her—she had guts. He couldn't think of many men who would have stood up to him the way she was doing. And her reckless challenge stirred something inside him, something too close to interest, something too close to anticipation for his liking. It was the kind of interest and anticipation no woman but Jo had ever stirred up inside of him.

Now he knew he was crazy. Or maybe he'd been dropped into the *Twilight Zone.* The woman before him, hissing and shivering, wasn't his type. There wasn't even a vague resemblance between her and Jo. Her hair was a deep, rich auburn, her skin as pale as porcelain, her eyes the brightest, clearest shade of blue he'd ever seen. She was small and fair and fragile and too...too damned fiery. And it was past time to shut her up and send her on her merry way.

"Actually, I mean me. I'm Mackenzie Harrow. I own the Whispering Wind, and as I just told you, I don't operate a dude ranch anymore. However, there are several nice motels in Bandera. I'm sure you'll be able to find accommodations there."

For just a moment Maggie was thrown off balance by his words. This...this *person* was Mackenzie Harrow? This cold, angry man was Elizabeth's father? And more important, why was he talking about motels in Bandera?

"Wait a minute, Mr. Harrow. Wait just one little minute. I have a reservation confirmation *and* I have a receipt indicating I've paid in full for two weeks at the Whispering Wind Dude Ranch beginning today, June 1."

Without waiting for a reply, she spun around, stalked into the dining room, picked up her purse and pulled out the appropriate papers. Eyes down, intent on proving her point, she turned and walked into Mackenzie Harrow's broad, bare chest. Instinctively she rested one hand on him, bracing herself. He was so hard, so incredibly... warm.... The crisp, dark hair covering his chest tickled her palm. And beneath her fingertips she could feel his heartbeat quicken. Just as hers did.

Without thinking, Mac wrapped his hands around her shoulders, holding her, steadying her. Through the cold, wet fabric of her pale blue silk blouse, her skin was soft, her bones fragile, the same soft and fragile quality of her hand on his chest. Her head barely reached his shoulder, yet he caught the scent of honey and lemon in her hair.

He flexed his fingers once, twice, very gently, breathing slowly, deeply. She tipped her face up to meet his gaze. Her bright, blue eyes widened with surprise, her lips parted. Oh, yes, she was small and fragile and... and... fiery. Releasing her as if he'd been burned, he stepped back.

"That's impossible," he muttered, shoving his hands in his pockets. "I canceled all the early reservations and refunded all the money in March."

"Well, I made a reservation and sent a check in February. All I've gotten from you since then is a confirmation and a re—"

"What's the matter, Daddy? I heard voices."

Maggie turned to see Elizabeth Harrow standing on the staircase at the end of the dining room. She had grown a couple of inches since August. Her long, brown hair hung loose and her wide, dark eyes sparkled with mischief. She wore a flowered nightgown, but her feet were bare like her father's.

Maggie started to speak, then saw the girl wink just before she turned her attention back to her father. As she gazed at the girl, a frown creasing her forehead, Maggie's jumbled thoughts began to fall together.

"Sorry we woke you, sweetheart. There's been a misunderstanding about a reservation." Everything about Mackenzie Harrow softened as he gazed at his daughter, his eyes and voice full of love.

The change was so swift, so complete, so utterly unexpected that it took Maggie's breath away. For just a moment, one crazy moment out of time, she wondered how she'd feel if he looked at her with love in his eyes.

"There's been no misunderstanding, Mr. Harrow," she snapped, suddenly angry with herself and her foolishness. It was late, she was tired, and she was determined to get to the bottom of this. "I have a confir—"

"His name's Mac. You can call him Mac. Everybody does, don't they, Daddy?" Elizabeth urged, as she walked down the remaining steps and crossed the dining room. Again she winked at Maggie, then shook her head slightly as if in warning.

"Yeah, everybody," Mac muttered, frowning at his daughter's rather odd behavior.

Then, turning on his heel, he stalked into the living room. He stopped at the rolltop desk, switched on the green-shaded lamp and began pulling out drawers. Maggie followed him, papers in hand, while his daughter spoke to Christopher in a low voice.

"Hi, remember me? I'm Elizabeth."

"I guess so."

"What's your name?"

"Christopher Connor."

"I'm eleven. How old are you?"

"I'm eleven, too."

"Oh, really. When's your birthday?" Elizabeth asked.

"May 5."

"Mine's March 3. I'm older."

"Big deal. Just a coupla months," Christopher retorted.

"Do you like to ride?"

"I guess so."

"Hah, I bet you've never even been on a horse, have you?"

"So what if I haven't? We're not going to stay. Your dad doesn't want—"

"Damn it, anyway, I can't believe I missed it." Mac pulled a crumpled reservation receipt marked "paid in full" from the back of a long, narrow drawer.

"See, I *told* you," Maggie prodded, unable to control her smug smile.

"And I told *you,* Miz Connor, we don't do dudes anymore." Mac glared at her for a moment, then yanked open another drawer and pulled out a thick book of checks. Plopping onto the desk chair, he picked up a pen. "Tell me how to make this out so I can refund your money. Then you can be on your way."

As if to punctuate his demand, a flash of lightning lit the sky, followed almost immediately by a crash of thunder that shook the house. The rain, which had abated somewhat, beat against the windows with renewed vigor.

"Daddy, it's storming outside. They can't leave. Not tonight." Elizabeth ran to her father's side and put a hand on his arm. "Please, Daddy...what would Momma say?"

He gazed at his daughter, his face dark and forbidding, his fingers gripping the pen so hard it was a miracle it didn't snap in two. "Elizabeth, go back to bed."

"But, Daddy—"

"It's okay," Maggie interrupted, her voice soft and reassuring. Placing a hand on the girl's shoulder, she forced herself to smile. "As your father has pointed out several times already, he doesn't want us in his house. And I'd rather ride through hell in a hatbox than impose on him any longer."

Her smile fading, she lifted her chin, meeting Mackenzie Harrow's eyes with steady defiance. "You owe me, Maggie Connor, $850, Mr. Harrow. Write the check and we'll leave."

He gazed at her in silence for several seconds, a silence broken only by the rattle of rain-heavy wind against the windows.

What, in God's name, is the matter with me? he wondered. Averting his eyes, he ran a hand through his hair. He had no good reason to be acting like such a son of a bitch. Maggie Connor had done nothing but ask for what she believed was rightfully hers. She'd made a reservation and paid in advance. It was his fault, not hers, that her reservation hadn't been canceled months ago.

But, damn it all to hell, there was something about her that had set his nerves zinging the moment he'd laid eyes on her, something that had set him off like kindling touched by a flame. Something he wasn't ready to acknowledge, much less accept. And if she didn't leave very soon, he could end up doing both.

But Elizabeth was right. He couldn't let her leave tonight. He couldn't allow her to drive back to Bandera in the dead of night during a thunderstorm. Not because he wanted her to stay, but because he was too tired to lie awake all night wondering whether or not some smart-mouthed, fiery little redhead had managed to find her way back to town or ended up roof down in a ditch somewhere along the way.

"Rosa and I have been cleaning the guest rooms on the second floor this week, Daddy. How about Number Five—two big beds and a big bathroom and windows facing the front?"

"I appreciate the thought, Elizabeth. And I . . . I understand." Maggie smiled softly as she smoothed a hand over the girl's straight, dark hair. "But we're leaving."

Turning on her heel, she started toward the dining room, her purse, her overnight bag and the side door. "Mr. Harrow, it was a pleasure. Put the check in the mail. Come on, Christopher. I surrender. You get your wish. Six weeks in River Oaks being treated like a little prince by your grandparents, and six weeks sitting in front of a PC at computer camp. As for me, I think I'm going to sign up for a trek through the Australian out—"

"You're not going anywhere tonight, Miz Connor," Mac growled, his voice low, as he wrapped one large, work-roughened hand around her upper arm, jerking her to a stop before she'd taken two steps. When she rounded on him, he tightened his grip just enough to let her know he meant business. Towering over her, his silvery gray eyes glittering, he tugged her toward him, narrowing the distance between them to mere inches.

"Number Five, Miz Connor," he purred, sliding his hand down her arm in one long, smooth stroke. Grasping her wrist, he turned her hand over, pressed a brass key into her palm, then closed her fingers around it. "Up the stairs to the second floor, down the hallway to the left, third door on the right. Better get out of those wet clothes. You don't want to end up with pneumonia. And you'd better get some sleep. You'll want to make an early start in the morning."

He held her for a moment longer with his hands and his pale eyes. Then, his face grim, he released her. Shoving his hands into his pockets, he spun away from her and strode into the living room without a backward glance.

Stunned into momentary silence by his honey-velvet drawl, not to mention the honey-velvet heat of his hands on her, Maggie watched him disappear. At the sound of a bottle hitting the rim of a glass, however, her temper blew with the full force of a dynamite explosion. She had spent three years, three long, hard years attaining physical and emotional independence, and no man, least of all a man such as Mackenzie Harrow, was going to give her orders and live to tell about it.

Her body rigid, her eyes narrowed, her naturally full lips pressed together in a thin, grim line, she started after him, intent on telling him, no, *showing* him exactly what he could do with the key to Number Fi—

"I've got your overnight bag. Come on, I'll show you the way to your room."

This time the hand on her arm was as small, soft and utterly feminine as the voice that offered instead of ordered. Maggie glanced at the young girl before her, then shifted her gaze to her son, standing to one side, tipping his head toward the staircase, his eyes hopeful.

In an instant she regained control of her temper, unable to ignore their mutual plea for peace. This wasn't the time or the place to make a point of how independent and self-sufficient she was. In fact, it wasn't really necessary at all. In the morning she'd do as Mackenzie Harrow suggested.

She'd make an early start, and if she had anything to say about it, she'd never see him again in her life.

"Thanks, Elizabeth. I think Christopher and I could use some sleep, right, buddy?"

"Right, Mom." He sidled over to her, welcoming the arm she slipped around his shoulders, as they followed the girl across the dining room and up the staircase. "And, Mom?"

"Yes, son?" Maggie glanced at him as she slid the brass key into the lock on the door of Number Five.

"I'm sure glad you didn't slug him."

"Me, too." Beside her, Mackenzie Harrow's daughter giggled with delight. "You looked mad enough to do it, and I'm not sure what my dad would have done if you did. I guess you're too old for a spanking."

"Oh, I don't know about that, Lizzie Beth."

Maggie whirled around to see Mac standing at the top of the steps. His eyes glittered with amusement as his lips twitched into something vaguely resembling a smile.

"Oh, yeah?" Maggie shot back.

"Yeah!"

Ignoring the deep, rich rumble of masculine laughter that was his last word as he turned to go up to the third floor, Maggie took the overnight bag Elizabeth offered, pushed Christopher into the room and slammed the door shut.

"He's got to be the most...the most...impossible...man I've ever met," she muttered, hurling her purse and key onto the dresser and dropping the bag on the floor. Then, as she caught sight of herself in the mirror, she groaned. No wonder he didn't want her in his house. She looked as though she'd been dragged through a ditch full of dirty water.

"You know, Mom, it was kinda fun watching you get mad at Mr. Harrow. You're always so cool. I can't remember you ever getting mad at Dad, and you never get mad at Grandma or Grandpa, at least not mad enough to yell. But,

Mom, a couple of times tonight you were yelling. It was neat."

"Neat?" Maggie stared at her son in amazement as he rooted through the overnight bag for his pajamas and toothbrush.

"Yeah, Mom, really neat," Christopher replied as he slipped into the bathroom.

As he shut the door, Maggie sat down on the edge of a double bed. It couldn't be true. It simply could not be true. Was her son telling her that after years of trying to be the perfect daughter, the perfect student, the perfect wife and mother, after years of schooling herself to be calm, to be patient, to be understanding, what he really admired about her was her ability to yell?

Or was he saying that he appreciated the fact that she wasn't so perfect after all? Now there was a thought worth thinking about. . . .

To be honest, yelling wasn't something she could remember doing before tonight. She had never questioned any of her parents' dictums. Nor had she ever gone jaw-to-jaw with Mitchell Connor. She had been too unsure of herself, of her thoughts and feelings, and too in awe of him. He had been so much older, and though she had loved him dearly as a husband, she had wanted to please him in much the same way she'd always wanted to please her parents.

But in the three years since Mitch's death, she had changed. She had finished college and moved to San Antonio. She had bought a small house and found a teaching job. She was a different woman. She was strong, self-confident and self-sufficient, and she had no intention of going under anybody's thumb ever again.

"So put that in your pipe and smoke it, Mister Harrow," Maggie muttered, unbuckling her once beautiful, now completely ruined sandals.

Without a moment's hesitation, she slam-dunked them into the trash basket beside the dresser. It would probably cost her a small fortune in dry-cleaning bills, but if she was lucky she might be able to salvage her skirt and blouse. Of course, after tonight, she had some serious doubts about her luck.

"Come on, Christopher, get out of the bathroom *now,* or I'll be forced to start yelling again."

Above the sound of running water, she heard him laugh. It was the free, easy laughter of a delighted child, the kind of laughter her son hadn't indulged in much since his father's death. For all the aggravation, all the annoyance, all the ultimate disappointment, Maggie Connor realized that their trip to the Whispering Wind really had been worthwhile.

Starting here and now, she'd stop trying to be so perfect, and maybe Christopher would stop trying, too. And if her son liked to hear her yell, well, just wait until the next time his room resembled an explosion in a toy factory. He'd hear some yelling then. Oh, yes, he'd definitely hear some yelling then.

Chapter Two

No matter how deeply she burrowed beneath the blankets, Maggie couldn't block out the sound of the falling rain. Nor could she block out the oddly musical beeps and tweets that were vaguely familiar yet impossible to identify. She stirred slightly and opened her eyes, focusing on the lace-curtained window a few feet from the edge of her bed. Water streamed down the steamy glass, and although the sky was a dark shade of gray, it had lightened enough to assure her that night had passed into day. And she had vowed to make an early start back to San Antonio.

But the bed was incredibly warm and comfortable, and despite what had to be hours of sound sleep, she wasn't really ready to get up yet. In fact, if it wasn't for the monotonous, tinny-sounding music that had replaced the beeps and tweets, she'd curl up and close her eyes again. Unfortunately there was no way she could sleep with that awful noise grating on her nerves. Pushing the blankets away from her face, Maggie rolled onto her back and turned her head.

"Morning, Mom. I was wondering if you were going to sleep all day." Christopher spared a moment to glance at her, then went back to the small electronic game he was holding in his hands. He was dressed in the navy blue sweatpants and Houston Astros T-shirt she'd packed in the overnight bag for him.

"I thought I told you to leave that thing at home," Maggie muttered, squinting in the pale glow of the bedside lamp he'd turned on. "You're going to end up blind as a bat if you don't stop spending hour after hour staring at one tiny screen or another."

"I've only been playing for twenty minutes. I thought it would be quieter than the television. But now that you're up..." He switched off the game, tossed it aside and slid to the end of the bed. "You don't mind if I watch cartoons, do you?" he asked as he reached for the knob on the small set atop the wide oak dresser.

"What time is it, anyway?" Still not ready to rise and shine, Maggie pushed herself to a sitting position, plumping her pillows against the headboard. She hadn't thought to unpack her travel alarm clock, and she'd left her watch in the bathroom.

"*Pee-Wee's Playhouse* is on, so it's after nine o'clock."

"After nine?" The last of her lethargy disappeared in an instant, as she swung her legs over the side of the bed. So much for her promise to make an early start. Mackenzie Harrow's bad opinion of her had probably worsened by several degrees. "But why should I care? I'm never going to see him again," she grumbled.

"What did you say, Mom?"

"Get your things together, Christopher. As soon as I'm dressed we're going to hit the road." As she passed the dresser, she grabbed the overnight bag, then walked into the bathroom, closing the door behind her.

She had stopped worrying about what other people thought of her a couple of years ago and she wasn't about to regress, especially where a man as determinedly disapproving as Mr. Harrow was concerned. From the moment he'd first laid eyes on her, he hadn't liked anything about her, and he'd made darn sure that she knew it. Well, he could just take his disapproval and put it where the sun didn't shine.

Rummaging through her bag she found a pair of pale gray leggings, an oversized kelly green sweatshirt, matching green socks and a pair of sneakers. She had traveled enough with her parents and then Mitch to know the importance of easy access to a change of clothing and some of her toiletries, so she wouldn't have to start the drive back to San Antonio in a damp skirt and blouse and ruined sandals.

Unfortunately, with the way it was still raining, she'd probably end up wet anyway, just running from the house to her car. But at least she and Christopher would be on their way home. And she would prefer to be slightly soggy in the privacy of her own car than to suffer any more of Mackenzie Harrow's begrudging hospitality.

Face washed, teeth brushed and clothes on, Maggie reached for her hairbrush. With a few quick strokes she tried, unsuccessfully, to tame her almost shoulder-length auburn curls. She thought about adding a touch of makeup to her pale face, then decided it would be a waste of time. The rain would only wash it off.

Resisting another glance in the mirror, she tossed her brush in the bag and zipped it. As she put on the small gold hoop earrings and the expensive gold-and-stainless-steel watch she always wore, she scanned the bathroom quickly, making sure she wasn't forgetting any of their things. She didn't want to have to contact Mr. Harrow at any time in the future, if she could help it.

Rejoining her son in the bedroom, she noted that he'd done as she'd asked. His wet clothing and game paraphernalia were neatly stacked on the dresser. Never comfortable with leaving a mess, Maggie took a few moments to straighten the beds and tidy the room while Christopher stowed his gear in the bag.

"Well, I guess we'd better get going." She glanced at her watch. It was just past nine-thirty. She crossed the room, drew one edge of the lace curtain aside, and peered out the window. It was still raining hard and steady, and the heavy, leaden sky offered no hope of it letting up any time soon. She wasn't fond of driving in bad weather, but at least it was day instead of night. And maybe it wasn't raining quite so much closer to home.

"There's a flood warning for San Antonio," Christopher advised as he joined her at the window. "They announced it during a commercial. Do you think we'll be able to make it home?"

So much for better weather ahead, Maggie thought. "Probably, if we leave now," she replied, trying to reassure herself, as well as her son.

The streets near her house rarely flooded, even during the worst storms, but she wasn't so sure about all the other roads she had to travel along the way. With it raining as hard as it was, however, she had no doubt that the longer she lingered at the Whispering Wind, the more chance she had of getting stuck somewhere down the line.

She picked up her purse and overnight bag as Christopher opened the bedroom door. Stepping out into the dimly lit hallway, she realized how quiet it was. As if they were all alone in the big house, she thought, settling the strap of her purse over her shoulder and starting down the narrow staircase. Maybe Harrow and his daughter were out in the barn doing chores. If so, then she and her son could slip away without a word. She didn't have to take her refund with her. He could drop it in the mail. That way she wouldn't have to see him or speak to him again.

"Hey, Mom, aren't those our suitcases over there by the door?"

A frown tugging at the corners of her mouth, Maggie followed her son across the dark, empty dining room. The two pieces of black-and-tan luggage dotted with drops of rainwater *did* belong to them. But what were they doing in the house, when she'd left them in the trunk of her car? She was going to end up wet just getting herself and her son into the car. She'd be soaked to the skin if she had to struggle with two suitcases, as well. Wrapping a hand around the knob, she pulled open the door, then drew in a sharp breath.

"Mom, where's our car?" Christopher stared at her with wide, frightened eyes. "Do you think somebody stole it? If somebody stole it, Grandpa is gonna be awful mad."

"Who would come all the way out to the middle of nowhere to steal a car? Especially in the middle of a storm," Maggie chided. "And why would they leave our suitcases behind?"

What had she done with her keys? she wondered, as she dug around in her purse. Probably left them in the ignition. She'd been in such a hurry to get inside last night. But surely she was correct in believing that nobody in his right mind would venture out in a storm to a place as nearly inaccessible as the Whispering Wind just to steal her car.

Closing the door, she bowed her head for a moment, trying to think. Then, surveying the dark room, she noticed the beams of light streaming through the glass panels in the swinging doors she had assumed led to the kitchen. She dropped her purse and overnight bag on the floor beside the suitcases, then started toward the light. There was only one way to find out what was going on. Ask someone who might know. And much as she hated the thought of confronting him again, she had a feeling *he* would know. With her luck, he was probably waiting for her just around the corner, a smirk on his dark, handsome face.

She stepped into the big kitchen and stopped, blinking in the glow of the bright fluorescent lights. Christopher, following closely on her heels, crashed into her back, sending her staggering a few steps farther than she wanted to go. Reaching out with one hand she caught hold of a piece of the long, wraparound counter and steadied herself as her eyes met Mackenzie Harrow's.

He was sitting at the table, finishing what appeared to be a hearty breakfast of eggs, bacon, toast and coffee. She might have imagined the startled look on his face, but he held her gaze two beats too long to leave any doubt in her mind. He hadn't been lying in wait for her, after all. Her sudden appearance had definitely taken him by surprise. And though she had come searching for him, she couldn't deny her own surprise when his pale gray eyes clung to hers much longer than necessary.

With his shirt buttoned, his hair combed and a day's worth of beard removed, he didn't seem quite so dangerous. Especially with half a length of kitchen floor and a wide, wooden table between them. In fact, she was almost ready to believe he wasn't so bad, after all, when he settled back in his chair and crossed his arms over his chest. His eyes chilling by measurable degrees, he gave her a very thorough once-over, his attitude infinitely more insulting than interested.

"What kind of getup is that?" he asked, his deep voice laced with sarcasm. Meeting her gaze, he lifted an eyebrow and stared at her, waiting for her to respond.

"The kind of *getup* that guarantees me a comfortable drive back to San Antonio," Maggie snapped, glaring at the man who was now smirking at her just as she'd envisioned he would. "If you'll tell me where my car is—"

"Hi! Ready for some breakfast?" Elizabeth interrupted, as she stepped through the swinging doors. She offered Maggie a tentative smile as she walked by. Stopping at the table, she picked up her father's empty plate and mug, then continued on to the kitchen sink. "Rosa can't get up the road because of all the rain, but I'm a pretty good cook. I can fix eggs and bacon and toast, and there's hot oatmeal or cold cereal. Daddy made the coffee, didn't you?"

"Yeah, I made the coffee." Pushing his chair away from the table, Mac stood up and turned away. "Sit down, Miz Connor, and I'll pour you a cup. How about you, son? Do you want milk or orange juice?"

With every outward appearance of calm and control, he opened a cabinet, all the while silently cursing whatever devil had loosened his tongue a few minutes earlier. He didn't give a damn if she pranced around in tights and a tutu. But, hell, for such a little thing she had the longest legs, legs that were shown off to their best advantage from mid-thigh on down by whatever it was she was wearing.

And that wild mess of red hair... surely she hadn't come all this way without packing a comb and brush. Maybe she'd been in such a hurry to leave, she hadn't bothered to use it, but Mac wished she had. Slamming a coffee mug and a glass on the counter, he turned to face her. She was still standing near the door and she had that hoity-toity look on her face again.

"Thanks for the offer, but I'd like to get on the road before the weather gets any worse. If you'll just tell me—"

"Weather's already about as bad as it gets. The road into Bandera is closed. So is the road from Bandera to San Antonio." Cocking his hip to one side, he dug into the side pocket of his jeans with his long, broad fingers and pulled out the keys to her car. "Looks like you're stuck here for a few days. At least until the water goes down. I brought in your suitcases and put your car in the garage out back.'' With a flick of his wrist, he tossed her keys at her. ''Mighty careless leaving those in the ignition of that fancy little car of yours.''

She caught the keys in both hands, her relief that her car was safe momentarily overriding her irritation at his last dig. ''Surely there's some way to get out of here,'' she murmured, her eyes on him as he poured a mug of coffee for her and set it on the table.

''Believe me, lady, if there was any way to get you out of here, you'd be gone. Unfortunately the roads are flooded, and unless that car of yours can float, you're staying here.''

He wasn't any happier about the situation than she was. He might be stuck with her two, maybe three days. That meant he'd have to face two, maybe three more sleepless nights like the one he'd *enjoyed* last night. He'd tossed and turned, afraid to close his eyes because every time he did, he'd seen her bright blue eyes and her wide, full mouth and felt the softness of her skin against his fingertips. Picking up the glass, he glanced at the boy.

''Milk or juice?'' he asked, as he opened the refrigerator door.

''Milk, please,'' Christopher replied, stepping around his mother and heading for the cereal boxes lined up in a row on the counter next to the sink. ''Mmm, Honey Nut Cheerios. My favorite.'' He reached for the box as Elizabeth pulled a bowl from the cabinet.

Maggie watched as Mac filled a glass for her son, then placed it and the milk carton on the table. Her gaze traveled to the steaming mug of coffee waiting for her. She ought to give in gracefully, especially since she seemed to have no choice. Because if what Mackenzie Harrow said was true and the roads were flooded, she certainly couldn't go back to San Antonio. And she could do a lot worse than accept a warm drink from the man. Still she lingered near the door, aware, as her son was not, of how truly unwelcome they were. Aware, too, that for some odd reason it hurt.

"I guess you'll want to call your husband, let him know you're all right. There's a telephone on my desk in the living room."

She wasn't wearing a ring, something he'd noticed last night, something he'd thought of more than once during the restless hours before dawn. But these days married women didn't always wear a ring, especially if they were looking for something they couldn't find at home. Being stuck with her for several days would be a hell of a lot easier if he knew for sure that she was out of bounds.

Mac's gruff voice drew her attention back to him. He was standing by the refrigerator, hands on his hips, studying her with cold, hard eyes. Waiting to pick a fight, she thought. Ready, willing and able to beat her down. But why?

"I...I don't have a husband," she replied, her voice soft and tentative, her gaze steady. If he wanted a fight, she'd give it to him, but only if he pushed her too far. He wasn't going to play macho man with her and get away with it, even if she was a guest in his house.

"Ah, a dee-vor-say, huh?" He slurred the word, deepening his drawl, making no attempt to hide his distaste.

The sneer in his voice was as unexpected and uncalled for as the sudden hostility in his pale eyes. He'd set himself up as judge and jury, and without waiting to hear what she had to say, he'd sentenced her to a spot in the gutter with the rest of what he obviously considered trash. She wanted to defend herself, but doubted it would change his opinion of her. He seemed so pleased with his assessment of her. Why spoil his fun? Anyway, if she told him she was a widow, he'd probably assume she'd driven Mitch to his—

"He died." At the kitchen table, Christopher glanced up, his eyes on Mac. When the man turned to look at him, he spoke again. "My dad died three years ago, Mr. Harrow. My mom's a widow, not a divorcée." Obviously pleased with his attempt to set things straight, he dipped his spoon into his cereal.

"My mom died, too, but it's only been a year and a half." Slipping into the chair next to Christopher's, Elizabeth reached for the milk carton. "We still miss her a lot, don't we, Daddy?" Without looking at him, she added milk to her cereal, then picked up her spoon.

Talk about feeling like two cents waiting for change, Mac thought, running a hand through his hair as he stared at the floor. He could feel his face burning a dull red, and the thought of meeting Maggie Connor's eyes made him cringe. He wanted to kick himself, but unfortunately he'd already planted both feet in his big mouth. *So spit 'em out and apologize to the lady.*

He raised his head and found her watching him. Rather than the anger he'd expected, there was something more like sympathy shadowing her bright blue eyes. Damn it, he didn't want her sympathy. And he sure as hell didn't want to ask for her forgiveness. But he owed her an apology, and Mackenzie Harrow always paid his debts.

"I'm sorry." As he held her gaze he realized that he meant it. He *was* sorry. Sorry for her loss, sorry for his loss, and sorry that he was acting like a real son of a bitch again when she'd done nothing to deserve it.

She was stuck with him just as surely as he was stuck with her, and it was his fault, not hers. Believing she was some sort of hussy would have made the next few days more bearable. But she wasn't a hussy. She was a nice lady with a little boy, and she'd paid good money for a two-week vacation that had been canceled without her knowledge. She had every right to rant and rave at him, yet she didn't.

In fact, she'd planned to slip away as quietly as possible, without a word to him. And she would have, weather permitting. She wanted as little to do with him as he wanted to do with her. He should be relieved rather than angry. And he should stop staring at her wide, full mouth. He should stop feeling so . . . so hungry. . . .

"I'm sorry, too," Maggie murmured as she moved away from the door. Stopping by the table, she picked up the mug of hot coffee he'd poured for her and cradled it in her palms, savoring its comforting warmth. "And I *will* use the phone later to call my parents. I don't want them to worry about us."

"Fine." He stuffed his hands into the side pockets of his jeans and rocked back on his boot heels. "Do you need some cream or sugar or sweetener for your coffee?"

"I drink it black." She lifted the mug and sipped the dark brew, glancing at him out of the corner of her eye. Sensing his sudden discomfort, she wanted to smile, but she didn't. No use doing anything that might have the same effect as throwing fat on a fire. Contrition had tamed him, but only slightly. "Mmm, this is great coffee." Mug in hand, she moved toward the cereal boxes on the counter.

Wheeling around, Mac pulled open the refrigerator door. "How about some eggs? There's bacon and ham, too. And some pancake batter." He was rattling like a bag of bones and making just about as much sense. But it was her fault, walking around in what she considered a pair of pants. If they clung to her bottom the way they clung to her legs . . .

With a muttered curse, Mac slammed the refrigerator door. He had to get out of the kitchen and he had to do it now. But she was a guest, and the least he could do after his shabby behavior was offer to prepare her breakfast. Gritting his teeth, he glanced at her over his shoulder. Bad move. She was smiling the warmest, friendliest smile he'd seen in a long time. It made him feel . . . funny. Not laugh-out-loud funny, but odd and...and uncomfortable. He shifted from one foot to the other as he realized exactly where the source of his discomfort was located.

"Eggs and bacon would be wonderful," Maggie replied, setting her mug on the counter. "But I can fix them myself, if you'll just show me where you keep the pots and pans."

"I'll help," Elizabeth offered. She finished a last spoonful of cereal and slid out of her chair.

"Great," Mac muttered. "I've got some work to do out in the barn."

He walked the long way around the table, grabbed his plastic poncho by the kitchen door and slung it over his head. Then he clapped his hat on his head. A moment later he opened the door, and without a backward glance, walked into the rain, welcoming its wet chill with grim determination.

Maggie felt her smile fading. So much for her hopes of easing the tension between them, she thought, as she mixed eggs and milk and dumped them into the pan Elizabeth had set on the stove for her. She was more than willing to accept his apology for misjudging her and let bygones be bygones. She was even willing to meet him halfway on the road to goodwill and cordial relations. Unfortunately, however, it seemed as if she was going to have to be satisfied with his apology. Considering the way he'd run out at the first opportunity, Maggie had no doubt that the only road Mackenzie Harrow was interested in traveling was the road that promised to take him as far away from her as possible.

And if anyone ought to understand how he felt, it was she. Going it alone had been her key to independence, an independence she cherished so much she swore she'd never give it up. Yet it bothered her that she wasn't welcome on Mac's road. At least, not for the remaining two or three days they'd be together. For one thing, he was still mourning his wife.

Maggie had known somewhere in the back of her mind that he was a widower. Elizabeth *had* mentioned her mother's death when they'd met the previous August. But Maggie hadn't realized how deeply the loss had affected Mac until his daughter had spoken of it a few minutes ago. The stricken look on his face had revealed the true depth of his pain and sorrow. It had also given Maggie a new understanding of why he didn't want her in his house.

The dude ranch must have been something special he'd shared with his wife, something he refused to carry on without her. Maggie's unexpected arrival had been tantamount to trespassing in forbidden territory he had been determined to defend. She would never forget his hostility nor his caustic comments. *We don't do dudes anymore.* He'd been dead set on driving her away. Had she been less sure of herself and her rights, he would have succeeded. Or had she understood his reason for behaving so badly, she would have gone without an argument.

There was more to Mac's animosity toward her than her unknowing invasion of his home, though. Something about her personally angered and upset him, something over which she had no control. She couldn't change her looks or her manner, her mode of dress, or the car she drove. She *wouldn't*. But she could stay out of his way for the next few days.

Even if she had to sit in her room, reading, she *would* stay out of his way. She didn't want to cause him anymore grief, and she certainly didn't want to suffer anymore of his ill will. Why ruin what was left of what was supposed to be a vacation when there was even a slight possibility of avoiding any further unpleasantries?

"Hey, Mom, is it okay if I go upstairs and watch cartoons?"

Maggie shifted her attention from the pan of eggs she was stirring to her son. "Why don't you carry the suitcases upstairs for me? I packed them light enough so I could handle them, and I know you're as strong as I am." She flashed a teasing grin at him.

"Sure, no problem." He returned her grin as he set his bowl and glass in the sink.

"There's a television in the living room." Elizabeth glanced at Christopher, then turned back to the toast she was buttering for Maggie. "And there's a player piano and a pool table and—"

"A pool table?" Christopher's eyes brightened with sudden interest.

"Do you know how to play?"

"Sort of."

"I sort of know how, too. Do you want to play a game?"

"Sure."

Maggie hid a smile as her son shrugged and headed for the dining room. Glancing at Elizabeth out of the corner of her eye, she realized the girl was trying not to smile, too.

"Thanks for mentioning the pool table. I was hoping to get him away from his computer, his electronic games and the television for a couple of weeks, but I only managed one out of three."

"You're welcome." Elizabeth handed her a plate for her eggs and bacon, then poured another mug of coffee for her. "I'm...I'm sorry about my dad," she murmured as she set the mug on the table.

Maggie settled into a chair, then paused for a moment, her fork poised over her plate. "Is there a reason why he acts like such a...such a..." The most appropriate word that came to mind couldn't be spoken aloud to an eleven-year-old girl. Backpedaling a bit, she changed tacks. "Is there a reason why he's so crabby?"

"He's not usually crabby, at all," Elizabeth explained. "If I'd known he was going to act the way he's been, I never would have..." Her face turning bright red, she ducked away from Maggie's probing eyes. Moving quickly, she headed for the swinging doors.

"Elizabeth?" Maggie hadn't planned to pursue the suspicion she'd had the night before. She'd planned to be halfway back to San Antonio by now. But the girl had offered an opening too tempting to ignore, especially since she was stuck in a situation not of her own making for several more days.

"Yes?" She stopped, one hand on the door, keeping her back to Maggie.

"Is there a reason why your father forgot to cancel our reservations other than he just forgot?" Maggie asked, her voice soft and encouraging.

Her shoulders sagging, Elizabeth dropped her hand to her side. "Maybe."

"Maybe yes or maybe no?"

"Maybe . . . yes. . . ."

Maggie had to strain to hear the whispered reply that wasn't very surprising, at all. "So, why wasn't our reservation canceled along with all the rest, Miss Harrow?"

"I . . . I took it out of the drawer and hid it. I put it back yesterday morning." Turning slowly, Elizabeth faced Maggie. Her dark eyes wide and pleading, she crossed the kitchen, stopping near the table.

"But . . . why?" Though her voice was still soft, Maggie couldn't hide the sudden note of confusion. "If your father doesn't want to operate a dude ranch anymore, why didn't you let him cancel our reservation?"

"It's not that he just doesn't want to have guests here. He wants to sell the ranch. He wants to sell the Whispering Wind and Windstorm and the mares and move to Dallas. It's because he misses my mom and he thinks it was his fault that she died. Because he was so busy with the ranch he didn't know she was sick, and she didn't tell him until it was too late. But he won't be happy anywhere except here. I just know it. He promised we could stay the summer. And when I saw your name on the receipt, I remembered how you helped Grandma and Grandpa. And I thought maybe you could help my dad, too."

Maggie listened to the girl's jumbled rush of words, trying to make sense out of what she was hearing. It seemed that her assumption about Mac's loss of interest in the ranch had been right on target. But she hadn't guessed at his intention to sell the place or his lingering guilt over his wife's death. In any case, without his wife beside him, he obviously wanted no part of the home and business they'd built together. Or was he forcing himself to give up one love because he blamed it for the loss of the other?

"How did you think I could help your dad, Elizabeth?"

"I . . . I don't know." Her face redder than ever, the girl stared at the floor as she gripped the table with one hand.

Ah, but you do know, Maggie thought, gazing at Mac's daughter with surprising fondness, considering her deception. Though she was still a young girl, Elizabeth had the ageless instincts and understanding of a woman. She had realized what was missing in her father's life and she had done what she could to provide what she thought was needed to make them one big, happy family again.

With the boundless faith of a hopeless romantic, she had believed that it might be possible for them to live happily ever after. Oh, the innocence of youth. How Maggie hated to be the one to disillusion her. But if Elizabeth Harrow was old enough to play matchmaker, she was also old enough to discover that you can't always get what you want.

"Your father loved your mother very much. And I think he still misses her a lot. I don't think he's ready to find someone to take her place. In fact, it might be a long time before he's ready to love someone as he loved her." *And I certainly won't be that someone,* she reminded herself silently.

"I know you meant well, Elizabeth. But surely you can see that my being here isn't helping your father at all. He's been angry since Christopher and I walked in the door, and he's going to be angry until the moment we walk out again. As for selling the ranch..." Maggie hesitated, choosing her words carefully. She didn't want to upset the girl, but neither did she want to offer false hope. "Maybe the only way he can find happiness in the future is by walking away from the past."

"He can be happy here. I know he can," Elizabeth cried as she raised her head and gazed at Maggie, her dark eyes shimmering with unshed tears.

"I don't know, Elizabeth. Anything is possible, and you've got the whole summer ahead of you. You love the Whispering Wind a lot, don't you?"

"Oh, yes. I don't want to live anywhere else...ever."

"And your father loves *you* a lot, too. He wants you to be happy, and he knows you're happy here. Maybe by the end of the summer he'll change his mind. In the meantime, what you need is some time alone together to share your thoughts and feelings. Christopher and I would just be in the way."

"I don't think so."

"Well, I do, and so does your father."

"Are you going to tell him about...about what I did?" Once again the girl ducked her head, as pink tinged her cheeks.

"No, I'm not. I think if anyone tells him, it should be you."

"He's going to be mad...*really* mad."

"Probably," Maggie agreed, trying not to smile. "But only for a little while. You've proven how much you love him and how much you want him to be happy. And in the end, that's what he'll remember."

"Do you think so?" Elizabeth asked, a cheerful note edging into her voice.

"I don't just think, I know," Maggie assured her, smiling affectionately.

"Hey, I thought we were going to play pool," Christopher called as he pushed through the swinging doors. Stopping a few feet away from Elizabeth, he studied her red face. "Are you in trouble?"

"She isn't in trouble," Maggie chided. "And, yes, you're going to play pool. So scat, you two. I want to warm up my breakfast in the microwave oven while it can still be salvaged."

"Okay, Mom." Christopher swung out the door without a backward glance.

"Maggie?" Elizabeth hesitated a moment longer. "Thanks."

"You're welcome."

She watched as the girl turned and followed Christopher. Then alone in the kitchen at last, she stood up and carried her plate to the microwave. As her food warmed, she rested a hip against the counter and, crossing her arms over her chest, stared out the window.

It was still pouring so heavily she could barely discern the outline of the big barn several hundred yards away from the house. In fact, had it not been for the soft glow of light spilling through the windows, she probably wouldn't have noticed it at all.

He was out there, doing whatever ranchers did in their barns on a rainy day. Probably something physical, she thought. Something mind-numbing and body-fatiguing. Something, she found herself hoping, that would eat up his pain and anger. Maybe then he might be able to tolerate the sight of her. But she'd planned to stay out of his sight, hadn't she?

Carrying her plate back to the table, she thought of all that Elizabeth had said. Staying on the ranch was so important to the young girl. And she had thought that Maggie could help make it happen. But she couldn't, could she? Not in a couple of days, and especially not when the girl's father couldn't stand to be anywhere near her.

"Don't you do anything crazy, Mary Margaret," she cautioned herself as she lifted a fork full of eggs to her mouth. "Don't even *think* about doing anything crazy like getting involved. Because if you get involved, you're going to get hurt. Just eat your breakfast and mind your own business."

Popping a strip of bacon into her mouth, she pushed away from the table and crossed to the counter. She peered out the window again and, contrary to every grain of common sense she possessed, she wondered just how long Mackenzie Harrow planned to hide.

Chapter Three

Glancing at his watch, Mac realized it was almost four o'clock. Beyond the small office window the sky was as dark and dreary as it had been all day, and the tap, tap, tap of rain against the glass was just as steady. With a sigh he reached across the papers scattered over the surface of the battered wooden desk and turned up the volume on the radio. Settling back in the equally battered wooden desk chair, he propped a foot against a partially opened drawer and folded his hands behind his head. He closed his eyes and tried to concentrate on the mellow strains of a Liszt melody, willing the soft, sweet music to take him away.

It took him as far as the ranch-house kitchen. Once more he saw her standing by the swinging doors, her chin tipped up at a dangerous angle as she tried to hide the hurt he'd caused in her when he'd accused her of being something she wasn't. As he had the night before and again that morning, he wondered why he behaved so badly whenever he was with her.

Because you're tempted, buddy, tempted in a way you haven't been since you first met Jo, his conscience prodded. Because you want to bury your hands in her wild mess of hair, you want to hold her fragile, fiery body in your arms. Because you want to crawl inside her and feel her explode around you. Because you want to eat her cries as she eats yours, giving and taking and giving again.

"Damn it, *no!*" Mac's foot hit the floor with a dull thud. Sitting forward in his chair, he propped his elbows on the edge of his desk and rubbed his face with his hands, trying to wipe away the erotic images that tormented him so unmercifully.

Twisting his lips in a painful grimace, he thought of how hard he'd worked all day to keep such images at bay. He'd cleaned stalls, groomed horses and polished tack with a vengeance, forcing himself to focus on nothing but the tasks at hand. The hard labor had eased some of his physical tension, yet he hadn't risked going back to the house for lunch. Instead he'd settled down to a long afternoon of boring paperwork in his office in the barn. It was the kind of paperwork that required all of his attention, and it had—until he'd let his guard down for just a moment.

"Damn it," he repeated as the music drifted away. What was he going to do? He hadn't budged from the barn all day, but he was going to have to return to the house soon. His growling stomach reminded him that he'd missed lunch, and with Rosa unable to get to the house somebody had to prepare dinner for his daughter and the Connors. Obviously that somebody was he.

Resigned to his fate, he began to gather his papers as the radio announcer launched into the hourly news and weather report. He had trusted Elizabeth to handle lunch. There was canned soup, ham, cheese and bread, as well as cookies and fruit on hand. But he couldn't expect her to cook a full meal, the kind of meal guests at the ranch deserved. And anyway, *he* was as hungry as a—

"... and locally, rain is expected to continue into tomorrow with another line of heavy thunderstorms expected in the area late tonight or early tomorrow. Flooding in low-lying areas is making travel extremely dangerous. The Texas Department of Public Safety urges motorists to use caution—"

With a short, extraordinarily succinct curse, Mac switched off the radio. He had hoped to get rid of her first thing Monday morning. Now it might be Tuesday or perhaps even Wednesday before she could leave. The roads would drain fairly quickly once the rain stopped, but it didn't sound as if the rain was going to stop anytime soon.

Cursing again, he filed the papers in the desk drawer, slammed it shut, then pushed his chair back and stood up. With a speed born of long practice, he fed and watered the horses one last time before shrugging into his rain poncho and settling his hat on his head. Standing in the doorway, he allowed his eyes to rove over the barn, assuring himself that everything was in place. Stop putting it off, he chided himself, as he reached for the light switch.

Moments later he clumped up the back steps and pushed open the kitchen door. Startled by the unexpected light and warmth, not to mention the savory smell of good, old-fashioned home cooking that greeted him, he paused just inside the doorway and surveyed the big, bright kitchen. The table had been set with their everyday dishes, but someone had added a gracious touch, complementing the simple white crockery with quilted red linen place mats and matching red-and-white checked napkins. The same someone had arranged a variety of brass candlesticks filled with red and white candles in the center of the table. Red candles... He hadn't even known that he owned red candles.

Inhaling the mélange of tempting aromas wafting around him, he shifted his gaze from the table to the oversized double ovens built into one wall. Beyond the smoky glass he could see two casserole dishes bubbling energetically. And on the wide counter that stretched toward the sink there was a layer cake covered with chocolate frosting, a plate of cookies, and a pan of yeast rolls waiting to go in the oven. On the other side of the sink, sitting on a high stool at the far end of the counter was Miz Maggie Connor, an odd pair of half glasses perched on her nose and Jo's favorite cookbooks spread out around her.

She was watching him over the top of her glasses, her bright blue eyes wary despite the faint smile lifting the corners of her mouth. He stared at her for several seconds, clenching and unclenching his jaw as he tried to quell the urge to shout at her, to shake her senseless, to sweep his arm across the table, to gather up the cookbooks and lock them away. She had no right, no right at all to come into his home and . . . and . . .

He moved away from the door, taking a step into the kitchen, his gaze as unwavering as hers, forgetting the heavy wooden door that still hung open. Caught by a sudden gust of wind, it slammed shut, the loud banging noise breaking the thread of tension strung tight between them and stopping him just short of saying or doing something stupid. Turning on his heel, he pulled off his hat and hung it on the rack near the door, then yanked his poncho over his head.

It was much simpler to tolerate her presence when he was angry with her, but he had no real reason to be angry with her now. In fact, he should be grateful that she'd taken the initiative to prepare a meal for them. He should appreciate the work she'd done, which was also work he wouldn't have to do.

He had to admit that his cooking wasn't anything to rave about, either. When Rosa was away visiting one of her grown children, he and Elizabeth often drove into Bandera for fried chicken or pizza. He'd do well to remember that they were going to be stuck together on the ranch for several days without Rosa. If Miz Connor wanted to cook, he really shouldn't give her any grief about it. And at least she wouldn't be bothering him if she was busy in the kitchen.

"You don't have to cook for us. You're a guest here." He had intended to simply let her know that he had no expectations where she was concerned. He hadn't intended to do it in such a begrudging tone of voice. Turning to face her, he ran a hand through his hair, then propped his fists on his hips as he met her gaze.

Her smile had faded and a hint of hurt shadowed the increasing wariness in her eyes. Looking down at her hands clasped in her lap, she shrugged and shook her head. "But I *like* to cook. I don't have much of an opportunity to do it during the school year, and usually putting together a big meal isn't worth it with just the two of us. Christopher can be so picky, and then we have leftovers for weeks...." Her voice trailed away as she glanced at him for a moment.

Then, shrugging again, she focused her attention on the cookbooks scattered over the wide tile counter. "The kids helped with the cake and cookies. What a mess." She smiled slightly as she tucked the books between the crockery pots Jo had used as bookends. "I hope you like King Ranch chicken as much as Elizabeth said you do. I tried a spinach recipe, too, and there's a green salad in the refrigerator. And rolls..." Again her voice trailed away.

Only one book remained on the counter. It was Jo's special spiral notebook, full of her favorite crowd-sized recipes, the dishes she and Rosa had prepared for their guests. He knew he should say something to Maggie, but he couldn't seem to find the words, and he couldn't seem to stop staring at the notebook as she closed it carefully and slid it among the others.

"These were your wife's cookbooks, weren't they?" she asked softly. "Elizabeth didn't think you'd mind if I looked through them. I'm sorry. I should—"

"Don't be sorry," Mac muttered, dropping his hands to his sides. "Of course I don't mind if you look at them. And I appreciate the help with dinner." Avoiding her gaze, he started across the kitchen. "Do I have time to take a shower and change clothes?" He tossed the question over his shoulder as he pushed through the swinging doors.

"Sure. I thought we'd eat around six o'clock."

"Great. I'll be down at six."

For just a moment Maggie heard the tinkle of the player piano, then with a whoosh the doors closed, leaving her alone in the quiet kitchen. Swiveling on her stool, she tossed her glasses aside, then propped her elbows on the counter. She cupped her chin in her hands and stared out the window.

Although it was just past five o'clock, the sky was a dull, dark shade of gray and the rain continued to fall. It wasn't as heavy as it had been earlier, but it was steady. She ought to go upstairs and catch the local news and weather reports on TV, but she had an idea that the weather report wouldn't be to her liking. With a sigh, she bent her head and massaged her forehead with her fingertips.

It had been a long day. It also should have been a relaxing day. Normally she loved to read when it rained, but she'd been too restless, mentally as well as physically, to settle down with any of the half dozen books she'd brought with her. And she'd lost patience completely with her current counted-cross-stitch project when she realized she wasn't counting, just stitching rather haphazardly. She'd ended up playing a board game with Elizabeth and Christopher until lunchtime.

She had prepared soup and sandwiches for the three of them. Actually she'd prepared enough food for four, but

Mac hadn't returned to the house. Then, as the children helped her tidy the kitchen, Elizabeth had suggested baking a batch of cookies. One thing had led to another and another, and before she knew it, the table was set, dinner was in the oven, and she was waiting for Mac.

"I wasn't *waiting* for him," she muttered as she slid off the stool. Angry with herself and the direction her thoughts were taking yet again, she glanced at the clock. It was almost time to put the rolls in the oven. With quick, efficient movements, she retrieved a pair of pot holders, moved the spinach au gratin from oven to microwave, slid the pan of rolls on the rack and reset the timer.

"But you were *so* happy to see him," she chided herself, picking up her one-sided conversation where she'd left off as she hurled the pot holders onto the counter.

He had blown through the door on a gust of wind and rain, bringing with him the warm, earthy fragrance of the barn and the musky scent of a man who had worked hard all day. He had been surprised by her preparations for dinner, but he hadn't been pleased. And he hadn't had any qualms about showing his displeasure.

"So, what else is new?" she quipped, as she reached for the coffeepot and began to fill it with water. Mackenzie Harrow had been showing his displeasure with her since the moment she'd arrived.

Just because he was stuck with her didn't mean he had to like it, or even act as if he liked it. It was his house, after all. And until twenty minutes ago, she *had* stayed out of his way for the entire day. But what she chose to do while she was staying out of his way was her business, as long as she didn't tear his house apart or steal the family jewels.

And if what she chose to do was cook a meal for them, he could have the common courtesy to be gracious about it. Darn it, she was a good cook. No, she was a *great* cook. It wasn't as if he'd have to gag down a serving of unrecognizable, inedible glop. Although she had no doubt he'd treat anything she offered him as if it *were* glop—

"Hey, Mom, is it time to eat yet?" Christopher asked as he and Elizabeth piled into the kitchen, falling over each other in their eagerness to be the first through the door. "We're starving."

"Mmm, it smells wonderful in here," Elizabeth said with a sigh. "King Ranch chicken is my favorite."

"I thought you said it was your father's favorite." Maggie plugged in the coffee maker, then turned to face the children just in time to catch her son heading toward the frosted cake finger-first. "Uh-uh, not until after supper."

"Oh, he likes it, too," Elizabeth said in reply to Maggie's comment.

"Good. Now, you two wash your hands. Then, Elizabeth, you can get the salad and, Christopher, you can put the rolls in a basket."

"What about me? Any orders for me, Sarge?"

The running water at the sink had disguised Mac's entry so effectively that Maggie hadn't realized he was in the kitchen until he growled his questions right behind her back. She came very close to dropping the casserole dish she'd just pulled from the oven, barely making it to the counter where she could set it down. Had it not been for the hint of teasing in his voice, she would have whirled on him, ready for a fight. As it was, she took a deep breath, then turned slowly, smiling softly.

"Sarge, huh? Do I sound that bossy to you?"

"And then some," he admitted, acknowledging her smile with a small one of his own.

It was the first time he'd looked at her with anything approaching warmth. Not a lot of warmth, but just enough to shift the cold, distant mask he seemed so determined to keep in place whenever they were together. It was also just enough to render her speechless for several seconds.

"I'll pour the drinks, all right? What do you want?" he asked, ducking his head and walking toward the refrigerator as Elizabeth and Christopher chorused their requests for milk.

What the hell was the matter with him, standing there grinning at her like a fool? Just because she'd looked so damned... appealing, bending over the oven door. Just because her bright green sweatshirt had ridden up over her bottom, revealing the excellent fit of her damned pants. Heaven help him, his hormones were getting out of hand. He was going to have to do something to satisfy his urges, and he was going to have to do it soon. Just as soon as Maggie Connor was on her way back to San Antonio. He'd find someone anonymous and he'd... he'd get it out of his system.

"I'll have iced tea. I made a fresh pitcher this afternoon. Why don't you get it while I pour the milk?" Maggie suggested as she took the carton from him.

Freed from his reverie by the brush of her fingertips against the back of his hand, Mac reached for the tea, then slammed the refrigerator door. As he filled glasses for Maggie and himself, he watched her light the candles on the table. Even though the kitchen was warm and cozy, the small, flickering flames cast a special glow over the simple setting, drawing the four of them together in a very close and intimate way.

How long had it been since he'd eaten by candlelight? Years ago, when he and Jo were newlyweds, when forever had been theirs to share...

"Oh, Maggie, it's beautiful. Can we turn the lights off?" Elizabeth asked.

"No!" Mac uttered the single word in a harsh, forbidding tone of voice, surprising himself almost as much as the others.

He met his daughter's wide-eyed gaze and shook his head. He was feeling as touchy as an aging tomcat and almost as antisocial, but he had guests and a sensitive young girl to think of. They didn't deserve another dose of his surly behavior.

Avoiding Elizabeth's steady stare, he set the pitcher on the table. "Not tonight, sweetheart. Maybe another time." He walked around the table and pulled out Maggie's chair for her.

"But, Daddy—"

"We'll do it another night, all right?" Maggie interrupted, touching the girl lightly on the shoulder before she slid onto her chair. "Let's eat before everything gets cold." She glanced up at each of the three faces gazing down at her, and smiled her brightest, most cheerful smile, then reached for the spinach au gratin as the others joined her at the table.

Within moments the silence that threatened to put a damper on their dinner was broken by the children's squabble over which way to pass the dishes. That argument quickly dissolved into another over who had won the game of pool, then another over how to beat the odds on one of Christopher's electronic games. Both Maggie and Mac were more than happy to let the kids carry the conversation, commenting only when their opinions were asked. They were also more than happy to avoid looking at each other.

Once again Maggie knew she'd done something to upset Mac, but by now she firmly believed *anything* she did would upset him, one way or another. Not that she'd gone out of her way to please him. She wouldn't go out of her way to please any man. But neither had she gone out of her way to displease him. She hadn't cooked dinner, set the table or lit the candles to anger him. She'd done it all because she wanted to and because she thought it was a small contribution toward making her presence more tolerable. Unfortunately it seemed that Mac would have found an empty kitchen, a cold oven and a bare table more to his liking.

Well, that was just too bad. Because for however many nights she'd have to stay at the Whispering Wind she was going to cook dinner, set the table and light candles for herself and for the children. And if Mac didn't like it, he could stay in the barn until they were finished with their meal. She speared a piece of chicken with her fork, popped it into her mouth and chewed it with the same vigor that she chewed on all the things she wanted to say to him but didn't dare. No use starting a war over a few candles and a chicken casserole.

Mac savored another mouthful of spinach au gratin and stole another glance at Maggie. He didn't even like spinach, but whatever she'd added to the droopy green stuff had turned it into a taste of heaven. He was already on his second serving and seriously considering a third. She was a good cook. No, she was a *great* cook, and he ought to have the guts to tell her so.

But the look on her face, not to mention the way she was attacking her food, warned him that whatever she was thinking, it wasn't anything nice. In her present frame of mind, she'd probably turn the kindest compliment against him. And so what if she did? He could take anything she had to dish out and serve it right back to her. Might as well keep her riled up. If she stayed mad at him, and he stayed mad at her, then there wouldn't be any danger of anything... happening. Right?

Wrong, wrong, *wrong,* he warned himself as he reached for his glass of tea. Her temper was as volatile as his, her emotions just as close to the surface. If they went at each other in anger, there was no telling what else would happen when they exploded. Given the thoughts he'd been having since last night, there was every possibility that a heated argument could turn into something else altogether, something equally hot and ultimately harmful.

Better to keep his mouth shut. Surely she'd know by the way he'd cleaned his plate not once but twice that he had enjoyed the meal she'd prepared. As he set his glass on the table, he caught her looking at him. She met his gaze for one long moment, a hint of waiting, of wanting in her bright eyes. Then she focused her attention on her plate with a barely discernible sigh. With an equally soft sigh, Mac split his third roll and slathered it with butter.

"Mom, may I be excused?" Christopher wiped his mouth with his napkin, then dropped the square of cloth on the table next to his plate as he pushed back his chair.

"Me, too, Daddy? I'm finished," Elizabeth added. "We want to watch—"

"Not so fast, you two. Since Maggie was kind enough to cook dinner for us, I think the least we can do is clean up the kitchen."

Ignoring their chorus of protests, Mac rose from the table. He picked up his plate, then reached for Maggie's, his eyes meeting hers over the glowing candles. "Thanks for the meal. It was very good." He hadn't planned to say the words aloud, but something in her solemn, almost sad expression nudged the compliment out of him. He even made an effort to smooth the normally rough edges from his tone of voice.

"You're welcome." Maggie stood up, too. Although she didn't gift him with one of her brilliant smiles, her expression softened a bit. "Well, I guess I'll go...relax for a while. Maybe everyone will be ready for cake in an hour or so."

"Sounds good to me."

"Me, too."

"Me, three."

"Great." Maggie turned, retrieved her glasses from the counter, then headed for the swinging doors, not quite sure what she was going to do to relax. She had planned to spend as many after-dinner hours as possible in the kitchen, but obviously Mac wanted her out of his way.

"I'll rinse and you stack." Christopher's voice rang with eleven-year-old me-Tarzan authority.

"No, *I'll* rinse and *you* stack," Elizabeth shot back.

"I'm the guest."

"But it's my house."

"All right, you guys, stop arguing," Mac interrupted. "Christopher, you rinse tonight. Tomorrow night Elizabeth can rinse. Fair enough?"

"We're still going to be here tomorrow night?" Christopher asked, unable to mask the hint of pleasure in his voice.

"I'm afraid so. In fact, I'm afraid you're going to be here for several nights, especially if it's still raining in the morning."

Several nights? Her shoulders sagging, Maggie barely restrained a groan of frustration as she pushed through the doors. What a way to spend a vacation. Trapped in a house with a man who couldn't stand anything about her except maybe her cooking. And hadn't she just sworn off cooking for him for the duration? No, she'd consigned him to the barn for the duration.

Unfortunately she had a feeling he was just as likely to spend the next few days in the barn as she was to punch another hole in her head. Ah, well, no sense worrying about it, she thought as she switched on the television set in the living room. It was Saturday night and if she wasn't mistaken, one of the networks offered a series of comedies between seven and nine. That's what she needed, she decided, flopping onto the deep, incredibly comfortable old sofa. A good laugh, maybe even a couple of good laughs.

Anything to beat down the futile, yet recurring urge to find a way to make Mackenzie Harrow happy. She'd spent too much of her life working to make other people happy.

And despite the withdrawal pains she'd suffered, she'd finally learned to channel her energy into making herself happy. This was neither the time nor the place to regress.

She had known Mac less than twenty-four hours, but if she knew anything about him, she knew that he was as used to running the show as her father was and her husband had been. She hadn't minded toeing the line with them because she hadn't really known any different. But she knew different now, and she liked being on her own. She'd be on her own again in a few days, she reminded herself, and she'd be glad of it. Sinking deeper in the sofa, she stretched her legs out in front of her and propped her feet on the scarred coffee table. She wouldn't miss the Whispering Wind or Mackenzie Harrow, not for a moment.

"Whatcha watching, Maggie?"

Elizabeth did a graceful somersault over the back of the sofa, plopping down next to her. Her face was red, her dark eyes shining with mischief, and strands of hair wisped around her face.

"Something silly. Want to watch it with me?"

"Me, too, Mom?" Christopher landed on her other side, as full of the devil as his newfound friend. Odd how in the space of a day he'd lost so much of his little-old-man attitude. Here was the boy she thought she'd lost forever.

"Of course, you can," she murmured, draping an arm around each child. Hugging one and then the other, she realized that she might miss the Whispering Wind, after all.

Several hours later Maggie rolled onto her side and stared at the lighted dial of her little alarm clock. It was almost eleven-thirty and she was no closer to falling asleep than she'd been ten minutes earlier. The chocolate cake and two cups of coffee she'd indulged in around eight o'clock were to blame. The combination of caffeine and sugar, especially after a physically inactive day, almost always guaranteed a major bout of insomnia.

Of course it didn't help that she also insisted on thinking about Mac and wondering why he'd disappeared after dinner. He hadn't joined them in the living room, nor had he come into the kitchen for dessert. He'd said that he was too full when Elizabeth found him in his third-floor bedroom. Well, it had been his loss. The cake had been delicious.

She shifted onto her back, staring at the ceiling she could barely see in the darkness, and listening to the rain tapping against the window panes and the gentle sound of her son's snoring. Was it her imagination or had the wind picked up again? Throwing back the blanket, she swung her legs over the side of the bed and padded barefoot across the room. She stopped at the window and peered out. The few trees near the house were bending and rustling at odd intervals. Off in the distance, lightning flashed in the sky. She counted to ten before she heard the distant rumble of thunder. Leaning against the wall, she waited, spotted another flash of lightning and counted to eight before she heard the thunder. The storm was definitely drawing closer.

"Well, that does it. I'll never get to sleep now. Might as well go downstairs and try to read," she muttered as she turned back to the bed. She slipped into the long, sleeveless white cotton robe that matched her gown. Then, ignoring her slippers, she reached for her glasses and the paperback mystery she'd started earlier and headed for the hallway.

The glow of a small light at the top of the stairs guided her way. She hesitated only a moment at the closed door leading to the third floor, then started down the stairs. If the door was closed he must be upstairs, so she'd have the living room all to herself. As she crossed the dining room she noticed a faint glow filtering through the glass panels in the swinging doors, but she assumed it was simply another light left on for safety's sake. Moving into the living room, she switched on a lamp, settled into a corner of the old sofa and opened her book.

The story was almost good enough to distract her attention from the approaching storm. She'd grown up in Houston so she'd been through her fair share of bad weather, including a couple of hurricanes. She didn't really mind thunder and lightning, high winds and heavy rain, but she couldn't sleep through a storm the way Mitch had. She had to be up and . . . ready for . . . whatever. The only thing that really frightened her was being alone late at night when the power went out. Somehow she always managed to be two rooms away from a flashlight or candles when it happened. Just as she was now, she realized as she took off her glasses and set her book aside. She should have stopped in the kitchen for a couple of candles and a box of matches just in case.

As if to confirm her thoughts, a bolt of lightning lit the sky beyond the living-room windows, followed almost immediately by a booming clap of thunder. A gust of wind hurled sheets of rain against the panes of glass. Better not to waste anymore time *thinking* about candles, she warned herself as she stood up. Better to head for the kitchen while she could still see where she was going.

As she rounded the end of the sofa, another flash of lightning streaked across the sky and another clap of thunder rolled after it. The lamp on the end table dimmed for a moment, brightened, and then, to Maggie's horror, went out completely.

"This is just great," she muttered, clasping the back of the sofa with one hand. Alone in the dark in an unfamiliar house with the great-granddaddy of all thunderstorms roaring around her. She wouldn't be surprised if a tornado was coming. The way her luck had been running the past couple of days, she wouldn't be surprised if she ended up in Oz. In any case, she had to get back to the room, had to check on Christopher. He had inherited Mitch's ability to sleep through the worst weather, but tonight was definitely the worst of the worst she'd ever seen.

Keeping a hand on the back of the sofa, she groped her way to the open archway leading into the dining room. The almost constant flashes of lightning assured her she was heading in the right direction. As she angled across the room toward the staircase, she stubbed her toe on a chair leg, bumped her thigh on the edge of a table, tripped over... something and ran smack into—

"Mac?" One of the shadows *had* been moving, she thought, as she gripped the front of his soft cotton shirt and rested her head on his chest.

"Maggie?" He *had* heard someone moving around earlier as he sat in the kitchen gorging on a hunk of chocolate cake and a glass of milk. Instinctively he wrapped his arms around her, steadying her. She shivered against him and he tightened his hold, rubbing the palm of his hand down her back. "What are you doing down here?"

"I couldn't sleep. I thought I'd read for a while, but then the lights went out." She hadn't detected the expected note of anger in his voice, so she relaxed a little, leaning into him, glad that he was there.

"Scared?" he asked softly, almost teasingly. As if it were the most natural thing in the world, he rubbed his cheek against the top of her head, savoring the soft brush of her curls against his beard-roughened skin.

"That depends. Are we going to blow away?" She could hear the strong, steady beat of his heart as his warmth seeped into her. It had been a long time since she'd felt so safe, so secure. It had been a long, long time since a man had held her in his arms so tenderly.... She shifted slightly, pressing close to him. She wanted the moment to last a little longer, even though she knew it wasn't wise.

"Not . . . tonight . . ." He knew he was going to hate himself in the morning, but if his life depended on it, he couldn't let her go. Not just yet. Groaning deep in his throat, he spread his legs, moved his hand to the small of her back and urged her closer still. He had forgotten how good it felt to hold a woman in his arms. And he hadn't even begun to imagine how good it could be if that woman was Maggie Connor.

As the storm spent its fury around them, and seconds beat into minutes, Maggie felt his body change, felt the hard throbbing against her belly as he moved against her in subtle invitation. Her body responded instantly with a swelling and a throbbing all its own, the wet heat between her thighs wanting, waiting to welcome him. She hadn't missed mating with a man, making love with a man, until now. And the urge to take this man inside her was almost overpowering. Still clinging to his shirt with both hands, she turned her head and pressed her lips against the hollow at the base of his throat.

As her mouth touched his bare skin, Mac stiffened. What the hell was he doing? He might be hungry for a woman, but he ought to have more sense than to try to satisfy his hunger with Maggie Connor. He had known her slightly more than twenty-four hours, but he knew enough about her to know that she wouldn't take it lightly. For her it wouldn't be a simple matter of scratching an itch. It would be making love, just as it had always been for him. And it would be a commitment, the kind of commitment he wasn't sure he could make anymore.

"The storm's letting up." He moved his hands from her back to her shoulders and gently drew away from her. "Come on, I'll guide you back to your room."

Silently cursing herself for being so forward, so...foolish, Maggie released her grip on Mac's shirt and stepped away from him. He was a stranger, a rather gruff, angry stranger who had said and done nothing to lead her to believe that he cared if she lived or died. Yet she had clung to him, enthralled by his physical desire for her, a desire that was more than likely born of desperation. He certainly couldn't go into town to take care of his needs tonight, she reminded herself.

In the dark she was just an anonymous female body. And in the light of day he could barely stand the sight of her. Two facts she'd do well to remember for the remainder of her stay on the Whispering Wind. At least in the dark he couldn't see the hot blush of embarrassment staining her cheeks.

"I think I can manage the stairs on my own." She pulled away from him, turned and stumbled on the first step. He caught her arm, saving her from falling, then wrapped his fingers around her elbow.

"And I can jump off the roof and fly," he muttered as he walked beside her.

"That I'd like to see."

"Oh, yeah? I get the feeling you'd rather see me crash and burn."

They paused at the door to the room she shared with her son.

"I don't want to see you hurt, Mac. But...but I don't want to be hurt, either. I just want to get through the next few days and go home."

It was exactly what he wanted her to say, but for some reason it didn't make him feel as good as it should. He might be anxious to get rid of her, but she didn't have to be quite so anxious to go, did she? Damn it, she was making him crazy again and she didn't even know it.

Without thinking, he reached out and touched her hair. Then, as if he'd been burned, he pulled his hand back and closed his fingers into a fist. "Good night, Miz Connor." He turned on his heel, not waiting for an answer.

"Good night, Mr. Harrow," she replied, sending her soft, sweet voice down the hall after him.

Chapter Four

Maggie spent most of what was left of the night rolling from one side of her bed to the other, alternately gazing at her soundly sleeping son and staring out the rainwashed window while her thoughts tumbled around inside her head. What had gotten into her? What wild and crazy demon had possessed her so completely that she'd dared to...to press her mouth against Mackenzie Harrow's bare skin...to *kiss* him? Granted, her sexual reawakening was long overdue, but why had it occurred with a man so thoroughly intent on disliking her?

He had growled or grumbled at her every time they'd met, his pale, silvery eyes cold and hard and distant on the rare occasions he'd deigned to meet her gaze. It didn't take an expert on body language to read the keep-your-distance signals he'd been sending. And yet when his arms had wrapped around her, his hold had been unbelievably gentle, his caresses soft and soothing. His growl hadn't been angry, it had been intimate. And when he'd shifted against her, she had known the extent of his arousal.

Rolling onto her back, Maggie rested her hand on her belly. He had wanted her, and he had wanted her to know it. But he hadn't wanted her enough to accept her wanting in return. He was hungry, darned hungry if she was any judge at all. But he wasn't willing to satisfy his hunger with her. Something else he'd wanted her to know, she thought, remembering the way he'd pulled away from her the moment she'd responded to his invitation.

Once again she told herself she should be grateful. He wasn't the kind of man she needed in her life. He was too much like her father, too much like Mitch, too used to laying down the law, to running the show, to getting his way regardless. And while she hoped to love and honor a man again some day, obey wasn't in her vocabulary anymore. Not that her father or her husband had ever forced her to do anything despicable. She had been loved and cherished, and she had loved in return. But because she had loved, she had spent thirty-two years setting aside her own wishes and desires in order to please them.

It was only after Mitch's death, when she'd realized how short life really was, that she'd found the courage to strike out on her own, to gain her independence. Breaking away had been a painful experience for her, as well as for her parents. But once they'd seen her determination to finish college, to move to San Antonio, to buy a small house, to teach school and raise her son on her own, they had begun to understand that where their only child was concerned, loving meant letting go. And Maggie had tried to understand how important it was to them to take care of her and Christopher. She knew that was why they had bought her an outrageously expensive foreign car for her thirty-fifth birthday.

With a groan of despair, Maggie turned on her side. Yes, she should be thankful that Mr. Harrow wasn't interested in pursuing a relationship with her. It would only end in grief. And, she thought, closing her eyes, she should be thankful that the rain was letting up. Maybe they'd be able to leave the Whispering Wind sometime tomorrow or the next day. How good it would be to sleep in her own bed in her own bedroom in her own house. How good it would be to put Mackenzie Harrow out of her life and out of her mind. Rubbing her cheek against the downy soft pillow, she wondered why she didn't feel better knowing that in a day or two she'd never have to see him or speak to him again. She should be thrilled. Unfortunately she was just plain tired, too tired to think anymore, she decided. Several seconds later she was sound asleep.

Much to her surprise she slept until after ten o'clock Sunday morning. She had needed the rest, especially after last night, but she hadn't thought she'd actually get it. Having gotten it, she felt lazy as a bum and just as unwilling to start what was left of the day. Maybe she ought to stay in bed, read, watch television, take the coward's way out and avoid facing Mackenzie Harrow.

"No way," she muttered, pushing herself up on her elbows. For one thing, she'd have to face him eventually, unless she planned to slip away from the ranch in the middle of the night. And knowing what little she did about him, she had an idea he was already hiding out in the barn anyway. She'd already missed breakfast, too. Her tummy wasn't going to allow her to miss lunch, as well.

With a sigh of resignation, she swung her legs over the side of the bed and surveyed the empty room. Christopher's bed was haphazardly made. One suitcase was open, half its contents, mostly her son's clothes, spilling onto the floor. She really must have been out of it to sleep through his ruckus, especially since it was so quiet otherwise.

"Quiet?"

She crossed the bedroom floor on bare feet, stopping at the window. Beyond the glass, the sky was as gray and heavy as it had been yesterday. But the air was still and the rain had eased from a steady downpour to a foggy mist. For the first time she could see the huge expanse of lawn rolling away from the front of the ranch house and dipping down into a shallow valley. In the distance she could make out a blurry rise of hills covered with scrub grass and small trees. And off to one side she could see the patio and pool area and the line of cabins they'd passed on their way in Friday night.

A nice place to visit, she thought as she bent to tackle her suitcase. But she wouldn't want to stay and wear out her welcome. Surely since it wasn't really raining any longer, the roads were draining. Surely she'd be able to get out of here soon. Grabbing a pair of worn, faded jeans and a blue plaid shirt, Maggie headed for the bathroom and wondered, as she had the night before, why she wasn't exactly thrilled that her escape from the Whispering Wind was imminent.

Thirty minutes later she found Christopher and Elizabeth side by side on the old sofa in the living room taking turns with her son's electronic game. They agreed to her suggestion of an early lunch, trailing into the kitchen after her to help. While Elizabeth flipped the grilled cheese sandwiches and her son stirred the chicken noodle soup, Maggie stood at the counter staring out the window. He was holed up in the barn again just as she'd suspected.

"Do you think your father would like some lunch?" She reached for a bag of potato chips, ripped it open, then poured a heaping portion on each of the three plates she'd set out.

"He's gone."

"Gone?" Maggie's head snapped up, her eyes on the girl standing by the stove. "Gone where? Into town? Are the roads open?" She couldn't remember hearing him drive away, but then she'd been sleeping so soundly she hadn't heard her son moving around the room.

"He went for a ride. On Windstorm. He said he was getting kind of ornery being cooped up for so long."

"Your dad or the horse?" Maggie asked, unable to stop herself.

Elizabeth glanced up, her mouth curved into a wide smile, and more than a hint of mischief in her dark eyes as she slid the sandwiches onto the plates Maggie held. "Both of them."

"What does ornery mean, Mom?"

"Cantankerous, crabby, short-tempered, grumpy..."

"Oh, right. But he wasn't real crabby this morning, was he, Elizabeth?" Frowning in concentration, he ladled soup into the bowls his mother had set on the table. "He made the best pancakes. And he asked a lot of questions about you."

Maggie paused halfway onto her chair. "What kind of questions?"

"Oh, I don't know. I can't remember...." He crunched into his sandwich, chewed slowly, swallowed. "May I have a glass of milk, please?"

She was tempted to pour the whole carton over his head. Instead she reached for his glass and filled it, then filled one for Elizabeth and one for herself. Then settling into her chair, she gazed at the girl. "I don't suppose you remember?"

"Just stuff about where you live and what you like to do." Elizabeth blew on a spoonful of soup, tasted it, then artfully changed the subject. "He went to see Juan and Rosa to make sure they're all right. He was going to check on the roads, too. He said he probably wouldn't be back until dinnertime. Can we make tacos tonight?''

For just a moment Maggie stared at the two children. They stared back, their eyes wide and innocent. Then shaking her head and smiling in spite of herself, she reached for her spoon. She knew enough about young people to know that eventually they'd remember every question Mac had asked, along with every answer they had given. And they'd offer the information in the worst possible place at the worst possible time. Unfortunately nothing but a cattle prod would get it out of them now, and even then, Maggie had her doubts.

At least she knew he was interested in her, if only in the mildest sort of way. Her smile widened just a bit as her spirits lifted. She knew nothing would come of it. He wanted her gone and she wanted to go. But in the meantime it was nice to know he wasn't quite as indifferent as he wanted her to believe. He had pushed her away last night, but if she stumbled into his arms again....

But she wouldn't end up in his arms again. For one thing, she didn't want to end up there. And long before the opportunity arose, she'd be on her way back to San Antonio, back to the safe, secure single life she'd chosen. A life she had enjoyed without regrets until—

"Hey, Mom, your soup's getting cold. Aren't you hungry?"

"I'm very hungry," Maggie assured her son, glad that he wasn't aware of the double meaning behind her words. Dipping her spoon into her bowl, she prepared to ease the gnawing in her stomach as she schooled herself to ignore the unexpected ache in her heart.

The dull gray sky had lightened considerably and the last of the morning mist had drifted away on the gentle breeze blowing in from the west, when Mac reined in Windstorm atop a low hill overlooking the ranch house. Though it was late afternoon and he still had several miles to ride before reaching home, he couldn't resist the urge to stop for a few moments and admire all that he owned. Speaking softly to the big chestnut stallion, he slid from the saddle. Slipping his hands into the back pockets of his jeans, he stood silently, surveying the peaceful scene below.

Elizabeth was right. He loved the ranch. It was more than just a place to live. It was a part of him. There had never been a time in his life when it hadn't been here waiting for him. Some of the land had been sold to pay his college tuition, and he had traded cattle for quarter horses and paying guests. But there was a timelessness about the place he couldn't deny. If he closed his eyes, he could almost imagine his father, his grandfather and his great-grandfather standing beside him on the ridge, as proud of their legacy as he. They had hung on through good times and bad, unwilling to sell. Because selling the Whispering Wind would have been akin to selling a part of their souls.

Back in February he'd been so sure that selling the ranch was the wisest thing to do for himself and his daughter. And he'd clung to his certainty for several months, ignoring his own doubts and her desperate pleas to stay. So why, all of a sudden, was he having second thoughts now? It wasn't a home without Jo. It was just a house and a piece of land. Maggie Connor blowing in his back door hadn't changed that. Maggie Connor with her bright eyes and her soft smile and candles on the table. Maggie Connor, warm and willing in his arms, her lips grazing the bare skin at the base of his throat, reminding him of what it was like to need, to want to lo—

"Damn it," he cursed, spinning on his heel, sending a handful of rocks scattering down the hillside, startling the horse.

He wasn't going to do it. He wasn't going to fall in love with any woman, no matter how much she reminded him of what he'd lost. And if, by some chance he did, he wasn't going to lose her to the Whispering Wind. It was a house and a piece of land that demanded hard work and sacrifice, and God in heaven, he'd sacrificed too much for it already. He and Elizabeth would be better off without it.

Grabbing the reins, he braced his left foot in the stirrup and swung his right leg up and over the saddle. The papers had been drawn up and lacked nothing but his signature. Dale Sherman had even upped the ante in an effort to insure against a change of heart. And Steve Elliott was still chomping at the bit to get his hands on Windstorm.

He had promised his daughter the summer, Mac thought, as he gathered up the reins. And he would keep his promise. But at the end of August he was going to sign the papers and move to Dallas. He already had several job interviews scheduled over the next few weeks, and Jo's mother had begun house-hunting for him. He wasn't going to change his mind, not today, not tomorrow.

Tomorrow, if the weather continued to clear, he was going to escort Miz Maggie Connor and her son down the dirt road leading to the highway into Bandera where he'd bid her goodbye. First thing in the morning, before he had a chance to discover something else to like about her. Before he was tempted to do something stupid like pull her into his arms again.

A schoolteacher, a *widowed* schoolteacher with overbearing parents, a loved and loving little boy...

"Guess she's got a boyfriend back in San Antonio, huh?"

"Nope."

"He doesn't live in San Antonio?"

"Who?"

"Her boyfriend."

"She doesn't have a boyfriend, Mr. Harrow."

Cursing roundly, Mac dug his heel into Windstorm's side, guiding the horse onto the narrow, muddy trail. He had given Christopher Connor the third degree, but why? Because he'd hoped to find Maggie lacking in some way, in any way. Unfortunately, she hadn't been lacking at all. She was a nice woman, living a nice, quiet life. And the sooner she got back to her nice, quiet life, the better. For him and for her.

Finding her in the kitchen an hour later when he came in from the barn wasn't quite the shock to his system that it had been the day before. In fact, he'd braced himself for the meeting he'd avoided all day, their first meeting since he'd held her in his arms last night. He was ready to see accusation in her bright blue eyes, to hear it in her soft, sweet voice. If she treated him the way he'd been treating her, he might be able to justify his bad behavior, not to mention his determination to send her away as soon as possible.

"Hi, Daddy. Guess what we're having for dinner tonight?"

Elizabeth stood by the stove, her smile wide and welcoming. The scent of highly seasoned meat wafted across the kitchen as she stirred the contents of the iron skillet on the burner. A wicker basket full of crisp tortilla shells and small dishes of *picante* sauce, sour cream and guacamole lined the counter. Once again the table was set, but instead of candles a crystal bowl filled with pastel tissue-paper flowers served as a center piece. In a far corner, her back to the room, Maggie chopped tomatoes into tiny bits, obviously focusing every ounce of her attention on the task at hand.

"Mmm, looks and smells a lot like tacos, sweetheart." He spoke to his daughter, but his gaze settled on Maggie and stayed there.

"Tacos and cheese enchiladas and Spanish rice and refried beans. Maggie and Christopher like Mexican food, too."

"Everything should be ready in about thirty minutes," Maggie advised in a neutral tone of voice. She set aside the bowl of chopped tomatoes, then reached for the block of cheddar cheese and the grater on the counter beside her without looking at him.

Mac stared at her back, willing her to turn and face him, but she seemed to be intent on ignoring him as completely as possible. Suit yourself, he thought, several seconds later as he spun on his heel, clumped across the kitchen and pushed through the swinging doors. It wouldn't last. Not through dinner when they were all seated around the table. She'd have to acknowledge him then.

But she didn't. Somehow she managed to offer him nothing on her own, not a look or a word, not a single smile, not a hint of laughter, and she did so without being rude or offensive. As they had the night before, the kids kept the conversation going, but Mac missed most of what they said. More than once he caught himself staring at Maggie, willing her to raise her eyes, to meet his gaze. And after a while he began to wonder if she was ill.

She looked smaller and more fragile in her faded jeans and blue plaid shirt. And though her wild red curls tumbled in shiny disarray, her face was pale and her eyes faintly shadowed with . . . hurt. He'd hurt her feelings, he thought with sudden clarity, as he toyed with a forkful of rice. The realization hit him like a punch in the gut. Taking a deep breath, he lowered his gaze to his almost empty plate.

He'd treated Maggie Connor to a full dose of his bitterness and anger, blaming her for things that were his fault, not hers. He'd been cold and distant, as remote as an iceberg in the Antarctic every time she'd been near. Until last night when he'd found her alone in the dark and taken advantage of her fear and uncertainty. He had drawn her close and he had thought of using her to satisfy his physical needs.

Yet when she'd responded to his overt invitation, he'd pushed her away.

Of course she was hurt. She had every right to be. But he didn't like being the one causing her pain. He had never hurt any woman intentionally. And Maggie didn't deserve to be hurt. Not by him or by any man. The least he could do was apologize, if only he could find the words. He'd have to think fast. She'd be gone in the morning.

"What's the matter, Daddy? Do you have a headache?"

Raising his eyes, Mac met his daughter's questioning gaze. He shook his head, barely managing to dredge up a smile for her. "I'm fine. Just...daydreaming." He glanced at Maggie, noted her total lack of interest, then turned his attention back to Elizabeth. "How was your day?"

"Okay, I guess. I wish we could have gone riding with you. Did you see Juan and Rosa? Are they all right?"

"Their power was off for a while yesterday, but the storm didn't cause them any problems otherwise. They'll be here in the morning." Although the old couple had earned the right to retire long ago, neither of them had any desire to give up their work on the ranch. Mac wasn't sure what he would have done without them, especially after Jo died.

"What about the roads, Mr. Harrow? Are they still flooded?" Christopher asked, tossing his napkin on the table.

"Unless it rains again during the night, the roads should be open by morning."

Again Mac glanced at Maggie out of the corner of his eye. For just a moment, her wide mouth turned down in a funny little frown as she stared at her plate. Then setting her fork down, she raised her eyes and met his gaze, a thin smile lifting her lips.

"We'll be on our way then, Mr. Harrow."

"Aw, Mom, do we have to go?"

"Do they have to go, Daddy?"

Mac turned to stare at his daughter. Maggie turned to stare at her son. Dead silence hung over the dinner table for several seconds. Then, as if drawn by a magnet, Mac glanced at Maggie. She met his gaze, but only for a moment. Ever so carefully she pushed back her chair and stood up. Picking up her plate with one hand, she reached for her son's with the other.

"Christopher, you know Mr. Harrow doesn't operate a guest ranch anymore. I think he's put up with us long enough. Now that the weather's clearing we really ought to be leaving."

Her tone was light, almost teasing, but there was nothing light or teasing about the expression on her face as she moved away from the table. Mac wasn't deceived by the tilt of her chin or the set of her shoulders. He had seen the hint of sadness and uncertainty in her eyes.

"But, Mom, Elizabeth thought—"

"Daddy, *please*—"

"Who wants dessert? The kids made cinnamon ice cream this afternoon," Maggie interrupted as she set the plates and silverware in the sink, then leaned against the counter, a too-bright smile lifting the corners of her mouth.

"Maybe later." Mac stood up, too. He wanted her to look at him again, but she avoided his gaze, focusing on something just the other side of his left shoulder. "Maggie, please..." *Please what? Please stay a while longer?* Mac shoved a hand through his hair, biting back the invitation, unwilling to allow his thoughts to become words. He couldn't ask her to stay. Not after the way he'd behaved the past two days. But suddenly he didn't want her to go.

"Well, then, if you don't mind, I think I'll go upstairs and get our things together. Come on, Christopher." She moved away from the counter, skirting the table the long way around as she walked across the kitchen.

"Aw, gee, Mom—"

"Christopher, please don't argue with me." She pushed through the swinging doors without a backward glance, her son trailing along behind her.

"Daddy—"

"Not now, Elizabeth." Mac picked up his plate and the basket of crisp tortillas and started toward the sink. "Are you going to help me clear the table or just stand there and pout?"

"I don't want them to go."

"We agreed that we'd stay on the Whispering Wind for the summer. We also agreed that we wouldn't have any strangers here."

"But Maggie and Christopher aren't strangers. They're our friends, now. At least they're *my* friends."

"Only because I screwed up and misplaced their reservation receipt. They never would have ended up here otherwise," Mac growled as he scooped leftovers into plastic containers. "Please finish clearing the table."

"Is that why you've been so grouchy the past couple of days? Because you think you screwed up?" Two empty glasses in each hand, Elizabeth hesitated for a moment, then continued in a soft voice. "Because you didn't screw up, Daddy."

Turning away from the sink, Mac gazed at his daughter. A pale rose blush climbed her cheeks and if she didn't look as guilty as a cat caught with the canary, he'd eat his hat. He closed the distance between them in three long strides, took the glasses from her hand and set them on the table. Then grasping her chin in his hand, he tipped her face up. "If I didn't screw up, Elizabeth, who did?" he asked, his voice equally soft yet steely.

"She helped Grandpa when he locked the keys in the car at Six Flags. She laughed and talked and made everything all right. I thought she'd make everything all right here, too. So... so I hid her reservation, so you couldn't cancel it. I didn't think you'd be so mad at her for coming. I thought she'd make you laugh and everything... everything would be... all right...."

Mac tried to make sense of the words she rattled off one after another as he tried to harden himself against the tears welling in her dark eyes. Tried and failed on both accounts. With a sigh, he sat on a chair and pulled her onto his lap. "Slow down, sweetheart. And don't cry. Please, don't cry." He wrapped his arms around her, hugging her close, waiting for her to settle down.

It was several minutes before she spoke in a very small voice. "I'm sorry, Daddy. I didn't mean to make you mad."

"What exactly *did* you mean to do?" Mac asked, his voice gently coaxing as he smoothed a hand over her dark hair. "Start at the beginning and take your time. I'm listening."

It was all the invitation Elizabeth needed. Taking a deep breath, she did as he'd asked, telling him everything and answering his occasional questions as honestly as she could. When she finally finished, he was very quiet.

"Are you going to give me a spanking?"

"Do you think you deserve a spanking?"

Pressing her cheek against his shoulder, she shrugged and shook her head, a *no* if he was any judge at all.

"You meddled in other people's lives, when you would have been wiser to mind your own business." Because she'd wanted to make everything all right and she'd thought Maggie Connor could help. Because there was something missing in their lives and she'd thought Maggie Connor could fill the gap.

She hadn't done it to be mean or spiteful. The meanness and spite had been *his* contribution to the past couple of days. He'd taken out his anger at himself on Maggie. He had thought that he'd made a foolish mistake, then he'd blamed her for his blunder.

"I think you're getting too old for spankings, Lizzie Beth. I also think you're old enough to know not to put your nose in where it doesn't belong." Taking her chin in his hand, he lifted her face, forcing her to meet his gaze. "Do you get my drift?"

"Yes...." Brushing at the moisture on her cheeks, she nodded her head.

"Just to make sure you do understand, you can spend the next two days in your room. While you're in there you can write 'I will mind my own business' fifty times." Harsh punishment for someone who'd been cooped up in the house for several days already and who hated putting a pencil to paper more than just about anything else. But what she'd done had been wrong, and he wanted her to realize it. Perhaps she already did. Instead of the argument he expected, she simply stared at him in silence.

"Also, we owe Miz Connor and her son an explanation and an apology. You're going to have to tell her what you did before she leaves." He tucked a wisp of dark hair behind her ear.

"She already knows," she mumbled in a tiny voice as she turned her face away.

"She knows?" Narrowing his eyes, Mac stared at the top of his daughter's head. How could she know unless... unless she had plotted her arrival with his daughter. She was a widow and she'd known he was a widower. "Are you saying there's more to your story, young lady? Are you saying Miz Connor came here knowing she wouldn't be welcome?" he demanded, not even trying to restrain the anger in his voice. Shifting Elizabeth off his lap, he stood up.

"Daddy, *no*." She grabbed his arm as he started for the swinging doors.

"Then how can she know when I just found out?"

"She...she kind of...guessed. On Saturday morning, after you left. We were talking and she...she guessed."

"She didn't say anything to me about it."

"She said it was my responsibility to tell you." She hesitated a moment, then ran across the kitchen and threw her arms around her father. "It wasn't your fault that she came, and it wasn't her fault. Don't be mad at her anymore, Daddy. Please don't be mad anymore."

Taking Elizabeth by the shoulders, he stepped back and hunkered down in front of her. "I'm not mad anymore." Lord help him, but he couldn't stand it when she cried.

"You're not?" She gazed at him, tears trembling on her thick, dark lashes.

"No."

"Then if you're not mad anymore, can they stay? Just for two weeks...."

For just an instant Mac wasn't sure if he wanted to laugh or cry. She was like a dog with a bone, where Maggie Connor was concerned, and he was running out of ways to deal with the situation. He hated resorting to blunt honesty, but suddenly he didn't seem to have any choice.

"Whether Miz Connor leaves tomorrow or two weeks from tomorrow, I'm selling the Whispering Wind to Dale Sherman at the end of August and we're moving to Dallas. Do you understand me?"

Her gaze was steady and her eyes suddenly dry as she stared at him for several seconds. Then a hint of a smile tipped up the corners of her mouth. "So they can stay for two weeks?"

He let go of her shoulders and stood up. Again he had the urge to laugh out loud, but he didn't. He moved across the kitchen, stopping at the sink. He was the adult, yet suddenly he felt very, very childish. She had never asked for much. And what she was asking now wouldn't cost him, not really. What could it hurt, if Maggie and Christopher stayed on the ranch for a couple of weeks. It would make Elizabeth very happy. And they weren't so bad. In fact, they weren't bad at all.

For just a moment, he remembered how good it had felt to hold Maggie in his arms. For just a moment, he remembered the pure pleasure that had surged through him when she'd pressed her lips against his bare skin. For just a moment, he was tempted . . .

"I'll think about it."

"Think about what?" Christopher swung through the door, then skidded to a halt in front of Elizabeth. His eyes widened as he stared at her. "Uh-oh. You're in trouble, aren't you? You've been crying," he crowed, temporarily sidetracked.

"I have not."

"Have too. Your eyes are red. Did you get a spanking?"

"Why don't you mind your own business. Anyway, I'm too old—"

"All right, you two. Stop bickering," Mac interrupted. He frowned at the pair of them, then spoke to Christopher. "Where's your mother?"

"In our room. She's reading. She said I could come downstairs until nine o'clock, as long as I don't get in anybody's way. Am I in your way?"

"Of course not. Especially if you've come to help Elizabeth clean up the kitchen."

"Sure, I can help her."

"When we're finished can we go outside for a little while?" Elizabeth asked, a fine note of pleading in her voice.

Beyond the window Mac could see that the sky was clearing, and off to the west, the sun was peaking through the clouds. "You can go out until dark." He met his daughter's eyes for a moment, then turned toward the swinging doors. "Just don't forget that you're grounded tomorrow and Tuesday."

"You're grounded for two days? What did you do?"

"Shut up, Christopher, or I'll punch you in the face."

Barely restraining a smile, Mac crossed the dining room and started up the stairs. They were good for each other, he thought, as he stopped on the second-floor landing and stared down the hallway. The door to Number Five was closed. For several long moments, he stood there, willing it to open, willing Maggie to walk out. If he ran into her in the hallway, he could apologize and get it over with. Of course, he could also knock on her door and offer his apologies.

Or he could just wait until morning, catch her before they left. He had to refund her money, too, and he hadn't written the check yet. He'd do that in the morning, also, he decided as he started up the steps to the third floor. He'd told Elizabeth he'd think about asking Maggie and Christopher to stay, and it was only fair to give it some thought. Actually, he really ought to sleep on it, he told himself as he strode into his bedroom.

Catching sight of his reflection in the mirror over the dresser, he paused for a moment. Instinctively he reached up and touched the place where she'd kissed him, tracing one long, broad finger back and forth across his skin. A couple of weeks. What could it hurt?

With a muttered curse, he dropped his hand and moved to the cluttered nightstand beside the big brass bed. What he really needed was to get his mind off Maggie Connor and onto something else altogether, he thought, as he searched for the science-fiction novel he'd picked up in the library a week ago. Thinking about her or anything to do with her only made his head ache. Among other things....

Chapter Five

Maggie stood by the bedroom window, one shoulder propped against the frame. Until today, heavy cloud cover and torrential rains had marred her view. Now, arms crossed over her chest, she watched the sky brighten from pale gold to clear blue, watched the light and shadows play across the wild, rugged landscape of the low hills in the near distance, and admired the natural beauty surrounding the Whispering Wind for the first and last time.

Her bags were packed. She was ready to go. And she was in deep trouble because her thoughts were mimicking the words of a sixties song. She smiled and shook her head. She had no intention of standing outside Mackenzie Harrow's door and waking him up to say goodbye. And she didn't expect a smile from him, much less a kiss. But in an odd way, the thought of leaving the Whispering Wind brought a hint of loneliness.

"Don't be silly," she chided herself, her voice whisper-soft. Only a masochist would miss Mackenzie Harrow. Elizabeth, on the other hand, was another story altogether.

In a very short time, the girl had gained a special place in her heart. Perhaps the thought of never seeing her again, the knowledge that she wouldn't be there to watch her grow and change from child to woman, was the source of the dull ache deep inside her. She could write to her, invite her to visit San Antonio, but not without Mac's approval. And Mac had yet to approve of her in any way.

Behind her, the bathroom door opened and a few seconds later her son joined her at the window.

"What are you looking at, Mom?"

"Sunshine and blue sky," Maggie replied, glancing at her son, then at her watch. "It's a beautiful sight, if I do say so myself. Ready to go?" It was almost seven o'clock and, with the sun up, it was light enough for her to find her way back to the highway on her own.

"But, Mom, remember what I told you last night? Elizabeth asked her father if we could stay, and he said he would think about it. She was pretty sure he'd say yes."

"Ah, Christopher, I wish you hadn't gotten your hopes up. As I've tried to tell you, he doesn't want us here. It's not . . . us, it's not personal. He just doesn't want anyone around." Pausing for a moment, she slipped an arm around his shoulders and hugged him, willing him to understand enough to stop arguing. "We've intruded on his privacy, and even though it was accidental, he isn't very happy about it. The best thing we can do is leave as quickly and as quietly as possible."

"But, Mom, she told him what she did. Now that he knows it isn't our fault that we're here, he won't be angry anymore and he—"

"Christopher, *please*. We had this conversation last night," Maggie interrupted, as she hugged him hard, then released him.

She admired his persistence even though it was irritating the heck out of her. And she was glad that he'd changed his mind about vacationing on a dude ranch. But she knew they weren't welcome on the Whispering Wind, and she refused to disappoint him further by offering even a faint hope that they were. Turning away from the window, she picked up the larger of the two suitcases resting on the floor, then crossed to the dresser to retrieve her purse and overnight bag.

"But, *Mom*..." Christopher wailed, not moving from his place by the window.

She walked to the door, fumbled with the knob, opened it and stepped over the threshold without a backward glance. Sometimes the best way to deal with her son's stubborn streak was to ignore it. Bribery often worked to dissuade him, too.

"We don't have to go home. We can drive to Houston and visit your grandparents. When I talked to your grandfather Saturday morning he told me he had a new Nintendo game for you." Gritting her teeth, she risked a look over her shoulder as she paused at the top of the staircase. When she saw him walking toward her, the other suitcase in his hand, she sighed with relief. He was frowning, but maybe he was just wondering which game her father had bought for him. Unfortunately she'd forgotten to ask.

Both the living room and dining room appeared to be deserted, but through the glass panels in the swinging doors Maggie could see that the lights were on in the kitchen. The good manners her mother had drilled into her tempted her to change course, to stop for a moment to say goodbye. Squaring her shoulders, she forced herself to head straight for the side door at the end of the dining room. If Mac's actions and attitude over the past couple of days were any indication, he didn't expect any fond farewells, and neither did she.

She opened the door and stepped out on the small porch. The air was early-morning cool, but the sun on her face promised a warm day ahead. The drive to Houston would be pleasant. They should arrive at her parents' house in time for lunch. Setting down her suitcase, purse and overnight bag, she turned to face her son.

"Why don't you wait here while I get the car?" Yesterday she had seen the big, three-car garage from the kitchen window. It was set back several hundred yards from the house, at the end of a wide gravel drive. If it was unlocked, she ought to be able to get away without another confrontation.

"I don't want to go to Grandpa's house. I want to stay here." Christopher dropped his suitcase on the porch and glared at her. "Aren't we even going to say goodbye?"

"No." Maggie glared back at him for a moment, then spun on her heel and strode toward the garage. She had a feeling the drive to Houston wasn't going to be quite so pleasant, after all.

In a matter of minutes she was in the car and had eased it to a stop near the porch. She shifted to park, released the trunk latch, then climbed out. Ignoring her sullen-looking son sitting on the steps, she grabbed a suitcase and the overnight bag. As she hefted one after the other into the trunk, the door to the house swung inward and Mac and Elizabeth walked out.

"Running off without saying goodbye, Miz Connor?"

Mac stopped at the edge of the porch, gazing down at her, a hint of amusement warming his pale gray eyes and lifting the corners of his mouth. Maggie glanced at him for one long moment, then picked up the second suitcase and turned away. He made her feel as if she were committing a crime. He *always* made her feel that way.

"Just getting out of your way as fast as I can, Mr. Harrow. I didn't think you'd want to be bothered with formalities." She swung the suitcase into the trunk. Pausing for a moment, she turned toward him. "After the past couple of days, I know how you feel about being...*bothered*." She slammed the trunk lid, pleased with the loud, final sound it made.

She was also pleased by the hint of color creeping up Mac's neck and spreading across his face. As he cut his eyes away from her, she allowed herself a tiny smile. At least he had the good grace to be embarrassed by his bad behavior, she thought, as she returned to the porch and reached for her purse.

"Touché, Miz Connor," he muttered, shoving his hands in the side pockets of his jeans. Then, he smiled, a real smile full of admiration and apology.

"You betcha, Mr. Harrow." Her eyes met his for several moments, as her heartbeat quickened.

The chill had gone from his gaze completely, replaced by something warm and inviting, something that reminded her of the way she'd felt when he'd put his arms around her and held her close. Something so teasing, so tempting that she wanted to go to him and put her head on his shoulder. Something so powerful that it scared the living daylights out of her. She could lose herself in him, lose herself for good and always, if she didn't get away.

"Come on, Christopher, we have to leave." Clutching her purse in both arms, she wheeled around and started toward the car.

He came off the porch in a single bound, catching her arm before she'd taken three steps, stopping her in mid-stride. She halted only because she had no other choice. Anger boiling up inside her, she turned her head and stared at him as she clawed at his hand with her fingers. Her nails were too short to do any damage, his hold on her too tight for her to wiggle free.

"Listen . . . I've been thinking—"

"Obviously a new experience for you," Maggie interrupted in a scathing tone of voice.

"I'll give you a new experience...." His voice low, he took a step closer, pulling her toward him.

"Daddy, I thought you were going to be nice." Elizabeth's soft voice cut through the sudden silence.

"I am being nice," he growled, glancing at his daughter and Maggie's son, standing wide-eyed on the porch, then turning his attention back to Maggie. He took a deep breath, hesitating for a moment before he continued in a gentler tone of voice. "What I'm trying to say is that you can stay if you want to. You can stay for two weeks." He released her arm and took a step back.

Of all the nerve. Offering to allow her to stay on the ranch for two weeks, two weeks she'd paid for in full, in advance. After the way he'd treated her.... "Don't do me any favors, Mr. Harrow." She moved away from him. "Two days of being treated as if I'm diseased is about as much as I can handle, thank you very much." She opened the car door and tossed her purse on the back seat. "Let's go, Christopher."

"But, Mom, he wants us to stay."

"He really does, don't you, Daddy?" Elizabeth chimed in. "And so do I. Please, stay, Maggie, please, please, *please*...."

Maggie stared at her son and Mac's daughter standing side by side on the porch. She didn't have the heart to refuse them, but spending two weeks in the same house with Mackenzie Harrow... Talk about suicidal, or even worse, homicidal. She didn't want to spend the rest of her life in prison.

"I apologize for my behavior the past couple of days. I had no right to act the way I did." Mac stood on the other side of her car. Resting his forearms on the roof, he gazed at her, his eyes steady. "If you agree to stay, I promise I'll mind my p's and q's."

"Why?" she challenged, not quite ready to hear what he was saying.

Because I want you to stay. Because I have to find out if what I felt the other night was real or just a figment of my imagination. Because I've been lonely too long.

"I don't know about you, but I'd hate to disappoint the kids," he said, beating back the thoughts he couldn't speak out loud. Better to use Elizabeth and Christopher as the lure. If she realized how much he wanted her to stay, he had a feeling she'd take off down the road so fast his head would spin.

Her eyes narrowed for a long moment, as if she were trying to ferret out the real reason for his sudden change of heart. He smiled what he could only hope was an encouraging smile, holding her gaze despite the children dancing around them, begging and pleading for a positive response. Finally, after what seemed like a very long time, she nodded her head slightly. A chorus of joyful cheers went up around them.

"All right. We'll stay for two weeks."

She switched off the ignition, retrieved her purse from the back seat and closed the car door. Mac met her at the trunk, took the keys from her hand and opened the lid.

"Okay, you two, how about a little help?" He handed the smaller suitcase to Christopher, the overnight bag to Elizabeth and took the larger suitcase himself. "We'll get you settled in Number Five, then we'll have some breakfast. If I'm not mistaken, Rosa said she was making waffles. Later on, before it gets too warm, I'll take you for a ride. If you want to ride. The horses need the exercise...." He was rattling worse than a handful of loose screws.

Actually he probably *had* a screw loose, asking her to stay on the Whispering Wind for two weeks. Before the time was up, he'd probably regret it. Within a day or so he'd probably be wishing he'd kept his mouth shut and let her go. But not now, not today. Today he wanted to make up for his surly moods, for the angry, hurtful things he'd said and done. Whether he was making a mistake or not, he wanted to erase the past couple of days and start over.

He stopped just inside the doorway of Number Five and set the suitcase on the floor. As the children sidled past him and raced down the hallway, he turned to face her. Standing close to her, he realized once again how small and fragile she was. And fiery, he reminded himself, damned fiery in more ways than one.

From the odd look on her face, he was sure he was grinning like a fool. He was *feeling* like a fool, but suddenly it didn't really matter. All that mattered was that she'd agreed to stay. And he vowed to make her time here as pleasant as possible. It was the least he could do for giving her two days of hell.

"Friends?" Still smiling, he held out his hand, wanting to touch her, wanting to seal their bargain.

"I...guess so." She hesitated a moment, then placed her hand in his. "Are you sure about...this? Are you sure you want us to stay here for two weeks? If you change your mind—"

"I won't change my mind." He tightened his grip, rubbing his thumb over the back of her hand, wanting to dispel the uncertainty lingering in her eyes and voice. "I'm sorry, Maggie. Sorry that I hurt you."

"But you didn't—"

"I promise I won't do it again, not intentionally."

She lowered her gaze, as if she wasn't sure what to say. He didn't blame her. He wasn't sure what else to say himself. In fact, he had the strangest feeling that at this moment actions might speak louder than words. He curled a finger under her chin, lifted her face, bent his head—

"Daddy, come on. Breakfast is ready."

As Elizabeth thundered up the staircase, he straightened. Releasing Maggie, he lowered his hands to his side and stepped away from her. "Guess we'd better..." He gestured toward the stairs where his daughter awaited them.

"Um, yes, we'd better go down." She turned and led the way, her shoulders stiff, her hips swaying gently.

He wanted to walk beside her, wanted to rest a palm on her small, round bottom, wanted to—

"What time are we going riding, Daddy?" Elizabeth gazed at him with huge, innocent eyes.

"You aren't going riding. Not today and not tomorrow. You're going to sit in your room and think about what it means to mind your own business."

"Oh, but please, Daddy—"

"I can add another day for every time you start to argue about it."

She stared at him for a moment, then stamped her foot, whirled around and ran back to the kitchen. Mac shifted his gaze from his daughter's retreating back to Maggie's smiling face as he joined her at the bottom of the stairs.

"I never thought of that," she said, a hint of admiration replacing the wariness in her eyes.

"What?"

"Adding another day for every argument. Of course, knowing my son's penchant for arguing about *everything,* he'd probably end up grounded for life plus twenty years."

As they walked through the swinging doors, Mac nodded in agreement. "I know what you mean, but so far it seems to work. Let me introduce you to Juan and Rosa." He took her hand in his and led her across the kitchen, stopping in front of the elderly couple standing by the counter. "This is my friend, Maggie Connor. She and her son, Christopher, will be staying with us for a couple of weeks. Juan works with the horses and Rosa helps out with the cooking and cleaning."

While Mac filled mugs with steaming coffee, Maggie exchanged greetings with the elderly couple. The glimmer of approval in their dark eyes and their warm, welcoming smiles touched her in a way she couldn't quite describe. For the first time in days, she didn't feel quite so...unwanted. And if they didn't mind that she and her son were staying on the ranch, she could always hope that maybe Mac wouldn't mind so much, either.

Had it not been for Elizabeth and Christopher, Maggie had no doubt that she'd be halfway to San Antonio by now. No matter what he said or did, she knew that Mac didn't want her on the ranch. He had been coerced into offering her an invitation to stay, just as she had been coerced into accepting it. Now, like it or not, they were stuck with each other for two weeks, and to keep their children happy, they'd have to make the best of it. They'd have to be reasonably nice to each other when the kids were present. And when they weren't...

Maggie thought of the moments they'd been together in the hallway. His voice had been soft and gentle, his hand holding hers hard and warm as he promised not to hurt her. She didn't doubt his sincerity for a moment. Nor did she doubt that it was as much her responsibility as his to make sure she wasn't hurt. Knowing what she did about Mackenzie Harrow, and aware of her growing attraction to him, it might be wise to stay away from him.

Had they not been interrupted, he would have kissed her and she would have let him and it would have been a foolish thing for them to do. Neither one of them was the type to engage in casual sex. Nor was either of them ready to commit to a more permanent relationship. Mac was still mourning his wife. And she wasn't ready to give up her independence for any man.

"Earth to Mom, earth to Mom...."

"Um, sorry. What...?"

"Here's your coffee. Just black, right?" Mac offered her a white china mug.

Smiling at the quizzical look in his eyes, Maggie accepted it gratefully. "Can I help with anything?" she asked, turning to Rosa.

"I have breakfast ready. You sit down and eat. Do you like waffles?"

"Love them." She slid into a chair at the table and took a sip of her coffee.

She knew what she had to do to make the best of the next two weeks, and she would do it. When the children were around she would enjoy Mac's company. And when they weren't, she'd make a special effort to avoid him. If they weren't alone together, if they couldn't give in to their physical needs and desires, neither of them would be a threat to what the other cherished most. And maybe at the end of two weeks, they really would be friends....

"This looks wonderful." Picking up her fork, Maggie dug into the plate of food Rosa set in front of her. Then, turning to Mac, she widened her smile. "Christopher and I would love to go for a ride. What time do you want us to meet you at the barn?"

Maggie found that it was surprisingly easy to avoid being alone with Mac, at least for the two days Elizabeth spent in her room. Since his new friend was unavailable, Christopher didn't seem to mind her constant presence. They hiked together in the low hills surrounding the ranch and swam in the large, L-shaped swimming pool, enjoying the hot, sunny weather. They played board games and table tennis and the player piano. And although he'd been less than enthusiastic about his first horseback ride, Mac had made the experience such a good one that her son willingly agreed to go again on Tuesday.

For his part, Mac seemed just as eager as Maggie to put some distance between them. Except for their rides and meals, she saw very little of him. When she did, he was usually working with one of the horses in the big corral by the barn. He did make an effort to sit with them in the living room for an hour or so in the evening after dinner, but aside from exchanging a few sentences, they mostly just watched television.

By Wednesday morning Maggie had begun to relax. Unfortunately she had forgotten about Elizabeth and how the two-to-one balance would change once the girl was allowed to leave her room again. She had also forgotten that two eleven-year-old children neither wanted nor needed full-time adult supervision. They had schemes and dreams of their own to pursue, places to go and things to do, and they wouldn't automatically include her in their adventures.

She was reminded of those painful truths as they guided their horses down the narrow dirt road that led to a small, secluded park about a mile from the ranch. Laughing and chattering, as if they'd been separated for years rather than days, Christopher and Elizabeth kicked their mounts into a gentle trot, taking the lead, leaving the adults several hundred yards behind. Though they weren't completely alone, it was the closest they'd been to it in several days, Maggie thought. And Mac didn't seem inclined to quicken their pace enough to catch up with the kids. In fact, Maggie had a sneaking suspicion he was holding his horse back, allowing the distance between them and the children to lengthen even more.

"Maybe we ought to ride a little faster," she suggested, glancing up at him.

"Why?" He met her gaze, his eyes steady. The brim of his Stetson shaded his face, making it impossible for her to read his expression.

"The kids..." She lifted one shoulder in a casual shrug as she focused her attention on the top of her horse's head.

"They're fine. They've got a lot of energy to burn. And Elizabeth knows her way around here almost as well as I do. They won't get lost. I thought you might want to take it easy again today. Still sore?"

Responding to the gentle note of teasing in his voice, she smiled and shook her head. "Just a little," she admitted. "Not as bad as yesterday, though. You were right about soaking in a hot tub of water. It really helped."

"Usually does."

They rode in silence for several minutes, the muffled clop and click of their horses' hooves blending with the drift of their children's voices. Maggie tipped her face up and closed her eyes for a moment, savoring the warmth of the sun on her skin, a warmth gentled by the lingering coolness of the morning breeze that whispered through the oak trees lining the road.

"The whispering wind," she murmured. "I wondered where you got the name."

"You can hear it early in the morning and late in the evening. It was one of the things my great-grandmother liked best about the place—the wind in the trees."

"I like it, too. And I like the wide-open spaces, the rugged landscape. It's so beautiful here, so very, very beautiful...."

"Don't romanticize it, Maggie. It's also a lot of work, hard work. A ranch takes everything you've got to give and then it asks for more."

The sudden roughness in his tone of voice surprised her. She glanced up at him, wondering if she'd angered him again. Since he wouldn't meet her gaze, she wasn't sure.

"Have you always lived here?" she asked after several moments of silence. After his last comment, she was more curious than ever about Mac and his relationship with the ranch. He seemed to love the place and yet, according to his daughter, he was determined to sell it at the end of the summer. Was it because he'd given it all he had to give?

"Always, except for a few years when I went to college in Austin, then worked for a company in Dallas. We'd probably still be in Dallas, if my parents hadn't been killed in an automobile accident. They were on their way home from a cattle auction. I thought about selling the place then, but Jo wanted to live here and I let her talk me into it."

"I'm sorry." She heard the note of bitterness and self-recrimination in his voice, and cursed herself for carelessly probing wounds that hadn't healed.

"It was a long time ago. I made my choice and I've lived with it." He paused for a moment, then continued, quickly changing the subject, giving in to his own curiosity about Miz Maggie Connor. "What about you? Have you always lived in San Antonio?"

They hadn't really talked to each other until now, and there were things he wanted to know about her. Questions needed to be asked and answered if he was ever to get a good night's sleep again. Questions he'd never have a chance to ask if she kept avoiding him as religiously as she'd done the past two days.

She had been giving him a taste of his own medicine, but he didn't think she had been doing it out of spite. She didn't seem like that kind of woman. Nor did she seem like the kind of woman who started something she didn't intend to finish. And she had to know exactly what they'd started the other night when he'd held her in his arms. Had it been nothing more than a weak moment for her? Or had she given in to loneliness and longing, the same loneliness and longing that had been eating him alive lately?

"I lived in Houston most of my life. But after Mitch died, I had to... get away, so Christopher and I moved to San Antonio."

"Running from the law?"

"In a way." She shrugged, keeping her eyes on the road ahead. "It's a long story."

He glanced at her for a moment, the rueful smile tugging at the corners of her mouth tugging at something deep inside of him as well. The thought of her running from anything or anybody bothered him more than he liked to admit. And more than ever he wanted to know what made Maggie Connor tick.

"Why don't we stop for a while? You can tell me all about it." He nodded toward a cluster of wooden picnic tables tucked under a stand of ancient oak trees where Elizabeth and Christopher had left their horses to explore a shallow cave nearby.

"It's an awfully dull story, especially if I begin at the beginning," Maggie advised as she slid from the saddle. "Are you sure you want to hear it?"

"All of it." Offering her one of the cans of juice he'd pulled from his saddlebags, he sat beside her on a bench.

"Well, then, don't say I didn't warn you." She smiled slightly as she sipped her drink. Then, taking a deep breath, she did as he'd asked.

"My parents were in their late twenties when I was born. They'd given up on ever having a child of their own. It was one thing my father's money couldn't buy. Then I came along. I was their miracle child. Not only did they give me all their love, they gave me everything else I could have wanted—clothes, toys, pets, private schools. I might have ended up spoiled rotten, but my father had rules he expected me to obey and standards he demanded I meet. Because I loved them, loved *him,* and because I wanted to make them happy, I lived up to his expectations. We had our arguments. I wanted to go away to college...." Her voice drifted away for a moment. "But in the end, I always did what he wanted. I knew that he only wanted what he thought was best for me, and I wanted to please him so much.

"When I was twenty, he had a mild heart attack. It scared all of us, but him most of all. And even though the doctor pronounced him fit as a fiddle after he had bypass surgery, he was determined to do something to guarantee my future. He introduced me to Mitchell Connor, one of the up-and-coming young executives in his oil company. Less than a year later, I quit school and Mitch and I were married."

"Did you love him?" Mac stared at her, trying to analyze the odd play of emotions that lightened, then darkened her bright blue eyes as he barely resisted the urge to put his arm around her. He could only begin to imagine how many of her own dreams and desires she'd given up to please her parents. Anger flared inside him when he thought of her marrying a man she didn't care for, to gain her father's approval.

"Of course," she replied, turning to face him, her eyes wide with surprise as she met his probing gaze. "He was a very attractive, eligible bachelor and his family was wealthy, so he wasn't after my father's money. He was twelve years older than I, but I'd grown up surrounded by adults so the age difference really didn't matter. He was a wonderful man and he was good to me and we had Christopher. He worked hard, too hard sometimes, but we had fun together, too. I would have gladly lived the rest of my life with him. But one night we went to bed and the next morning he didn't wake up. During the night a blood vessel burst in his brain, and he just ... just died...."

Giving in at last, he put his arm around her shoulders, watching her out of the corner of his eye as they sat in silence for several moments. She didn't seem nearly as surprised as he was by his sudden show of tenderness. Neither did she pull away. She simply sat and stared at something off in the distance.

"So you went to San Antonio after your husband died?" he asked after a while, his voice unusually rough and low.

"I hadn't planned to do it. But a few months after Mitch . . ." She shrugged and shook her head, a wry smile lifting one corner of her mouth. "My father invited Christopher and me to dinner. It was supposed to be a quiet evening at their house. Shortly after we arrived, the doorbell rang. It was another rising young executive from Chase Oil come to join us. I had no doubt about what was going on. Something in me . . . snapped. I was thirty-two years old and what I wanted was a life of my own, not another husband.

"I'll spare you the gory details of the arguments that followed, but two months later Christopher and I went to San Antonio. Luckily I could afford to buy a house and take the time to finish college. Then I got a teaching job at the neighborhood elementary school."

"How did your folks handle it?"

"Not very well, at first. But after three years, I think they've begun to understand and to let go a little. They'd still prefer to see me married, but I can't see it happening anytime soon."

"Why not? I thought you said you were happily married."

"I was, but I've lived on my own for three years now and it's been good, too. I can take care of myself and my son, and I don't have to answer to anyone but me." She turned to look at him, her eyes steady. "You were happy here with Jo, weren't you? But you haven't remarried. In fact, you've decided to sell the ranch, move to Dallas and start a new life. If you think about it, you'll realize we're really a lot alike.''

"How do you know what I'm going to do?" he asked, moving his arm away from her as he averted his eyes and rested his elbows on the table.

"Elizabeth told me." Standing up, she brushed the seat of her jeans. "Speaking of your daughter, not to mention my son, I think I'll take a little walk and see if I can find them. Want to come?"

"Follow that trail up the hill. They're probably in the cave about halfway up and to the left. Tell them I'm ready to head back. I'll wait for you here." He stretched his legs out in front of him and tipped his hat down over his eyes. From beneath his lowered lashes he saw her hesitate, a faint frown marring her brow. For just a moment she looked as if she might say something more, but she didn't. She turned on her heel and walked away.

As he watched her weave her way among the shaded tables, then move out into the sunlight, he thought of all she'd told him about herself. It hadn't been exactly what he'd wanted to hear. She wasn't man-hungry or husband-hunting, that was for sure. In fact, she didn't want a man, *any* man, in her life in any way, shape or form. And that was fine with him, because he didn't want a woman, *any* woman, in his life. At least not on a permanent basis.

So why had her vow of independence hit him like a smack in the chops? Why would he have preferred to hear her longing for someone, *anyone,* to take Mitchell Connor's place? Because something had happened between them the other night, and he wanted her to admit it. But why? So he could run the other way? It would certainly be the wisest thing to do.

He wasn't the type to settle for anything less than a permanent relationship, and that was the one thing neither of them wanted or needed right now. Getting tangled up with her would only lead to heartache. He knew it in his head, he could feel it in his bones. Ten days... Ten days and she'd be gone. Could he make it that long without touching her, holding her, kissing her? He'd have to, for her sake as well as his. Because if he touched her, if he held her in his arms, if he kissed her—

"Daddy, wake up. Maggie said you were ready to go."

Elizabeth hopped on the bench beside him, jarring him out of his reverie not a moment too soon. A few more minutes of fantasizing about Miz Connor, and a horseback ride back to the house would have been one very painful experience. As it was, his jeans were already a tad tighter than they'd been an hour earlier.

"We better hit the trail. I told Rosa we'd be back for lunch and it's almost eleven-thirty."

He pushed back his hat and stood up, his gaze going to Maggie where she waited beside her horse. She offered him a wide, sweet smile as she swung into the saddle. He groaned silently as his body responded with a will of its own. One very painful experience coming right up. He groaned again as he settled into his saddle. He hated puns.

Holding his horse back, he waited while Elizabeth and Christopher started down the road toward the ranch. Would Maggie ride with him or with them? He half hoped, half feared that she'd choose him. She didn't. She kicked her horse into a gentle lope, joining the children without a backward glance, leaving him to eat her dust. Avoiding him as he should avoid her for the next ten days.

"I'll be damned if I do," he muttered, nudging his horse forward at a walk. He had ten days. And he planned to make the most of them.

Chapter Six

"You've been avoiding me. Why? Scared I might bite?"

Though she was half asleep, Maggie had no doubt who was questioning her. Mentally cursing herself for dozing on the chaise lounge she'd moved to a shady spot near the pool, she blinked her eyes open. Where was he? And, more importantly, where were her chaperones, Christopher and Elizabeth?

Lying on her stomach, with her head propped on her folded arms and her face turned to one side, she viewed the wide expanse of lawn rolling away from the house. The whole place appeared to be deserted. And except for the gentle early evening breeze riffling through the leaves of the nearby oak tree and the occasional twitter of a bird, all was quiet. Maybe she'd been dream—

The chaise lounge shifted under her as he sat on the far side. The fabric of his worn jeans brushed against her bare leg. A moment later he leaned over her, resting one palm on the cushion just inches from her left hip. He smelled of hard work and horses, not an unpleasant combination at all. And he was warm, wonderfully warm. She could feel the heat radiating from his body through the thin fabric of her modest royal blue one-piece bathing suit.

"Playing possum, Miz Maggie?"

"No, I'm not playing possum, Mr. Harrow. And I'm not scared of you, either." Nudged into action by the teasing tone of his voice, she rolled onto her back and met his gaze for a moment. Then, averting her eyes, she quickly scanned the pool area, searching for the children.

They were nowhere to be found. How had they managed to slip away without a sound? She must have been more tired than she realized, to fall so deeply asleep. And now, without them around to act as a buffer, she felt completely... vulnerable.

She had stuck to them like glue for the past couple of days, ever since Mac had begun to look at her with more than a hint of interest in his pale gray eyes. Some strange sixth sense had warned her that he was biding his time, waiting to get her alone. But why? She had a feeling she was about to find out, whether she wanted to or not.

He had her trapped, flat on her back, between the length of one denim-clad thigh and one broad hand and bare forearm. Between a rock and hard place, she thought, barely restraining the urge to smile. That might encourage him, and the one thing he didn't need right now was encouragement. Not looming over her the way he was, his chambray shirt unbuttoned almost to his waist, his Stetson tipped low on his forehead.

He had a dangerous look about him, the kind he'd had the night they'd arrived. Yet she'd told the truth when she'd told him she wasn't afraid. Fear wasn't at all what she was feeling. What she was feeling was more like... anticipation.

"They're gone."

"Who?" she asked, her voice low. She had been staring at his bare chest, the curve of his jaw, the almost smiling slant of his mouth. For just an instant she had no idea who he was talking about.

"Your son and my daughter."

"Oh." That's right. She'd been looking for them before she got . . . distracted. Levering herself up on her elbows, careful not to get any closer to him than she already was, she focused on a point somewhere over his left shoulder. "Where did they go? Back to the house?"

"Yes."

"I'd better go back, too. I promised them I'd fix burgers and fries for dinner, and it's getting late."

Rosa had gone to Corpus Christi for the weekend to visit her youngest daughter, who was expecting her first baby in August. Maggie had assured the older woman that she didn't mind taking care of meals for a few days. And she didn't. Not when it gave her an excuse to get away gracefully. Which she could do only if he moved.

She eyed her white shorts and lemon yellow shirt lying on the ground beside the chaise. She'd have to sit up and swing her legs over the side to get to her clothes. And she could do neither as long as Mac stayed where he was. Unfortunately he didn't seem the least bit inclined to move.

"It's not that late."

"Late enough. What time is it, anyway?"

Mac turned his head, squinting his eyes as he studied the distance between the lowering sun and the western horizon. "About six-thirty, maybe seven."

"Oh, well, then I really should—"

He nailed her with his eyes, stilling her fussing and fidgeting with one long look. "You're avoiding me," he repeated. "I want to know why."

"Because I thought that's the way you wanted it. You made it clear from the very beginning—"

"Is that the way *you* want it, Maggie?"

"It doesn't matter what I want. I'm staying in *your* house. It's up to me to play by *your* rules to keep the peace, and that's what I've been trying to do. You know as well as I do that you didn't ask us to stay so you and I could spend time together. You didn't even want us here in the first place." She glared at him in exasperation, her limited patience at an end. Resting all of her weight on one elbow, she pushed against his chest with her hand. "Will you please let me off this damned chair?"

Before she had time to pull away, he covered her hand with his, holding it still, his eyes steady as he met her gaze. He didn't say a word, but she could feel the thump, thump, thump of his heart beneath her palm. Each beat stole a little of her thunder until it was all but gone, and still the silence stretched between them.

"Mac, please, let me go," she asked at last, her voice barely above a whisper.

He held her gaze a moment longer, then released her hand. Moving away from her, he stood up, shoved his hands into the back pockets of his jeans and turned his attention to a crack in the concrete pool deck. Maggie scrambled to her feet, grabbed her clothes and began to pull on her shorts and shirt, more anxious than ever to get back to the relative safety of the house.

"I admit I didn't give you the warmest welcome," Mac muttered, still staring at the ground. "But I apologized for my bad behavior Monday morning. I thought..." He shrugged one shoulder as he tipped his head up to look at her. "I thought we agreed to try to be friends. Friends usually spend some time together."

Maggie paused in the act of tying her shirttails into a knot at her waist. "We have spent time together." She finished with her shirt, then bent down to retrieve the book she hadn't opened. "We've ridden every day and we see each other at meals and for a while in the evening. Considering how busy you've been with the horses, I didn't think you'd appreciate my intruding on your free time anymore than that." She hesitated for a moment, then placed a hand on his arm. "I don't mind hanging out with the kids. That's why I'm here—to keep them happy."

Before he could stop her, she turned away, walking quickly toward the house. He caught up with her in three long strides, falling into step beside her.

"I didn't ask you to stay on the ranch to baby-sit my kid," he growled, a trace of anger in his voice.

"I'm not saying you did."

"Then what are you saying?"

"That you invited us to stay to please your daughter. I don't have any quarrel with that, because I'm here to please my son. So, we're even. Right?"

Not waiting for a reply, she opened the kitchen door, leading the way into the dark, quiet room. As she reached for the light switch, the door closed and Mac caught her hand. Spinning her around, he drew her toward him. He took off his hat and tossed it on the counter.

"Wrong . . ."

He bent his head and covered her mouth with his so quickly, so completely that he took her breath away. Her lips parted in surprise and an instant later his tongue curled against hers. She closed her eyes, leaning into him as he wrapped his arms around her. With a soft sound somewhere between a sigh and a moan, she buried her fingers in the shaggy hair at the nape of his neck, savoring his taste as he pulled her closer until the soft, worn fabric of his jeans brushed against her bare legs.

She should do something to stop him, to force him to let her go. He hadn't asked to kiss her, he'd simply done it. But she couldn't have pushed him away if her life depended on it. There was something so tender about the way he touched her, something so incredibly gentle beneath the fierce possessiveness of his kiss. Something she hadn't realized she needed until the moment he gave it to her. Knotting her fingers in his hair, she arched against him as heat and hunger flared through her body.

As suddenly as the kiss had begun, it ended. Much too soon for Maggie, Mac raised his head, moved his hands to her shoulders and took a step back. She wanted to protest, but only for an instant. Then common sense returned with a vengeance, warning her not to say or do anything stupid. Silently she met his steady gaze, waiting for him to speak.

"I asked you to stay on the ranch because *I* wanted you to stay."

"Why?" she asked, genuine curiosity in her soft voice.

"I...I'm not really sure." He squeezed her shoulders gently, then let her go. "Something happened between us the other night during the storm. And just now..."

He'd felt it, too, she thought. It hadn't been her imagination. But neither of them was ready for it. No matter what they said or did, they simply weren't ready.

"I know what you mean," she admitted, wanting him to know that he wasn't alone in his thoughts and feelings. "However, I don't think it would be wise for either one of us to get...involved with...anyone...now."

"I didn't say anything about getting involved, Maggie. But you're going to be here for another week. Why can't we just relax and try to enjoy the time we have left together?"

"But the kids...I don't want them to get the idea that we're...we're—"

"We're what? Friends? Nothing wrong with that. But we're also adults and we're entitled to some privacy. What we do if and when we're alone together shouldn't affect them."

"Oh, Mac, I don't think—"

"I'm not going to ask you to do anything you don't want to do. I'm not going to do anything to hurt you, and I'm certainly not going to do anything to hurt Christopher and Elizabeth. But damn it, Maggie, I want to be with you. Don't shut me out the way you've been doing. I have feelings, too. And I get lonely sometimes. Don't you get lonely, too?"

The sincerity she saw in his eyes and heard in his voice touched her deeply. He wasn't asking for much. Just to be with her on her terms on a temporary basis. How could she deny him? She couldn't, she *wouldn't*. It was as simple as that. Or was it? If it was so simple, why did she suddenly feel so shaky inside?

Unable to meet his questioning gaze any longer, she turned away from him and walked across the kitchen. Stopping by the table, she wrapped her hands around a chair back, hanging on to it as if for dear life. It wasn't that she didn't trust him. He had promised not to hurt her, and she knew enough about him now to know that he wouldn't. Maybe it was herself she didn't trust. It would be so easy to care about Mackenzie Harrow. And she didn't want to care about him any more than she already did. She didn't want to give him that much power over her, not now, not ever. Yet when all was said and done, she didn't have the heart to refuse his request.

"Yes," she admitted at last. "I get lonely, too." She hesitated a moment, then let go of the chair and turned to face him.

He met her gaze but didn't speak. Nor did he smile. He simply nodded his head once, as if to seal a bargain.

Releasing the breath she'd been holding, Maggie headed for the refrigerator. "If you switch on the light, I'll get started on the burgers. Do you want to put them on the grill or should I pop them under the broiler?" Glancing at Mac over the refrigerator door, Maggie blinked in the sudden brightness.

"I'll put them on the grill." He turned to go back outside but paused with his hand on the doorknob. "Um, I was wondering...do you have any plans for tomorrow?"

"Nothing special."

"I thought maybe the four of us could take a ride to Fredricksburg. Actually, Elizabeth suggested it. But if you'd rather go somewhere—"

"I love Fredricksburg, and we haven't been there in over a year. It would be a lot of fun."

"What would be a lot of fun?" Christopher and Elizabeth asked in unison as they bounced through the swinging doors.

"Fredricksburg," Mac replied.

"Are we going there tomorrow, Daddy? Are we, are we?"

"Yes."

"All of us?"

"All of us," Maggie assured her as she set a package of ground beef on the counter. "Now why don't you help me with the burgers so we can eat before midnight."

"And you can help me get the grill started, Christopher. Unless you want to hang around with the ladies."

"Oh, no sir. I'd rather go with you."

For no longer than a heartbeat or two, the two adults gazed at each other. Then they smiled. And then they turned away.

"Oh, Daddy, you look so cool."

"Think so, Lizzie Beth?"

Mac stared at himself in the full-length mirror on the bathroom door. He'd shucked his usual attire of faded jeans, boots and a work shirt for something a little more...young, urban professional. He couldn't quite believe he *looked* cool in a pair of tailored white shorts, a navy blue knit shirt and leather deck shoes, but he knew he'd *be* a hell of a lot cooler walking around Fredricksburg in the casual clothing than he would be in jeans and boots.

He also had to admit that he wanted Maggie to see him as something more than an unsophisticated country bumpkin. He wasn't ashamed of being a hardworking rancher, nor did he have any intention of pretending to be something he wasn't. But it couldn't hurt to let her know there was more to him than normally met the eye. Like a nice pair of legs, he thought, grinning with masculine pride as he took one last look at himself before turning away from the mirror.

"Do I look okay?" Elizabeth asked, spinning around in front of him.

"You look better than okay, sweetheart." Dressed in pink shorts and a pink-and-white checked blouse, her long, dark hair tied back with a narrow pink ribbon, she looked more like a young lady than the rough-and-tumble tomboy she often pretended to be. However, Mac didn't dare tell her that. "Think Christopher will like the new you?"

"Daddy!" She glared at him for a moment, then matched his teasing grin with one of her own. "Think Maggie will like the new *you?*"

"I hope so," he replied, more seriously than he'd intended.

"Me, too." For a moment her smile faded. Then, her spirits rising again, she turned away from him and started down the hallway. "Come on, Daddy. They're probably waiting for us downstairs."

He let her go on ahead of him, hesitating for one long moment while he wondered for the umpteenth time what exactly he was doing. Probably making a damned fool of himself. Whether it was one extreme or another, that was all he'd seemed able to do since Maggie Connor blew into his life. He'd been angered, then enticed by her all within the space of a week and without any encouragement from her. And now not only had he committed himself to spending a day with her, he was actually looking forward to it.

"Like a crazy kid," he muttered, as he started down the stairway. Just as he'd felt yesterday after he kissed her. Just as he'd felt last night when she'd lingered in the living room long past her usual hour to do so.

They hadn't said much to each other and, of course, the kids had been there, too. But she hadn't seemed quite so tense and standoffish as she had the previous few evenings. And when she'd finally said good-night, she'd said it with a warm, sweet smile. Just like the one with which she greeted him as he walked into the kitchen. Assuring him that he'd been right to confront her with his thoughts and feelings. Assuring him that she wanted this special day together as much as he.

And it was a special day, the kind of day he'd never forget despite the lingering uncertainty in Maggie's eyes and the occasional hesitation in her voice. She wasn't quite sure of him yet, and he couldn't blame her. But he could go all out to reassure her that the ogre was gone for good. He could and he did.

As agreed the night before, they stopped for breakfast at a little café in Bandera, then headed north toward Fredricksburg. Maggie insisted that they take her car because it was more comfortable than Mac's pickup truck. She also insisted that he drive, which gave him the opportunity to put the sporty foreign car through its paces on the winding back roads to his heart's content. Needless to say, they made the hour's drive in something less, with Mac as well as Maggie thanking their lucky stars that the state patrol obviously prowled another stretch of highway on Saturday mornings.

The old German town had been reborn within the past few years. Most of the buildings along the main street had been renovated and now housed a variety of shops, antique stores and restaurants that catered to the myriad tourists who flocked there year-round for a special taste of Texas. Several historic homes had been restored and reopened as bed-and-breakfast hotels, and the Nimitz Museum, devoted to World War II memorabilia, was housed in a large building on a quiet street corner.

After a quick conference, they decided to park near the museum, start there, then walk up one side of the main street and down the other, stopping for lunch whenever they were ready. It was late afternoon by the time they turned down the street where they'd parked the car, and if Mac had learned anything by then, it was that Maggie loved to shop. Not just shop—*buy*.

He groaned silently under the burden of packages she'd piled into his arms along the way. She hadn't spent a lot of money, and of that, she'd spent very little on herself, yet she'd had such fun doing it. And he'd had fun watching her.

She'd bought chocolate chip cookies at one bakery, peanut butter cookies at another. She'd bought books and magazines for herself and the children at the bookstore. She'd bought a linen blouse with a fine lace collar for her mother and a gaudy brass belt buckle with "Boss Man" emblazoned across it for her father. And she'd bought candles to replace the ones they'd used the previous night at dinner, much to Christopher and Elizabeth's delight. Thank God they hadn't come in the truck, or she probably wouldn't have stopped buying when she did.

"Oh, Daddy, look—puppies," Elizabeth squealed.

She ran past the car, Christopher at her heels, and turned into the driveway of a house half a block ahead. A woman sat on a lawn chair under an umbrella next to a small wire pen with a "Puppies For Sale" sign tipped against it.

"They're beautiful. Come and see them," she called as Mac and Maggie stopped by the car.

"You, too, Mom. There are two of them. One for each of us."

Mac groaned again as Maggie took the car keys from him and unlocked the trunk. He had promised Elizabeth a new puppy almost two years ago when Nellie died. But then Jo had gotten sick, and somehow he'd never gotten around to it. Probably because Nellie had been Jo's dog and he'd never had the heart to replace her.

"I think we'd better decide about the puppies before we join them." Maggie lifted the packages out of Mac's arms and set them in the trunk.

"What?" Frowning slightly, Mac glanced at her as he closed the lid.

"The puppies, Mac. I promised Christopher he could have one this summer. If you get one for Elizabeth, I'll have to get one for him. But if you don't, I can put him off until we get back to San Antonio."

"I promised Elizabeth one, too. It's been a couple of years since our old dog died." He hesitated for a moment, then took her by the arm and started up the sidewalk. "Might as well take a look. If they're healthy—"

"And not too big..."

"We're a couple of pushovers, aren't we, Miz Connor?" He traded smiles with her, as he took her hand in his.

"We are, indeed, Mr. Harrow," she replied, squeezing his fingers once before she turned her face away.

Fifteen minutes later they were on their way back to the ranch, each child holding a four-month-old Australian shepherd puppy, a red-and-white female for Elizabeth and a merle male for Christopher.

"I hope they don't get carsick." Mac glanced at Maggie out of the corner of his eye.

"Carsick? Oh, no..." Maggie swung around in her seat. So far they seemed to be all right. In fact, they were busy gnawing on each other and their respective owners with great enthusiasm. Too busy to be sick. "Don't let them chew on the upholstery, okay?"

"Okay, Mom."

"Have you thought of any names yet?" she asked, facing forward again.

"How about Nellie, like Momma's dog? She doesn't look like—"

"How about something else, Elizabeth?" Mac advised, his voice rough and low as he tightened his fingers on the steering wheel. Maggie turned to look at him, but he kept his eyes on the road.

"How about Bonnie and Clyde?" Maggie suggested after several seconds of silence. Her tone light and teasing, she directed her attention to the two in the back seat. "I have a feeling those pups are going to grow up to be a couple of outlaws."

"Hey, neat, Mom. What do you think, Elizabeth?"

"Yeah, neat."

"But mine's Clyde."

"And mine's Bonnie."

They finished the rest of the drive in relative peace and quiet. Mac stopped at the grocery store in Bandera to pick up a sack of dog food, leaving Maggie in the car to supervise the kids and pets. As he started the car a few minutes later, Maggie turned to him.

"What is that place over there across the street? I didn't notice it when we drove through town earlier."

Mac followed the direction of her pointing finger, his gaze settling on an old building with a Wild West facade and a pink neon sign in the window. "Blue Coot's Saloon? It's a bar and country-western dance hall."

"It looks kind of . . . interesting."

"Oh, it is. Gets pretty rowdy on a Saturday night, too." Mac turned to look at her, a wicked grin lifting the corners of his mouth. "We could come back later and check it out.

The owner is a friend of mine. We went to high school together.''

"What about . . . ?'' She tipped her head toward the back seat.

"Oh, yeah. I forgot that Juan and Rosa are gone this weekend. Maybe we could stop in next Saturday night, before you go back to San Antonio.''

"Sure, why not?'' She lifted one shoulder in a casual shrug as she turned to stare out the side window of the car. "You know, if you wanted, you could go tonight. I wouldn't mind staying with the kids.''

"I don't think so.''

"Would you mind if I went there by myself?''

Mac turned and stared at her for several seconds, wondering whether or not she was serious. But the way she was sitting, he couldn't see her face, and the tone of her voice had been undeniably neutral. He couldn't think of anything he would mind more, but he had a feeling that saying so wouldn't be wise. She was used to being on her own, used to doing what she wanted when she wanted. Who was he to try to set limits on her behavior? If she decided to go to Blue Coot's tonight, however, he had every intention of doing his best to dissuade her.

"If that's what you want to do, it's fine with me. I'll be here for the kids,'' he replied, his tone of voice as neutral as hers had been as he guided the car onto the dirt road that led to the ranch.

"I don't think so. I'm sort of tired. And it wouldn't be much fun to go alone, would it?'' She flashed a quick grin as he stopped in front of the gate. Then she hopped out to open it, without waiting for his reply.

He watched her walk up the road, remove the chain and swing the gate out of the way, the skirt of her simple white sundress swishing against her bare legs. In a way, he was relieved that she didn't want to go out alone. But in another way, he was disappointed. He'd already begun to think of ways to divert her, very interesting ways. Now he wouldn't have any excuse to use them. And unfortunately he was still at a time and place in his life when there were certain things he wasn't quite ready to do without a good excuse.

Maggie sat at the kitchen table, her chin propped in one hand, drumming her fingers on the wooden surface as she stared into space. It was late Sunday afternoon and she was bored and restless and . . . and lonely. Frowning, she leaned back in her chair and crossed her arms over her chest. What was the matter with her? She couldn't expect a three-ring circus everyday. But yesterday had been such fun, and today she'd been deserted by one and all.

After a day away, Mac had work to do. And Elizabeth and Christopher had taken the puppies for a walk, obviously a long all-day walk. She pushed away from the table and stood up. She ought to be grateful for the time alone. She could read or swim or simply sit in a shady spot by the pool. But she really didn't want to be alone.

Wandering around the kitchen, she trailed a finger over the countertops, stopping for a long moment by the row of cookbooks. Jo's cookbooks . . . Jo's house . . . Jo's husband, dressed in white shorts and navy blue shirt, looking good enough to— She pulled her hand back, spun on her heel and headed for the swinging doors.

She crossed the dining room quickly and stepped into the wide, empty living room. She had been staying in Jo's house with Jo's husband for over a week, yet she knew nothing about the woman. And it was beginning to bother her. If only she could see a picture of the woman, she thought, scanning the bookshelves and the wide mantel above the fireplace.

But there were no pictures, not down here. He probably kept them upstairs in their private quarters. And private was private. She couldn't go up there without an invitation, which she didn't think he'd ever offer. Just as he hadn't offered any real information about the years he'd spent on the Whispering Wind with his wife and daughter. He hadn't wanted to talk about it, though he'd probed her past to his heart's content.

Well, fair was fair, she thought, as she turned toward the side door. There were things she wanted to know, things she needed to know. Because he'd kissed her again last night when they met in the hallway just after dinner. A long, slow, deep kiss that had left her wanting more as she watched him walk up the steps to the third floor. But what more could she have with him in the few days they had left together?

Something was happening between them. Something was drawing them together. Yet something, *someone,* was keeping them apart. As long as Mac refused to talk about her, as long as he refused to accept the fact that she was dead, *Jo* would keep them apart.

The afternoon sun beat down on her as she crossed the distance between the house and the barn, but inside the long, wide building it was pleasantly cool. Most of the horses had been turned out early in the morning, but the few who remained in their stalls greeted her with soft whickers, poking their velvety noses at her as she walked down the aisle separating one row from the other. In the stillness she could hear the whir of the window air conditioner in his office at the opposite end. That was where she knew she'd find him. Hadn't he said something about catching up on paperwork?

She tapped on the closed door without hesitation, opening it when he called to her to come in. He shifted his gaze from the ledger on the desk to her and started to smile. But the look on her face must have warned him, because his smile faded fast.

"What's wrong, Maggie? Are the kids all right?" He pushed away from the desk, stood up and took a step toward her.

"The kids are fine." She closed the door, then leaned her back against it, pausing for a moment as her eyes adjusted to the bright, fluorescent light.

The small, square room carved from a back corner of the barn was filled to overflowing. A battered wooden desk, covered with books and papers, and a couple of chairs had been shoved against one wall. Two tall metal filing cabinets stood on either side of the window, channeling the flow of the air conditioner straight ahead. An odd assortment of bridles and halters and what appeared to be a medicine cabinet hung on another wall above a huge, old trunk.

"I just...just wanted to talk to you. If you're not too busy."

"Just clearing up some odds and ends and waiting for a phone call. Come on, sit down." He moved a stack of catalogs off the extra chair, then rested a hip on the edge of his desk as she sat. "What do you want to talk about?"

She took a deep breath, staring at her fingers as she twisted them together in her lap. Suddenly she wasn't quite so sure about confronting him. Maybe she'd be better off minding her own business. Maybe she'd be better off packing her bags and going back to San Antonio. Maybe she ought to forget about how good it felt to have his arms around her, his lips kissing her. Maybe... She raised her eyes, meeting Mac's questioning gaze as her heart beat a little faster. Maybe she shouldn't run away, after all.

"I want to talk about Jo," she said, her voice soft but steady.

His eyes widened with surprise, then narrowed as he turned away from her and started sorting through the papers on his desk. "Jo's dead." He offered the simple statement in a flat tone of voice.

"Is she?" she asked. When he didn't reply, she continued. "How did you meet her?"

"We met at the university in Austin."

"She didn't live in Bandera?"

"She lived in Dallas."

It was like pulling teeth, but Maggie refused to give up. Although he wouldn't look at her, he was answering her questions. And though he continued to stand by the desk, he'd given up any pretext of sorting papers.

"When were you married?"

"Just after graduation. Both of us had gotten job offers with different companies in Dallas. We found a little apartment in a nice neighborhood...."

As if he couldn't stop once he'd started, Mac paused for just an instant, then continued, his voice so matter-of-fact that he might have been relating a stranger's personal history rather than his own. He told her about the early years of their marriage, his job with a major corporation and Jo's work with social services. He told her about their move to the ranch after his parents were killed and the birth of their daughter a year later. He talked about the hard work they'd done and the sacrifices they'd made to build up the Whispering Wind's reputation as a dude ranch, as well as his own reputation as a breeder and trainer of prize quarter horses.

Maggie listened to every word he said, barely restraining the urge to go to him as the bitterness, the anger, the longing and loneliness he couldn't hide cut into her heart and clung to her soul in an unexpected way. She wanted to put her arms around him, to rest her head against his rigid shoulders, to offer him some kind of comfort. But when he paused again, flattening his palms on the desktop and tipping his head down, she stayed where she was. Instinctively she knew that he wanted neither her sympathy nor her solace. There was nothing she could say, nothing she could do to ease the pain she'd stirred up inside him.

"Everything seemed to be going our way," he muttered, breaking the silence stretching between them. Stepping away from the desk, he dropped his hands to his sides, walked to his chair and sat down. He glanced at her for a moment, his eyes full of confusion, then leaned back, crossed his arms over his chest and focused on a spot on the wall. "Almost two years ago Jo suddenly seemed tired all the time. She kept saying it was because we were having our best summer ever. We were completely booked until the end of August. And then she seemed to be putting on weight. We thought maybe she was pregnant, but she...wasn't.

"By mid-September, when things began to quiet down, I realized something was wrong. She was having trouble sleeping and she wasn't eating, but she could barely zip her jeans. She kept insisting she was all right, but I finally talked her into going to the doctor." He rubbed a hand over his eyes, then pinched the bridge of his nose between his thumb and forefinger.

"The diagnosis was...ovarian cancer," he said, his voice barely above a whisper. "And when they opened her up..." He took a deep breath and let it out. "The cancer had spread. There wasn't anything they could do to make her well again, and she knew it. So I brought her home. She hung on through the holidays. She wanted one more Christmas with Elizabeth. But then she...she just...let go. She didn't want to be a burden. She died that February, almost eighteen months ago. Aw, hell..." He sat forward, propping his elbows on the edge of his desk, rubbing his forehead on his clasped hands as if he could wipe away the reality of what had happened.

Maggie brushed the tears from her cheeks with the back of her hand, silently cursing herself for poking and prodding at Mackenzie Harrow's private pain and sorrow. But she wanted to know where he was coming from, when he took her in his arms and kissed her. Well, now she knew.

He'd come from the edge of love lost forever, from long days and lonely nights, from a need he didn't want, with wounds that hadn't healed.

She crossed the narrow space separating them, stopping near his chair, resting her hand on his shoulder. "I'm sorry, Mac." And she was. Sorry for him, sorry for herself, sorry for what could never be.

Pulling her hand away, she turned to go, but he caught her wrist and stopped her before she'd taken a stop. "I'm sorry, too, Maggie. I shouldn't have dumped on you like that, but once I got started..." He tugged on her arm, forcing her to turn and face him as he stood up. With his free hand he tucked a strand of hair behind her ear, then brushed his thumb over the dampness lingering on her cheeks. "You didn't even know her."

"But I *wanted* to know her, and now I feel as if I do." She smiled softly, reassuringly. "You loved her very much, didn't you?"

"Yes," he uttered the single word with soul-deep certainty as he let go of Maggie's arm.

"And you don't want to stay on the ranch without her."

"It's just not the same."

"No, of course not." She bent her head, pretending to study the toes of her boots for several seconds. Then lifting one shoulder in a casual shrug, she raised her eyes, meeting his gaze once again. "Guess I'll see what the kids are doing."

"Maggie, wait." He grabbed her hand as she moved to go. "I want to..." He hesitated as he curled his fingers around hers. "I want to thank you for listening. I haven't talked about Jo in...in a long time."

"Oh, Mac, you shouldn't thank me," she replied, her smile edging up into a grin. "You should be sending me to my room to write 'I will mind my own business' fifty times."

"Somehow I have a feeling that writing sentences wouldn't work any better with you than it does with my daughter. You care about people too much." He returned her smile with one of his own, as the shadows darkening his pale gray eyes began to fade.

"Only sometimes," she replied, reaching up to trace the edge of his jaw with her fingertip. "With very special people like you and Elizabeth. I'm glad we stayed." Leaning forward, she brushed a quick kiss on the tip of his chin.

"I'm glad, too." He slid his fingers into her hair and tilted her head back, gazing at her for several moments. "I've had a chance to find out what Elizabeth knew the moment she met you. You make everything all right, Maggie. More than all right...."

She wanted to tell him that she'd made her share of messes, as well, but he was drawing her closer and bending his head, and suddenly what she really wanted was—

"Damn it!" Mac eased his hand out of her hair and let her go.

"What?" she asked, grabbing the edge of the desk as she tried to regain her balance.

"Phone's ringing." He reached around her, pulled the offending instrument out from under a pile of papers and lifted the receiver. "Whispering Wind. Harrow speaking."

Maggie backed away from the desk, her eyes on Mac as he listened to the voice on the other end of the line.

"Sure, Bobby, I'd be happy to help you out. Can you hold on a minute?" He cupped his hand over the mouthpiece and turned his attention back to her. "I'm going to be on the phone for a while," he advised, real regret in his deep, soft voice.

"I'll get out of your way, then." She wrapped her hand around the doorknob and pulled it open.

"See you later?"

"Sure." She smiled as she stepped through the doorway. "See you later." She pulled the door closed and started up the aisle separating the rows of stalls. In the distance she could hear young voices and yapping puppies. Her smile widened, and she quickened her pace as her spirits lifted. She *was* glad that she'd stayed. Very, very glad . . .

Chapter Seven

"Are you sure you don't want to go with me?" Mac tossed his duffel bag on the front seat, then turned to check the hitch hooking the horse trailer to the back of his pickup truck one more time.

Maggie tagged along beside him, her hands tucked into the back pockets of her faded jeans, the early morning breeze ruffling her hair. "I'd love to go, but..." She tipped her head toward her son and his daughter, rolling around with the puppies on a patch of grass under an oak tree several yards away. "They want to stay."

"Yeah, I know," he muttered. Trying to hide his disappointment, he bent down and readjusted the wiring for the trailer taillights. They'd discussed it at least a half dozen times the night before, and her final decision had remained the same. But he had been hoping that she'd change her mind about the trip to the Bar Y Ranch.

When Bobby Dawson had called yesterday afternoon, Mac had agreed to drive to Alpine to take a look at his friend's new gelding, but only because he'd thought that Maggie and the kids would make the overnight trip with him. Unfortunately he'd forgotten about Bonnie and Clyde.

Both Christopher and Elizabeth had been more than a little upset about the possibility of being parted from their pets for two days. And Mac had refused to spend eight hours on the road with a couple of young pups. Not only was it unfair to the animals, but just thinking about the mess they'd make in the back seat of the double cab had been enough to make him shudder.

Leaving the kids and dogs with Juan and Rosa, who had returned Sunday night, should have been a viable alternative. In fact, it had seemed like a very good idea to Mac. But Maggie hadn't agreed. Firmly believing that the elderly couple had enough to do, she had insisted on staying at the ranch to look after the children while he was gone.

He had been tempted to call Bobby and tell him he couldn't make the trip, after all. But he was a man of his word. And if the gelding looked as promising as he sounded, Mac would bring him back to the ranch and work with him for six or eight weeks. His training fee would see them through the rest of the summer.

Still, he didn't like the idea of being away for the two days the round trip would take. Not because he didn't trust Maggie on her own, but because their time together was dwindling fast. More than ever, he wanted to be with her. He wasn't sure why, but he did.

Perhaps it had something to do with the way she'd poked and prodded at him to talk about Jo. Somehow she'd known it was time for him to let go, and she'd been tough enough to goad him into it. She had dug at him with one question after another until he couldn't hold back any longer. Before he could stop himself, he had laid all the pain, the anger and the frustration that had been eating at him for years at her feet.

Not to gain her sympathy, though he'd never forget how deeply he'd been touched by the tears in her eyes. He had wanted something more from her. He had wanted her understanding and her acceptance. He had wanted her to know how little he had left to give. And he hadn't wanted her to hold it against him.

She had understood all right. And she had slipped away from him much too easily. She hadn't given him an opportunity to pick up where they'd left off when he'd answered Bobby's call, either. He shouldn't mind. In fact, having so little to give, he should be grateful. But he wasn't. He was mad as hell.

Maybe it was just as well that he was going to be gone for a couple of days. He needed some time to think—about the past, the present and the future. About what he wanted and what he needed. About Miz Maggie Connor and how she might, or might not, fit into his life.

Talking about Jo had helped ease the pain of his loss in a way he'd never imagined it would. Talking about her had been a tentative step toward putting the past behind him. And with the past behind him, maybe the future would be easier to face. He might even have more to give than he realized. Someday he might be ready to love again. Only time would tell. But time wasn't exactly on his side, where Maggie was concerned. With a muttered curse, he stood up and brushed his hands on the seat of his jeans.

"We'll be all right, Mac. Don't worry."

At the sound of her soft, sweet voice and the touch of her hand on his arm, he turned to look at her. She tipped her face up and smiled at him, her bright blue eyes full of warmth and reassurance. It was all he could do to stop himself from pulling her into his arms.

"You've got the telephone number for the Bar Y?" he asked, his voice rougher than he meant it to be.

"Committed to memory, sir." Her smile widening into a teasing grin, she offered a mock salute as she repeated the number he'd posted in several places throughout the house and barn.

"Good." He nodded his head once, then glanced at his watch. Directing his attention over her right shoulder, he raised his voice. "I'm leaving."

"Bye, Daddy."

"Bye, Mr. Harrow."

"Nothing like playing second fiddle to a puppy," he growled. "Keep them out of the house, all right?" Turning on his heel, he opened the door of the truck.

"The kids or the puppies?" she asked, as he climbed in and closed the door.

"I'll leave it up to you." He paused for a moment, his hand on the key in the ignition. He gazed at Maggie through the open window, the corners of his mouth finally twitching into a smile. "Come here a minute."

She did as he requested, taking the few steps necessary to close the distance separating them. Standing on the balls of her feet, she leaned forward and propped her forearms on the edge of the window frame. "I'm here, Mr. Harrow."

"I'll call you tonight around eight or eight-thirty."

"I'll be waiting," she cooed, batting her eyes at him.

"You'd better be," he muttered. Then, unable to restrain himself any longer, he caught her chin in his hand, tilted her face up, and kissed her. Slowly, deeply, deliberately...

"Only because Blue Coot's Saloon is closed on Monday nights," she added a little breathlessly as soon as he released her.

"Oh, yeah?"

"Yeah." She stepped away from the truck and crossed her arms over her chest, her eyes full of playful defiance.

"One of these days, Maggie..." One of these days she was going to drive him round the bend, he thought as he switched on the ignition.

"Mac?"

"Yes?"

As he faced her again, she uncrossed her arms and moved closer to the truck. "Take care, Mac." She reached through the window and rested her hand on his arm. "I'll...we'll miss you." Not giving him a chance to reply, she withdrew her hand, spun around and started toward the house.

"I'll miss you, too, Maggie. More than you'll ever know," he murmured, his voice too low for her to hear. Then pressing down on the clutch he shifted gears, heading the truck down the drive without a backward glance.

"I saw you kissing Daddy. He's nice, isn't he? When he's not crabby."

Maggie just managed to catch the lamp before it fell off the table she was dusting. "Actually he was kissing me," she replied, risking a glance at Elizabeth. The girl was busily wiping one of the little cabin's front windows with a damp paper towel.

"What's the difference, Mom?" Christopher poked his head out of the bathroom, a soapy sponge dangling from one hand.

Maggie could have sworn she'd heard the water running in there just a minute ago, but then she'd always suspected her son had bionic hearing. "It's hard to explain, but I have a feeling you'll understand in a few years," she muttered. Tucking the dust cloth in her back pocket, she turned to face him. "Are you about done in there?"

"I'm doing the floor now." He disappeared through the doorway.

"How about you, Elizabeth?"

"I have one more window to do. Do you like my dad, Maggie?"

"Of course, I like him." She twirled around, quickly surveying the inside of the cabin, checking to make sure they hadn't missed anything. "Guess I'll go ahead and run the vacuum." She plugged in the machine and pressed her foot on the start button, thankful that it was too noisy to allow them to continue their conversation.

She wasn't in the mood to discuss her feelings for Mackenzie Harrow with anyone, not even with his precocious daughter. In fact, as soon as they finished with the last of the five guest cabins, she planned to slip away for some quiet time to herself. She needed to think, and thinking was impossible in the company of a couple of chatterboxes such as Christopher and Elizabeth.

Granted it had been her idea for the three of them to help Rosa with the bimonthly cleaning of the cabins. And she hadn't minded most of their nonsense. Being with them had been a lot of fun. Until Elizabeth mentioned the kissing. She had thought that their public display of affection had gone unnoticed, since neither child had said anything about it during the morning and most of the afternoon. She should have known better. Not only did children hear everything they weren't supposed to hear, they saw everything they weren't supposed to see. And now she was afraid that Elizabeth and maybe even Christopher might get the wrong idea about her relationship with Mac.

His kisses offered infinitely more than friendship, but she didn't want them to know it. She didn't want to know it herself. Because she was going back to San Antonio, to her own life, in less than a week, come hell or . . . or high water.

She switched off the vacuum, her mouth curving into a wry smile. Okay, so high water had stopped her once. But last night the local weather forecaster had predicted hot, dry days and cool, dry nights for the remainder of the week. And since she could think of nothing else that might prevent her from leaving as planned, she'd be home safe on Sunday.

Safe? She stopped coiling the cord around the vacuum handle for a moment. Why was she seeking safety? She wasn't in any danger on the Whispering Wind, at least not any physical danger. And emotionally she was stronger and more secure than she'd ever been. There certainly wasn't any danger of her falling in love with a man like Mackenzie Harrow, a man who reminded her more and more of Avery Chase and Mitchell Connor. No danger, at all, when their time together was measured in days. Especially if she didn't get close enough for him to kiss her senseless again.

She finished winding the cord, as Christopher and Elizabeth gathered up buckets, mops and cleaning supplies. Glancing at her watch she saw that it was almost four o'clock. They had more than enough time for a swim before dinner. She crossed to the window air conditioner and turned it off. Then pushing the vacuum in front of her, she herded the kids out the door.

"Look, Maggie, someone's coming." Elizabeth dropped her bucket and curved a hand over her eyes. "Maybe it's Daddy."

Blinking against the sudden, bright sunlight, Maggie followed the direction of Elizabeth's pointing finger. In the distance she saw a faint cloud of dust rising in the air as the sound of tires crunching on the dirt and gravel road drifted toward them. A few seconds later a bright red mini-van followed by a white station wagon topped the last low hill on the road leading up to the cabins and the main house.

"Do you know who it is?" Maggie asked, shifting her attention to the girl standing beside her as she tried, unsuccessfully, to quell her rising apprehension. Maybe they were friends of—

"Nope." Elizabeth shook her head as first the van, then the station wagon scrunched to a halt a few feet away.

Then again maybe they were ax murderers, she thought, as she looped one arm around Mac's daughter and the other around her son. For the first time since she'd arrived, Maggie realized how isolated they were on the ranch, especially with Mac away. Yet she wasn't completely alone with the children. From the corner of her eyes she saw Juan walking toward them, a squirming puppy under each arm, while Rosa waited near the house. More thankful than ever for the older couple's presence there, she pasted a smile on her face as the middle-aged, heavyset man climbed out of the van and started toward her.

"Howdy, folks. Is this the Whispering Wind Dude Ranch?" He stopped a few feet from the porch, an amiable grin on his florid face, as a woman and three children tumbled out of the van and were joined by another couple with two children from the station wagon.

"Yes...." Maggie replied, studying the nine eager faces gazing up at her. Just a couple of families on summer vacation, she thought as she relaxed her hold on Christopher and Elizabeth.

"We heard about you all from some friends of ours. We were wondering if you had any vacancies. We're on our way to old Mexico, but we thought we'd stop here for a few nights if you can accommodate us. I'm Dewey Welles, my little woman, Milly, and the kids, Little Dew, Molly and Fred. And that's Eddie Stevens, his wife, Jen, and their kids, Ricky and Ronnie." Mr. Welles gestured toward his family and friends as they smiled and offered friendly greetings of their own.

"Mr. Welles, it's nice to meet you. But I don't think—"

"We'll have to check the book," Elizabeth piped up, cutting Maggie off without hesitation. She jumped off the cabin's tiny porch before Maggie could stop her, and gazed up at Dewey Welles for one long moment, a died-and-gone-to-heaven smile tipping up the corners of her mouth. Then whirling around, she started toward the house with long, determined strides. "Come on, Maggie, we have to check the book."

"Elizabeth!" The girl didn't even falter. Forcing herself to keep smiling, Maggie stepped off the porch. "Excuse me, Mr. Welles. It seems I have to check the book. Why don't you make yourselves comfortable." She indicated a cluster of chairs several yards away in a small grove of trees. "I'll be right back." Dragging Christopher along with her, she hurried to catch up with Elizabeth.

"Is this another one of your schemes, young lady? Because if it is, your father is going to blister your bottom. And when he's done, I'm going to ask for a turn." She grabbed the girl's arm, pulling her to a stop as she started through the side door of the house.

"I didn't know they were coming, Maggie. I swear I didn't. But since they're here, and since the cabins are clean, I thought we could let them stay."

"Think again. There are nine people out there."

"I know." Elizabeth gazed up at Maggie with huge, innocent eyes. "And my dad could really use the money."

Having no immediate answer to that, Maggie ushered the children into the kitchen in silence. Juan and Rosa followed close behind them. "What about meals?" she asked at last, turning to face Rosa, hoping for some support.

The older woman shrugged, a smile in her eyes. "The freezer is full. So is the pantry. We can restock bread, milk, eggs, fresh fruit and vegetables on a daily basis, depending on how many are here. I'll need a little help with the cooking and serving, but don't worry. We can do it."

Don't worry? Talk about famous last words. "What about riding? They're going to want to ride and we can't use

Mac's quarter horses, can we?'' She glanced at Juan as he set the puppies on the kitchen floor.

"Oh, no, we can't do that. But if they want to ride, I'll call the Triple Z and make arrangements for them to ride there.''

"So they can stay, can't they, Maggie?'' Elizabeth asked, almost pleading.

She shouldn't even consider saying yes. In fact, the word should have been stricken from her vocabulary a week ago. But four pairs of eyes were watching her and waiting, four pairs of eyes full of eagerness and anticipation. And Mac needed the money.

"Please, Mom? Please say yes? It'll be fun. And we'll help, won't we, Elizabeth?''

"Oh, yes, we'll help a whole, whole lot.''

"All right, they can stay.''

Whooping with delight Elizabeth and Christopher threw their arms around her, hugging her quickly while the puppies yapped at her heels. A moment later, they were chattering like magpies as they started toward the door.

"Whoa, wait a minute. We've got to get organized.'' Maggie glanced at her watch. It was nearly four-thirty. "We'd better plan to serve dinner at six-thirty instead of six o'clock.'' Rosa nodded in agreement as she started toward the freezer.

"Elizabeth, you help me figure out where to put them and how much to charge. Then we can make up the beds and put out fresh towels. Christopher, can you keep an eye on the puppies while you set up one of the long dining room tables with nine places?''

"Of course.''

"Let's get busy, then....''

He didn't like what he saw. He didn't like it one damn bit. Shifting into first, he brought the truck to a crawl as he passed by the row of cabins, which should have been dark, *empty* cabins. Lights blazed in Number Two and Number Three, brightening the early evening as they reflected off the sides of a mini-van and a station wagon he'd never seen before. Lights blazed around the swimming pool, as well, and in the water almost a dozen people laughed and splashed and shouted as they batted an enormous beach ball into the air. He recognized only two of the children and none of the adults.

Pressing down on the clutch, he shifted into second and focused his attention on the house and the red-haired woman silhouetted in the kitchen window. He was hot and tired and dusty. And all he'd thought about for the last fifty miles was how he might lure her into the pool for a very private late-night swim. Privacy was the last thing they'd have tonight, he thought, as he muttered a string of swear words that would have made a sailor blush.

No wonder she hadn't said much when he'd called last night. For her sake, he hoped she had something to say now. "And it better be something good," he muttered as he pulled up to the barn.

Quickly, efficiently, he opened the trailer, backed the gelding down the short ramp and led him into a stall. In an hour or so, when the animal was used to his new surroundings, he'd come back to feed and water him. And meanwhile... He covered the distance between the barn and the house in record time, his anger mounting with each step he took.

Passing the kitchen entry, he climbed the steps and opened the side door. He wanted to make sure they were alone. He stepped inside and—

"Aw, hell." Stopping dead, he looked down, any doubt about what had squished under his boot eliminated by the odor of something better left outside. He heard a whine, then a scrabbling of tiny claws as Bonnie crawled out from under a chair. "Did you do this?" he growled at her, his voice low.

She whined again and wagged her tail, as Clyde crawled out beside her. "Bad dogs." He shook a finger at them, then reached behind him and opened the door. "Out, both of you." With playful yips, they scampered past him.

Shaking his head, he closed the door and leaned back against it. He lifted his foot and tugged off his boot. Holding it in one hand, he started for the kitchen again, this time watching where he walked.

Ready to do battle, yet wanting the element of surprise on his side, he eased open one of the swinging doors, then paused for a moment, surveying the scene before him. She was standing at the counter, her back to him, humming to herself as she stirred a large bowl of something. Probably cookie dough, since several empty cookie sheets covered the kitchen table. For just a moment, he wanted to take her in his arms and kiss the living daylights out of her. He took a deep, steadying breath, then grimaced as he looked at the boot in his hand. Suddenly the thought of turning her over his knee was infinitely more appealing.

"What the hell is going on around here?" He shoved the door open all the way, allowing it to crash against the wall. She shrieked and almost dropped the bowl as he hobbled, one boot on, one boot off, into the room and headed for the sink.

"Mac! You scared me." She set the bowl on the counter and turned on him, hands on her hips.

"I'm going to do a hell of a lot more than scare you," he muttered as he yanked a wad of paper towels off the roll, wet them under the faucet and went to work on the bottom of his boot.

"What are you doing?" She took a tentative step toward him, then stopped as he turned his head and stared at her for the space of several heartbeats.

"Wiping dog mess off the bottom of my boot. What does it look like I'm doing?"

"Oh, no, I forgot about the puppies." She whirled around and started toward the swinging doors.

"I put them out. You can clean up what they left when I'm done with you."

"What do you mean when you're done—"

"Just tell me one thing," he said, cutting her off before she could start on him. "When I drove up, I saw lights on in a couple of the cabins. I saw a mini-van and a station wagon parked nearby. And I saw almost a dozen people in the swimming pool. Was I hallucinating, Miz Connor? Or are we entertaining guests at the Whispering Wind?"

"Would you believe you were hallucinating?"

"Would you believe it's a good thing I can't remember where we keep the butcher knives?" He glared at her as he wadded up the soiled paper towels and tossed them into the trash can. Refusing to acknowledge the teasing glint in her eyes, he pulled on his boot, then washed and dried his hands. "Who are those people and why are they on my property?"

"They...they heard about the ranch from friends. They stopped here yesterday and asked if they could stay for a few days."

"You should have told them the ranch was closed."

"I thought about it. But...but Elizabeth said you needed the money. And the cabins were clean. And Juan and Rosa seemed to think it would be all right. So, I..." She shrugged one shoulder and lowered her eyes, her soft voice trailing away.

"So you what?" he demanded. His hands on his hips, he took a step toward her.

"So I told them they could stay," she shot back as she met his gaze. "It didn't seem right to turn them away. It seemed like such a waste leaving the cabins empty, when they could be used as they were meant to be. You and Jo worked so hard to build up this place. Just because she's dead you don't have to let the Whispering Wind die, too. She wouldn't have wanted you to do that. And I don't think you want to do it, either."

"You don't know what I want," he muttered, turning away from her as he wished he could turn away from the pain that sliced through him. She was right. Jo wouldn't have wanted him to give up the ranch. But Jo was gone and he had to get on with the life he had left to live. He had given all he could to the Whispering Wind.

"Maybe not," she replied, her voice softening as she brushed past him and grabbed a handful of paper towels. "I . . . I did what I thought was right. I'm sorry you're angry about it."

"When are they leaving?"

"Thursday morning. They paid in advance for three nights. But if you want, I'll tell them they have to go tomorrow and refund their money." She wet the paper towels as Mac had done, then turned away from him.

"They can stay until Thursday morning." He spoke the words in a grudging tone of voice as he caught her arm. "What are you doing?"

"I'd better clean up the mess on the dining-room floor before someone else steps in it."

"I'll take care of it."

"It's my fault. You told me to keep the puppies out of the house." She sniffed and blinked her eyes, turning her face away. "So if you'll just get out of my way, I'll do it."

"Are you going to cry?"

"She said you needed the money. . . ." Her bottom lip quivered.

"Aw, Maggie. . ." He did what he'd thought about doing all the way home. He pulled her into his arms and rested his cheek against her silky curls. "I'm sorry."

"You're always...always mad at me." Her voice qua-
vered as she took a long, shaky breath. "I think I want to go
home."

All of a sudden he couldn't remember why he'd been so
upset about a few strangers staying on the ranch. It seemed
so silly, especially since he'd known all along that she hadn't
asked them to stay to spite him in any way. Thanks to Elizabeth, she had probably thought that the only thing standing between him and debtors' prison was the group of
people paddling around in the pool.

"I think I've just been mad at life lately, and I've been
taking it out on you. I'm sorry." He tightened his hold on
her as he took a deep breath then let it out. "Don't go,
Maggie. Don't leave me here alone with all those people."

"Oh, Mac, I wouldn't do that." She stepped back and
raised her chin. "It's not so bad. Really, it isn't. We're all
helping out, even Christopher and Elizabeth."

He rubbed a thumb across her cheek, collecting the single tear that marred her pale face. Now that he really looked
at her, he could see the shadows under her eyes. "It's a lot
of work, isn't it?"

"Yes." She breathed the word on a soft sigh. "But it's
been fun, too. And they're really very nice, even the kids."
She smiled at some memory he couldn't share.

"You're lucky. We've had some real terrors here in the
past, adults as well as children."

"Speaking of real terrors, I'd better..." She eased out of
his arms.

"I said I'd take care of it, and I will." He pulled the damp
paper towels out of her hand. "What time does the pool
close?"

"Oh, I forgot." She glanced at her watch, then walked
over to the row of light switches near the door. "It closes in
ten minutes." She flicked one of the switches up and down
several times, blinking the lights illuminating the pool area.

"Need any help in here?"

"I'm almost finished."

"In that case, I guess I'll check on the horses after I finish with the dining-room floor. Then I'm going to head upstairs. See you in the morning?"

"Bright and early. Rosa's going to teach me how to make cinnamon rolls—lots and lots of cinnamon rolls."

"You're supposed to be on vacation."

"Compared to a classroom full of third-graders, this *is* a vacation."

"You're crazy, Maggie."

"I know, Mac."

He didn't want to smile, but as he pushed through the swinging doors he caught himself doing it anyway. For the first time in a long time, he realized how good it was to be alive and well and living at the Whispering Wind. In fact, despite the dog mess on the dining-room floor and a couple of cabins full of unanticipated guests, it was damned good to be back home again. But how long would he feel that way about the ranch once she was gone?

His smile fading into a frown, he finished wiping up the floor and headed out the door. When he'd promised Elizabeth that they'd stay the summer, he hadn't wanted anyone else around. Now, to his surprise, he wanted Maggie and Christopher to stay, not just until Sunday but for the rest of the time he had left on the ranch. But how could he ask her to stay?

Well, he could just plain *ask* her. Getting her to agree would be the hard part. What if she had a summer job lined up, or plans for another vacation trip somewhere else? What if she simply didn't want to be within a fifty-mile radius of him any longer? He wouldn't blame her for feeling that way. He'd promised to behave himself once, a promise he hadn't lived up to very well tonight.

But if she stayed he'd have time to prove to her . . . what? That he wasn't such a horse's ass, after all? Among other things. . . Yet how could he get her to stay? He glanced at the two families straggling out of the pool and heading toward the cabins, and the beginning of an idea began to take shape.

She thought that he needed money and she thought that she'd helped him earn it be accepting guests. And after the past couple of days, surely she had to know he couldn't handle guests as well as horses on his own. People had been calling for reservations off and on for the past few months. He'd turned them away, but it was a good bet he'd get more calls during the remainder of the week, not to mention the rest of the summer. And of course the ranch got its fair share of drop-ins. There were people who planned ahead and people who waited until the last minute.

They didn't have to entertain a full quota of guests. And they could accommodate them in the cabins only, not in the house. He grinned as he stepped off the side porch and headed toward the barn, the puppies nipping at his heels. It might work. It just might work. Whether or not it did, it was worth a try.

A last summer on the Whispering Wind with Maggie and her son would be so much better than a last summer alone with Elizabeth. And if it meant having a few strangers on the ranch, he'd live with it. Just for a few weeks. To give them all something to remember when he and his daughter were settled in Dallas and Maggie and her son were back home in San Antonio. . . .

Chapter Eight

"It's about time you crawled out of bed. I was getting ready to send up a search party."

"Good morning to you, too." Maggie grinned at Mac as she crossed the kitchen. Stopping by the counter, she pulled a white china mug from the cabinet and reached for the coffeepot.

"It's almost eight-thirty, Mom," Christopher chided.

"We thought you might be sick," Elizabeth added.

Cupping her steaming mug in her hands, Maggie turned to face the three people sitting at the table. "Well, I *am* on vacation. I didn't think it would matter if I slept in, now that our guests are gone." She took a sip of the hot brew, savoring its dark taste and rich aroma. "Have you eaten yet?" With her encouragement, Mac had given Rosa the day off, leaving them to fend for themselves.

"We're just about finished," Christopher replied, as he and Elizabeth dug into their bowls of cereal.

"What about you, Mac? More coffee?"

"No, thanks. I've had enough." He gazed at her with what Maggie could only call a speculative gleam in his pale gray eyes. "You going to sit down or just stand there, hovering over us?"

"In a minute."

She turned back to the counter and popped a slice of bread into the toaster. As she waited for it, her back to the table and its occupants, she sipped her coffee and listened to the silence surrounding her. Something was going on, something she wasn't sure she wanted to know about in any great detail. Three against one wasn't her idea of a fair fight, and she had the strangest feeling that some sort of battle was brewing behind her back.

She took her time buttering her toast and refilling her mug, relishing the slower pace she hadn't really missed until she'd been faced with the demands of the nine guests, two children, two puppies, an elderly couple and, of course, Mackenzie Harrow himself. It had taken all of her organizational skills and most of her energy to assure decent meals were served on time, cabins were cleaned and fresh sheets and towels were readily available. Late nights had been followed by early mornings, with all the hours in between filled to overflowing.

Mac had been right when he'd said that running a dude ranch, even on a small scale, entailed a lot of work and worry. It also took two people. Mac had horses to train and a house, a barn and fences to maintain. She knew now that he couldn't handle guests as well. And she knew, too, that doing it together didn't necessarily mean spending time together.

They hadn't seen much of each other over the past couple of days, but she hoped they'd be able to make up for lost time today and tomorrow. After that she and Christopher would be heading back to San Antonio, and there was a good chance she might never see Mac and Elizabeth again. Frowning slightly she picked up her plate and mug, turned and joined the others at the table.

"Something wrong, Maggie? Are you feeling all right?"

Startled by the sudden concern in Mac's voice, she raised her eyes, met his gaze and forced herself to smile. "I'm fine. A little tired, maybe, but I'll survive now that our guests are gone."

"Why, Miz Connor, don't tell me you've changed your mind about operating a dude ranch. I thought you were enjoying yourself. And you seemed to take to all that cooking and cleaning and washing like a duck takes to water." His concern disappeared behind a teasing grin that should have ruffled her feathers but didn't.

Though he liked to pretend he was a prize specimen of male chauvinism, she knew that he wasn't. He'd stood beside her late Wednesday night and helped her scrub crusted chicken casserole off six huge metal pans, then offered to empty the double dishwashers so she could go on up to bed. He'd carried sheets and towels to the cabins, loaded the washing machines, emptied the driers and even mopped the kitchen floor when she'd dropped a full pitcher of orange juice.

"I *was* enjoying myself, Mr. Harrow." She picked up her mug and took a sip of coffee. Out of the corner of her eye she saw Christopher and Elizabeth exchange a smile and a thumbs-up signal.

"Good, because I've got three families coming on Sunday, six adults and seven children all together. We can decide where to put them when you finish your breakfast. That is, if you want to stay on till the end of the summer and give me a hand. As Elizabeth said, I could use the money, and by now you know I need the help."

Maggie's mug hit the table with a loud thump, sending hot liquid splashing over its side and onto her fingers. Her thoughts tumbling one over another, she grabbed a napkin and blotted up the mess, as she avoided Mac's probing gaze. Two weeks ago he'd wanted nothing more than to see her gone. Now, out of the blue, he was asking her to stay until August, and she couldn't help but wonder what had prompted such a thorough change of heart.

Maybe it had something to do with the kisses he'd stolen at the oddest moments, when she was standing over a sink full of dirty dishwater, when he relieved her of an armload of clean linen or caught her all alone in the second-floor hallway. Just the thought of those kisses was enough to tempt her to say yes. They were courting kisses, both pleasing and promising. Each one had left her wanting, *needing* more in a way she hadn't wanted or needed in years.

But she couldn't stay, she warned herself, as she felt the heat of a blush climb her neck and stain her cheeks. She had a life of her own, on her own. And she had to be nuts to even consider giving it up to spend the summer with Mackenzie Harrow, scratching an itch that was better left alone.

"I . . . I don't think—"

"Please, Mom, *please* say yes. I want to stay. And we'll help, too. We promise."

"We promise," Elizabeth echoed, her dark eyes shining with excitement. "Please stay, Maggie."

"But I . . . we can't." Maggie eyed her son and Mac's daughter and wished for a way to convince them—and herself—that what they were asking was impossible. Because if she was around Mac much longer, she was going to do something rash like rip off his clothes and—

"Why not?" Mac asked, his deep voice cutting through the children's chorus of pleas as well as her flight of X-rated fantasy. "Do you have a summer job lined up already? I can't pay much over room and board, but I don't expect you to work for nothing." He paused for a moment, holding her gaze. "If you've already made plans, I'll understand. But if you haven't..."

She lowered her eyes, picked up a piece of toast and bit into it. She didn't want to answer Mac's question, because if she did she'd have to do so honestly. And in all honesty she didn't have any plans for the rest of the summer. She'd thought about running an ad in the paper when they got home, offering special tutoring to students who couldn't fit into the regular summer-school schedule due to jobs or travel. She'd also thought about picking up a course or two at the university. But she hadn't committed to anything definite, at least not for herself.

However, she *had* made plans for Christopher. He was supposed to spend several weeks at computer camp and several weeks with her parents. Swallowing her toast, she turned to her son.

"We can't stay, Christopher. You've got computer camp and we're supposed to visit your grandparents." She glanced at Mac and smiled apologetically.

"I don't want to go to computer camp anymore. I want to stay here. If you call right away and cancel my reservation you can get your money back, can't you?"

"But your grandparents—"

"We decided we could visit our grandparents for a week or so in July," Elizabeth added, nipping Maggie's protest in the bud. "Daddy said it would be all right if we're both gone at the same time because he won't plan on having many guests then."

Maggie turned to look at Mac, her eyes narrowing slightly. She wanted to believe he'd had a spur-of-the-moment idea, but she wasn't that stupid. He had planned this confrontation very carefully and he'd made sure that he had not only his daughter but her son on his side. She couldn't imagine how he'd convinced Christopher to give up computer camp, much less settle for just a week or so with her parents, but he had.

A week when Elizabeth would be gone, too. A week when they wouldn't have many guests on the ranch. Interesting. Very, very interesting, she thought, her heartbeat accelerating as he smiled a smile that was much too full of the devil to set her mind at ease. Her initial assessment of him had been right on the mark. He was definitely a dangerous man.

"What made you change your mind about having strangers on the ranch?" she asked at last, not only to prolong the moment when she'd have to say yes or no, but because she was genuinely curious. Although he'd helped her with the work involved, he hadn't socialized at all with either the Welles family or the Stevens family. He had left what he termed "customer relations" to her.

"I thought about what you said, about it being a waste not to use the place the way it was meant to be used. I . . . I think you're right." He shrugged one shoulder as he toyed with his empty coffee cup. "Since I promised Elizabeth we'd stay until the end of the summer, I figured we might as well go ahead and open up the cabins. And as I said, I could use the money. But I need you here to help me," he admitted, his eyes steady as he met her gaze. "Just for the summer."

Just for the summer . . . So that hadn't changed. Obviously he still planned to sell the ranch at the end of August. Maggie glanced at Elizabeth, expecting some sort of protest. But the girl sat quietly, a soft smile lighting her eyes. For the second time in two weeks, Maggie considered the innocence of youth.

Elizabeth still believed that everything would work out in the end, and why shouldn't she? So far, everything had worked out as she'd planned. And who was she, Maggie wondered, to throw a monkey wrench in the works?

It wasn't as if she had anything else better to do for the summer. And maybe, just maybe, by the end of August Mac *would* change his mind about selling the Whispering Wind. If she proved to him that he could make a go of it with someone's help, then surely he'd realize that he didn't have to give it up. He could hire an assistant to help him next summer. Surely he'd be able to find a woman, perhaps a widow like herself, who would be willing to work for him in exchange for room and board and a small salary. Why he might even decide to marry her—

Averting her eyes, she pushed away from the table and crossed to the counter, her coffee mug in one hand, her empty plate in the other. What he needed was a wife, but she didn't want to be a wife—not his or anybody else's. So why did she suddenly want to smash a plate against the wall at the thought of him married to another, albeit unknown woman? *Because you're in too deep, Mary Margaret, and you're about to get in even deeper...*

"I guess you've discussed this with Rosa already?"

"She's agreeable."

Turning slowly, Maggie crossed her arms over her chest and gazed at her son. "If I cancel your reservation at computer camp and any part of the deposit is nonrefundable, *you* will refund it out of your allowance. Understood?"

"Then we can stay?" He jumped out of his chair and started toward her, his eyes bright.

"Just a minute. I'm not finished yet. You will also be the one to call your grandparents and explain why you won't be spending five or six weeks with them this summer."

"I'll call right now."

"You'll call this evening so you can talk to your grandfather, as well as your grandmother."

"Yes, ma'am."

Maggie shifted her gaze from her son to Mac. He was watching her, a soft, knowing smile curving the corners of his mouth and brightening his pale eyes. She wasn't sure whether she wanted to slug him or hug him for being so good at getting his way. She might be able to turn her back on her own needs but not on another's, and he seemed to know it.

"I've got to go back to San Antonio to check on my house and make arrangements to have my mail delivered here. I might as well do it today."

"I'll go with you," Mac offered, his smile widening.

"I'd rather go alone." She wanted the time to think about what she was doing. And she needed to give herself a chance to change her mind. She wouldn't be able to do either with Mac around. "If I leave now, I should be back by early afternoon. Then you can show me the ropes," she added, trying to ease the sudden uncertainty from his eyes.

"Will you bring back my computer and my game file?" Christopher asked.

"Of course. Do you want anything else?"

She planned to pack another suitcase with extra clothes for both of them and she also wanted to bring back the materials necessary to prepare for the coming school year. New books had been approved for several of the subjects she taught and she wanted to get a head start on new lesson plans if she had time.

"I don't think so."

"Well, I guess I'll get going, then."

As she moved away from the counter, Mac stood up and caught her hand in his. "Be careful," he advised, turning her around to face him.

"I'm always careful," she replied, squeezing his fingers for a moment. *Except where you're concerned,* she added to herself as she crossed the kitchen and walked through the swinging doors. Where he was concerned, rash and reckless behavior seemed to be the order of her day.

She should be in bed, asleep, yet once again she was standing by the window, gazing into the darkness. She was restless. Restless in a way she had no right to be, considering how busy she'd been over the past three weeks, she thought, as she fingered the buttons on the front of her plain white cotton nightgown.

When she'd returned from San Antonio, Mac had barely given her enough time to catch her breath before he'd begun her crash course in operating a dude ranch the Harrow way. She'd had to learn the system of charts and books that were used to keep reservations straight and avoid double bookings, as well as how to record income and expenditures. They had also gone over the standard daily menus for a week so she would have an idea of how much to order from the grocery and the meat market depending on the number of guests staying on the ranch. By Sunday, when the first three families had arrived, Maggie had been suffering a bad case of cold feet. But it had been too late to cut and run, so she'd pasted a smile on her face and gone to work.

Since then every cabin had been full almost every day. The names and faces changed, but the chores stayed the same. Even the Fourth of July holiday hadn't been a day off, since they'd decided to have an outdoor barbecue for their guests, followed by a small fireworks display. However, by establishing a routine and assigning jobs to Juan and Rosa and Christopher and Elizabeth on a rotating basis, she'd managed to eliminate some of the drudgery while giving everyone, including herself, a fair share of free time.

Mac had his own work schedule, but several times, when she'd been especially busy, and without her asking, he'd helped out in the kitchen or laundry early in the morning or late in the evening. Aside from the hasty meals they shared with Juan and Rosa and the kids in the kitchen, it was almost all she'd seen of him.

In fact, they'd shared very few private moments, and when they were alone, she was often too preoccupied to know it until Mac dropped a kiss on her cheek or smoothed a hand over her hair on his way out. With a sigh, she rolled her forehead against the cool glass of the windowpane. What was wrong with her? She wasn't here to spend time alone with Mac. She was here to help him run the ranch. And it was running very well.

Even with her small salary, which she didn't really need but had been wise enough to accept, Mac was making money. And so far, the guests had seemed pleased with the hospitality they received. There had been complaints, of course, but they had been minor, and the problems easily solved. Now, if only she could do something about *her* problem....

Maybe a glass of warm milk would help her get to sleep. Better yet, she could go for a swim, she thought, as she gazed out the window once again. Though the house and grounds were quiet, the cabins, huddled in the shadows, were dark and still, the pool, shimmering in the bright light of the full moon, offered an irresistible invitation to come and play. She'd have it all to herself for as long as she wanted. And twenty laps ought to cure whatever ailed her. At the very least, she'd be so worn out she wouldn't be able to stay awake even if she wanted to.

Padding across the room on bare feet, she dug out her suit, slipped into the bathroom and shed her gown. Moments later, she pulled the bedroom door closed as quietly as possible, not wanting to disturb her sleeping son. Detouring through the empty kitchen, she pulled a flashlight out of a drawer, picked up a beach towel in the laundry room, then headed out the door.

Since the rainstorm that had stranded her at the ranch, the days had been hot and dry, the evenings pleasantly cool. Tonight was no exception, Maggie thought, as she followed the narrow path from the house to the pool, the beam of her flashlight leading the way, the puppies yipping playfully as they nipped at her heels.

"Hush, you guys," Maggie ordered in a stern tone of voice as she switched off the flashlight, then dropped it on a chaise lounge along with her towel.

Feigning obedience, both pups gazed up at her for a moment, then scampered toward the edge of the pool, sat down and waited for her. Though intrigued by the wide expanse of water that was usually filled with people, Bonnie and Clyde had yet to wet their little paws, and Maggie had no intention of encouraging them to do so now.

"Stay put." She wagged a finger at them and frowned, just to let them know she was serious. Then pivoting gracefully she arched her body and dove into the pool.

Though the pool wasn't heated, the water was several degrees warmer than the night air. As she stroked to the surface, it rippled over her body, subtly clinging yet caressing. Taking a deep breath, she tilted her head back and smiled at the moon, hanging fat and full over the treetops. For several moments, she savored the special peace and quiet of the ranch as she tried to count the myriad stars sparkling in the sky. Then rolling onto her stomach she began to swim, her pace slow and steady.

After ten laps she had to stop and rest. Though she wasn't badly out of shape, she had to admit that twenty laps after a hard day of work was too much for her. Closing her eyes, she floated on her back, allowing her aching arms and legs to sway with the gentle motion of the breeze-ruffled water. She should get out of the pool and go back to the house, but she wasn't quite ready to give up her warm, comfortable cocoon for even a short walk in the cool night air.

"What are you doing out here all alone?" Mac's deep, low voice startled her as it cut through the stillness somewhere up above her head.

With a quick twist, Maggie turned to face him, moving her arms and legs back and forth to keep herself from sinking. He was standing on the edge of the pool closest to her,

wearing nothing but a modest pair of swimming trunks, his
hands on his hips as he gazed down at her. In the moonlight, he was more shadow than substance, but even at a
distance and in the darkness he appeared to be a smiling
shadow.

"I couldn't sleep," Maggie replied, her voice soft and
tentative as she drifted away from him.

"Me neither," he admitted. A moment later, he dove into
the pool and surfaced right in front of her. Shaking his hair
out of his face, he scattered drops of water over her.

"Mac, you're getting me wet," she chided, backing away
from him.

"You're in a swimming pool, Maggie. You're supposed
to get wet." With a grin that reminded her of a big, bad
wolf, he grabbed her around the waist and pulled her under
the water with him.

"You rat," she sputtered, as they surfaced.

Bracing her hands on his shoulders, she couldn't help but
return his grin. He seemed so proud of his boyish prank.
And in the moonlight, he looked so young and carefree, as
if all the pain and anger and frustration of the past two years
had been washed away. She wanted to hold the moment in
her heart forever. She wanted to—

"Maggie..." Her name no more than a murmur, he bent
his head and covered her mouth with his as he drew her into
his arms.

She clung to him as the water rippled around them,
burying her fingers in his dark, wet hair, wrapping her legs
around his waist, pressing her barely covered breasts against
his bare chest as his tongue curled around hers. His hands
roamed over her body, caressing her back and her buttocks, spanning her waist, then moving up her rib cage.
Sliding his thumbs under the edges of her suit, he stroked
the sides of her breasts, then brushed the hard peaks of her

nipples as he slanted his mouth first one way, then another over hers.

Moaning softly, she arched into him, savoring the rough texture of his hands against her smooth skin, following the plunging rhythm of his tongue with a gentle rocking of her hips as she knotted her fingers in his hair. When at last he lifted his head, she buried her face in his neck with a murmured protest.

This was what she had longed for when she had stood at her window, unable to sleep, and she didn't want it to stop. Her body throbbing with desire, she clung to him more tightly as he moved into shallower water, her panting breaths matching his as she pressed her lips to his shoulder, the side of his neck, the line of his jaw, the tip of his chin.

She was spinning out of control, but she didn't care. It had been such a very, very long time since she'd even thought of making love. But Mac was here with her now, holding her, kissing her, caressing her, and she didn't want to think, she wanted to do. Sliding her legs along his until she stood before him, she ran her hands down his back and around his waist, smoothing her palms over the flat plane of his stomach in ever widening, lowering circles until she cupped him in her hands.

Leaning back against the side of the pool, Mac groaned deep in his throat as he braced his feet on the bottom. Her hands on him, holding him, caressing him, tempted him to the limits of his self-control. He wanted to be inside her, but not here, not yet. It was too soon for them. Neither the time nor the place was right. Making love with Maggie would require a commitment he wasn't sure he could make. And though he wanted to take all that she seemed so willing to give, he couldn't do it until he *was* sure.

"Mac, please, I want—"

"I know, sweetheart," he whispered, tracing the outline of her ear with the tip of his tongue. "So do I." He moved against her, showing her just how much he wanted as he smoothed his palms over her breasts. Ever so gently he teased her nipples with his fingertips as he bent his head and claimed her mouth for one last, deep kiss. "But not here, not . . . yet . . ." Releasing her, he took her hands in his and brought them up out of the water. "Not yet, Maggie. I want it to be special for us, very slow and very special."

His mouth, hot and damp against her fingers, sent shivers racing through her body.

"Are you cold?" He pulled her into his arms, holding her close, smoothing her wet hair away from her face as the warm water lapped at her shoulders.

"No." She rubbed her cheek against his chest, secure in his gentle, undemanding embrace. "I'm really kind of . . . hot," she laughed softly, shyly, as she rested her head on his shoulder.

"Well, this ought to cool you off," he offered, his voice suddenly teasing as he wrapped his hands around her waist, lifted her out of the water and set her on the edge of the pool.

"Mac!" she cried, giggling like a schoolgirl when he gazed up at her, a sheepish grin curving the corners of his mouth.

"Quiet, Miz Connor, or we'll end up with an audience."

"We already have an audience." She nodded toward the puppies creeping toward them on their bellies, their little bottoms wiggling playfully.

"You know what I mean." He moved closer to her, propping his forearms on her knees.

"Uh-huh." She glanced at the cabins several hundred yards away, but they were dark and still.

"I've missed you."

"I've missed you, too," Maggie admitted, threading her fingers through his wet hair, spiking it up in a hairstyle that made him look more like a wild rock 'n' roll singer than a conservative rancher. "You got your hair cut."

"A couple of days ago. Don't tell me you've been too busy to notice."

She leaned forward and kissed his cheek. "It's been crazy around here, but I can't say you didn't warn me."

"It'll settle down in a couple of weeks . . . when the kids are gone. . . ." He moved her legs apart so he could step between them, then leaned forward so he could run a trail of quick, light kisses from her belly to the hollow between her breasts.

His mouth was incredibly hot against the cool, wet fabric of her suit. She wanted to rip it off and slide back into his arms. Instead, she closed her fingers around his hair and tugged his head up. "Why did you do it?" she asked, her voice more than a little unsteady.

"What?"

"Cut your hair. I liked it long and shaggy." She rested her hands on his shoulders and tipped her head to one side, a frown wrinkling her forehead.

"I don't think Bates and Carswell or Jackson Enterprises would approve."

"Who are Bates and Carswell and Jackson Enterprises?"

"The companies I'm interviewing with tomorrow, or rather today. Don't tell me you forgot."

"Completely." She shook her head ruefully, unable to believe she'd had such a major memory lapse. He'd mentioned the interviews several times, and she'd made a point of marking the date on her calendar, but until he'd mentioned it, she hadn't realized today was the day. Or maybe she'd purposely put it out of her mind, hoping he'd do the same. "So, I guess you haven't changed your mind about selling the ranch?"

"You're beginning to sound like Elizabeth. You're also scowling at me just like she's been doing since I walked in the door with short hair."

"I'm scowling at myself because I've been too busy to notice until now," she replied in a breezy tone of voice. He hadn't actually denied the possibility of a change of heart, but she knew better than to push him on it, at least right now. Considering how he griped about the traffic in San Antonio whenever he had to go there, Maggie had a feeling that his trip to Dallas would do more than she could to convince him that he belonged on the ranch anyway.

"We'll have to see what we can do about that as soon as I get back."

"But I thought I was supposed to be busy. I thought that's why you asked me to stay—to look after your guests."

"That was only one reason, Miz Connor." He wrapped an arm around the back of her neck and pulled her forward for a long, slow, deep kiss.

"Aha, I'm beginning to suspect ulterior motives, Mr. Harrow," she whispered breathlessly when he finally released her.

"Suspicions confirmed," he growled, gripping her hips in his hands as he kissed her neck, her shoulder, the swell of her breast, his mouth hot and wet against her cool, dry skin. Finally, unable to resist any longer, he dipped his head down and stroked first one tight, hard nipple and then the other with the tip of his tongue.

"Mac...if you don't...stop..." Tilting her head back, she buried her fingers in his hair again and despite her warning words held him close, her thighs pressed against his sides. "I'm going to..." She shuddered as his teeth grazed her with infinite yet possessive care, the aching and the emptiness inside her almost more than she could bear.

"I'm...stopping," he muttered. "And you're going to go back to the house...now." He eased away from her, his hands sliding down her thighs as he stepped back.

"What about you?"

"I'm going to stay here and...swim." He made the simple exercise sound more like a wicked witch's curse.

"Are you sure?" Maggie asked, swinging her legs out of the water and standing up. A small breeze slipped down her bare back and around her legs, making her shiver.

"It's the only thing I'm sure about tonight." He was almost halfway across the pool, the deeper water covering his broad shoulders. "See you in the morning, Miz Maggie."

"See you in the morning, Mac." She turned away from the pool, scooped up her towel and flashlight, and headed for the house, only vaguely aware of the puppies trotting along beside her.

She wasn't sure if she wanted to laugh or cry, but she was absolutely positive she didn't want to go to bed alone. Unfortunately Mac wasn't giving her any choice. She should be grateful that he cared enough to want their lovemaking to be special. And she was. Yet she couldn't help wishing he was a little less chivalrous. Of course, if he were a callous brute, she wouldn't have looked at him twice.

"Which all goes to prove you can't have your cake and eat it, too, Mary Margaret," she muttered, as she climbed the side porch steps.

Her hand on the doorknob, she paused for a moment and glanced over her shoulder. Mac cut across the pool much as she had done earlier, his strokes slow and steady. He touched the side, turned gracefully and started in the opposite direction. She wondered how long he planned to stay in the water. She was tempted to wait just inside the doorway and find out. But he wouldn't appreciate it, and she really did need to sleep. With a murmured good-night to the puppies crowding around her ankles, she opened the door and stepped across the threshold.

Though it was after one o'clock when she finally crawled into bed, Maggie didn't expect to get much sleep. But shortly after her head hit the pillow, she drifted into dreamland and stayed there until her alarm went off at six. By six-thirty she was in the kitchen, a mug of hot coffee on the counter beside her as she started the first of several batches of biscuits.

"What are you doing up so early?"

"If it's Tuesday, I'm baking biscuits for twenty-five hungry people." Smiling softly, she turned to face Mac as he joined her at the counter. "Oh, wow, you look..." *Wonderful,* she thought, gazing at him for several moments, her eyes wide with surprise, her smile suddenly full of uncertainty.

Dressed in a well-tailored gray suit just a few shades darker than his eyes, a crisp white shirt and a maroon-striped tie, he looked nothing like the man who owned the Whispering Wind. He looked like the high-powered corporate executives who worked for her father. He would have no trouble fitting in at Bates and Carswell or Jackson Enterprises. And if that was what he wanted, she should be pleased for him.

But she wasn't pleased, at all. She didn't want him going to Dallas and interviewing for jobs. She wanted him to stay on the Whispering Wind...with her. And that was a dangerous kind of wanting. It would mean giving up so much more of herself than she'd done so far. It would replace temporary with permanent, and she wasn't ready for that kind of permanence yet. She might never be.

"Something wrong? Have I got a spot on my shirt or something?" He poured a mug of coffee, then rested a hip against the counter, watching her.

"Nothing's wrong." Carefully she measured another cup of flour into the mixing bowl in front of her. To save her life she couldn't remember how many she'd added already, but one more wouldn't hurt, and it gave her an excuse to avoid Mac's probing gaze. "I was just going to say you...you look nice."

"You look nice, too," he teased, reaching out to rub a thumb over her cheek. "Flour can be so becoming."

"I thought it might hide the shadows under my eyes." Moving away from him, she reached for the carton of buttermilk. "Will you be home tonight?"

"Maggie, what's wrong?" He caught her arm and pulled her around to face him.

"Just tired, I guess." She gazed up at him for one long moment, offering what she hoped was a reassuring smile. She didn't want to worry him with problems only she could solve. "And I really wanted to have the biscuits started before Rosa gets here."

Taking her cue, he released her arm and stepped back, giving her room to work. "I'll try to make it back tonight, but it might be late when I get in. If I decide to spend the night in Dallas, I'll call you, all right?" He finished his coffee and set his mug on the counter.

"All right," she agreed, trying to concentrate on getting the buttermilk into the measuring cup instead of on the countertop.

"You've got the numbers where I can be reached?"

"Yes, of course."

"Then I guess I'd better get going."

"Goodbye, Mac." She poured the buttermilk into the bowl.

An instant later, he took the cup from her hand, set it on the counter and grabbed her shoulders. Before she could protest, he bent his head and kissed her, his mouth claiming hers quickly yet so completely that when he released her she had to grab on to the counter for support.

"Goodbye, Maggie." He turned on his heel, strode across the kitchen and walked out the door.

A few minutes later she heard the sound of his truck starting, then the scatter of gravel as he headed down the drive. "Hurry home," she murmured as the silence settled around her once again. "I'll be waiting for you."

Chapter Nine

"Mom, *Mom!* Guess who's here!" Christopher cried as he skidded through one of the archways separating the living room and dining room. Elizabeth and the puppies were close on his heels.

Maggie tossed her pen on the desk and removed her reading glasses, then eased back in her chair. For one mad moment she thought that Mac had changed his mind about spending the night in Dallas, but then her common sense kicked in. Whoever was coming, Maggie knew it wasn't Mac.

He had called shortly after lunch to tell her that Jo's mother had arranged for him to meet with a real-estate agent who had several houses to show him the following day. He hadn't sounded happy about the house-hunting expedition, but Mrs. Andrews had gone to a lot of trouble to make arrangements that coincided with his job interviews, and she'd done so at his request. Knowing Mac as well as she did now, Maggie had no doubt that he'd spend most of the following day tramping through every house the agent had to show him—even if his heart wasn't in it. And Maggie hoped against hope that his heart wasn't in it.

But if Mac was still in Dallas, who on earth had arrived at the Whispering Wind? From the way her son was jiggling from one foot to the other next to her chair, his bright eyes full of excitement, her first guess would be Santa Claus. She shifted her attention to Elizabeth, standing off to one side. The girl met her gaze, her eyes unusually solemn and full of uncertainty as the side door opened and closed, and two sets of footsteps started across the dining room floor.

"Oh, no," Maggie muttered as the other name for Santa Claus clicked in her head. Flattening her palms on the desktop, she pushed out of her chair and stood up. "I'm going to wring his neck."

"It's Grandma and Grandpa," Christopher crowed. Spinning around, he ran to join the elegantly dressed elderly couple as they walked into the living room. He hugged his grandmother, then his grandfather, then turned to face Maggie. "Can you believe it, Mom? It's Grandma and Grandpa."

"I can believe it," Maggie murmured, hanging on to the edge of the old desk with one hand and trying, *trying* to hang on to her temper, as well.

She was thirty-five years old, an adult, an independent single mother with a job and a home of her own. But they were her parents. And although that didn't give them the right to meddle and manipulate, she was wise enough to know that their only motive for doing so was their boundless love for her and Christopher.

"Are you going to go away with them?" Elizabeth asked, her voice whisper-soft.

Maggie glanced at the girl, reading very real concern in her wide, dark eyes. "No, we're not," she assured her, her voice equally soft as she slipped her hand into Elizabeth's for a moment and gave it a quick, hard squeeze.

Then she turned toward her parents, a very real yet very wry smile tipping up the corners of her mouth. "Mom, Dad, this is such a surprise." Three steps took her across the space separating them and into their welcoming arms.

"Maggie, darling, you look...wonderful." Deborah Chase held her daughter at arm's length, gazing at her as if it had been years instead of months since she'd last seen her, then pulled her back into her arms. "We've been so worried about you."

"You're the one who looks wonderful." She returned the warm embrace with deep and genuine affection. They had become more than mother and daughter over the past three years. They had become the best of friends. "And I'm fine, Mom, just fine."

"I don't know about that, Mary Margaret," Avery Chase growled, enveloping her in a big bear hug the instant her mother released her. "You sounded mighty tired when I talked to you last week. And you've got shadows under your eyes." He, too, held her at arm's length and studied her closely, eyeing her faded jeans and wrinkled shirt with disdain.

"Working on a dude ranch for the summer." He shook his head as if the mere thought of it was too much for him. "And you, young man," he continued, focusing his attention on Christopher though he hadn't let go of Maggie. "You're brown as a berry, you're dressed like a beggar boy and you need a haircut." The twinkle in his bright blue eyes, eyes Maggie and her son had inherited, belied the harshness of his criticism.

"I want to know exactly what's going on around here." Barely missing a beat, he turned back to his daughter. "You take off for a two-week vacation on a dude ranch, and the next thing I know, you're working on the darned place. My

little girl and my only grandchild *working* on a ranch. Tried
to mind my own business, like your mother said I should.
Figured you'd get it out of your system after a week or so.
But it's going on six weeks and you're still here. I want some
answers, Mary Margaret, and I want 'em now."

"I forgot the question," Maggie teased. Rising up on her
toes, she kissed his lined and weathered cheek, then stepped
away from him as he released his hold on her arm. Turning
back to her mother, she slipped an arm around her waist and
hugged her again. They were almost the same height and
once Deborah's hair had been the same deep auburn as her
daughter's. Now it was as white as new-fallen snow. "Let's
go in the kitchen. I've got a huge pitcher of iced tea in the
refrigerator. Actually I've got *several* huge pitchers of tea in
the refrigerator. We can have a drink while I help Rosa get
dinner started. You're staying, aren't you? Why don't you
take off your coat and tie, Dad?"

"Now just a darn minute, Mary Margaret. What the heck
is going on—"

"She's helping my dad, um, save our ranch," Elizabeth
cut in, her voice soft but steady as she faced Avery Chase.

"And just who are you, missy?" Maggie's father gazed
at the girl, arching a thick, shaggy, gray eyebrow as he
tipped his head to one side.

"I'm Elizabeth Harrow. My father is Mackenzie Harrow. He owns the Whispering Wind," she replied, her dark
eyes meeting his without wavering. "He needs Maggie's
help. *We* need Maggie's help."

"I see." Avery Chase glanced at his daughter, a new and
very speculative light in his eyes. "Well, in that case..." He
let his words drift away as he moved to join Maggie and her
mother. "Iced tea sounds nice, but I think I'd rather have a
glass of bourbon. And I'd sure like to meet Mr. Mackenzie
Harrow."

"Don't even think about it, Dad," Maggie warned, as she led them through the dining room and into the kitchen.

"Think about what, little girl? A glass of bourbon or a meeting with your Mr. Harrow?"

"You know what I mean. But just to be on the safe side, let me clarify a couple of points. You can have a glass of bourbon. As for meeting Mr. Harrow...maybe another time. He's in Dallas and he won't be back until tomorrow night. Since you're leaving in the morning—"

"Who said anything about leaving in the morning, Mary Margaret?"

"I did, Daddy. I did."

With a sigh of relief Mac closed the long metal gate barring the road to the ranch house and looped the safety chain over the fence post. Pausing for one long moment, he tipped his head back and gazed at the dark night sky, hung with the fullest, fattest moon he'd ever seen, and sparkling with starlight. Then, a cool, gentle breeze ruffling his hair, he walked back to his truck and climbed inside. It was good to be home, so very good to be home.

The two days in Dallas had seemed more like two years. He couldn't count the number of times he'd wondered what he was doing there. Six months ago he'd been positive that a job with a big corporation and house in the suburbs were exactly what he wanted. Now he wasn't quite so sure.

The job interviews had gone well, but would he accept a position with Bates and Carswell or Jackson Enterprises if one was offered? Would he actually buy one of the houses he'd looked at earlier today? Or would he stay on the Whispering Wind? It was a decision only he could make, and it was a decision he'd have to make sometime soon. Sometime after he'd had a chance to talk to Maggie....

He pressed down on the accelerator, sending dust and gravel flying as he topped the last low hill separating him from the house. The cabins were dark, the swimming pool deserted, but there were lights glowing in the living-room windows. His heart beat a little faster, his lips curved into a smile. It was past ten o'clock, but maybe, just maybe she was waiting for him. She hadn't teased him about going to Blue Coot's Saloon either yesterday or today, when he'd talked to her.

In fact, she'd sounded more reserved than usual when he'd called to tell her he was taking a later flight to San Antonio than originally planned. But surely she would have told him if she was having a problem of some sort, he thought, as he rounded the curve in the drive. Then again, she might not. She was so damned independent, refusing to ask for help even when she really needed it. *Especially* when she really needed it, he amended, eyeing the big, brand new Cadillac parked near the side door of the house.

With a muttered curse, he pulled up behind the strange car, switched off the engine and cut the lights. A few seconds later he walked into the house and moved quietly across the dining room, heading toward the soft murmur of voices and the faint drift of a symphony coming from the living room. She wasn't waiting for him, after all. She was enjoying someone else's company, thoroughly enjoying it, if her light, teasing tone of voice was any indication. And she was doing it in the privacy of *his* home. Well, he'd just see about—

"Mac, you're home," she cried, her eyes bright, her smile wide and welcoming as she jumped off the old sofa and started toward him. For just a moment he thought she might hurl herself into his arms, but she stopped a few feet away, her expression suddenly shadowed by uncertainty. Behind her, still seated on the sofa, an elderly couple gazed at him, their expressions full of interest and amusement.

He stared at her for the space of several heartbeats, willing away the angry frown furrowing his forehead. When would he ever learn to stop misjudging her? From this day on, he promised himself, closing the distance between them and taking her into his arms. "Maggie...I missed you," he murmured, rubbing his cheek against her soft curls as he held her.

"I missed you, too," she sighed, tightening her hold on him to emphasize her words. Then, easing away from him, she tipped her head up, her smile back in place again. "And I was beginning to worry. It was getting late and the kids decided to go on up to—"

"Well, well, well...you must be Mackenzie Harrow. Heard a lot about you. If you let loose of my little girl for a minute, I'd like to shake your hand."

"Mr. Chase, I've heard a lot about you, too." Without a moment's hesitation, Mac settled Maggie under his left arm, then extended his right hand to her father. "Nice to meet you, sir." He met the man's eyes as they shook hands, refusing to be intimidated by him, at least outwardly.

"My wife, Deborah." The older man nodded toward his wife.

"Mrs. Chase." Mac acknowledged the introduction, reassured by the woman's encouraging smile, as well as Maggie's arm around his waist. Not only did he want her parents' approval, he wanted hers, too. "You came to check up on your daughter, didn't you?"

"Yes, we did," Avery Chase replied. "Came to get a look at you, too," he added, his eyes narrowing as he stared at Mac. "Wanted to see just exactly what Mary Margaret was getting herself into."

"Dad!" Maggie protested.

"It's all right," Mac assured her, squeezing her shoulder. "I understand your father's concern. Would you like to take a walk out to the barn to see the horses, Mr. Chase?"

"Mac, it's almost eleven o'clock at night and my father has already seen the barn and the horses several times to-day." She looked at him as if he had rocks in his head.

"Sounds like a fine idea, Mr. Harrow," her father agreed, ignoring her completely. "Why don't you ladies go on up to bed?"

"I think we should *all* go up to bed," Maggie argued. "You can see the—"

Turning Maggie around to face him, Mac bent his head and kissed her full on the mouth, quickly but completely silencing her protests. Smiling at the stunned expression on her face, he dropped a kiss on her cheek, then the tip of her nose. "Good night, Mary Margaret," he murmured, his pale eyes full of mischief as he released her.

"Come along, dear. It's been a long day, and I know you have to get up early in the morning. Mr. Harrow, it was a pleasure meeting you." Deborah Chase offered him another encouraging smile, then glanced at her husband. "Thirty minutes, Avery, and don't forget to mind your manners."

"Yes, ma'am."

Mac stood to one side, watching as the old man kissed his wife and daughter. He could see the rebellion brewing in Maggie's bright eyes, but when she looked to him for support, he simply smiled and shook his head. Though he had no reason to cater to Avery Chase, Mac was willing to do so for Maggie's sake. It was obvious that her parents loved her and wanted to protect her, and Mac wanted them to know he had no intention of hurting her. In fact, his intentions toward Maggie Connor had been and always would be honorable.

"I don't know about you, Mr. Harrow, but I'd settle for a bourbon-and-water at the kitchen table."

"Call me Mac. And a bourbon-and-water sounds good to me, too."

As Avery Chase pulled out a chair and sat down, Mac poured their drinks, then joined the older man at the table.

"What do you think of the Whispering Wind?" Mac asked, honestly interested in Maggie's father's opinion of the place.

"I think it's worth saving." He took a long swallow from his glass, holding Mac's gaze over the rim.

"Saving?" Mac frowned as he turned his glass in his hands. "Saving from what?"

"I thought you might tell me. According to your daughter, Maggie's helping you save your ranch. Elizabeth says you need her."

"Elizabeth has a very vivid imagination. Actually I'm thinking of selling the ranch at the end of the summer. Since my wife died . . ." Mac glanced at Avery, then took a sip of his bourbon-and-water. "It's a lot to handle on my own."

"You're not handling it on your own now, are you?"

"Maggie's only staying for the summer."

"You ever think about asking her to stay permanently?"

Mac raised his glass and swallowed the last of his drink in a single gulp. Pushing away from the table, he stood up, crossed the kitchen and set his glass in the sink. He rested his palms on the countertop and stared out the window. Somewhere in the back of his mind he *had* thought about it, but not seriously. Not yet. He shrugged and shook his head.

"She has a life of her own, a job and a home in San Antonio. And if anyone should know how much she values her independence, it's you, Mr. Chase."

"A lot of bluff and nonsense, if you ask me. Anyway, I've never seen her or my grandson happier than I have the past two days. And I'd be willing to do just about anything to make sure my little girl's happy."

"I'm not for sale, Avery." Mac gripped the countertop, his knuckles turning white as he glared at Maggie's father over his shoulder. "I don't want or need your money."

The two men exchanged long, measuring looks. Finally Avery nodded his head once, his sharp, steady eyes gleaming with approval. "Well, then, I wish you luck, son." He raised his glass in a toast, then swallowed the last of his drink. "Knowing my daughter the way I do, I know you're going to need it. Gets an idea in her head and has a hard time turning it loose, but then I suppose you've found that out already. Maybe I ought to talk to her, put in a good word for—"

"No!" Mac spun around and took a step toward the old man. "Please, Mr. Chase...Avery, don't say anything to her at all about me...about...us." If her father pushed him on Maggie, she'd run back to San Antonio so fast his head would spin. And Mac didn't want her to run away. He wanted her to stay, at least until the end of the summer. That was as far ahead as he was willing to think at the moment.

"You telling me my putting a bug in her ear is the same as the kiss of death?" Avery challenged, a hint of amusement accentuating the approval in his eyes. "How do you know I'm not going to order her to pack her bags and get out of here? Wild horses wouldn't drag her away then."

"I think you gave up giving her orders a few years ago," Mac replied, a wide grin on his face as he retrieved his glass and the bottle from the counter and returned to the table. He poured two fingers of the dark, smooth liquor in each glass, capped the bottle and set it aside. Then, his grin disappearing, he met Avery Chase's steady gaze. "I'm not going to make any promises about the future that I might not be able to keep, but I swear to God I won't do anything to hurt Maggie and Christopher. I...I care for her...for them."

"She cares for you, too, son. And don't you forget it." Again Maggie's father nodded his head once, as if confirming all that he'd said and some things he hadn't. Then he glanced at his watch. "Deborah gave me thirty minutes.

Time's almost up.'' He picked up his glass and swallowed a mouthful of bourbon.

"I thought Deborah and I would take off tomorrow afternoon," he continued, his eyes sparkling with meddling-old-man mischief as he traced a finger around the rim of his glass. "Thought maybe we'd take those two young rascals with us, if you don't have any objections. We can stop in New Braunfels for a couple of days. They've got some sort of water park there, slides and swimming pools, stuff like that. We can stop at Six Flags for a couple of days, too, then drop Elizabeth off at her grandparents' house. Save you and Maggie the long drives to Houston and Dallas. Give you some time alone together." He arched one bushy brow as he glanced at Mac.

Mac stared at him for several seconds, the corners of his mouth twitching into a grin that was half admiration, half aggravation. The man didn't know when to quit. For the first time, he could understand Maggie's desperate desire for independence. Her father had run her life for thirty-two years, and even after three years on her own, he was still bound and determined to do whatever he thought necessary to secure her future, even if it meant throwing her into the waiting arms of a widowed rancher ten days ahead of schedule.

She'd probably see right through the ploy and she'd probably be mad as hell, not only at her father but at him for going along with it. Because Mac intended to go along with it. It might be incredibly selfish, but much as he loved his daughter and cared for her son, suddenly he wanted Maggie all to himself—and the sooner, the better.

"What about Bonnie and Clyde?" There had been grumblings about leaving the puppies on the ranch while the children visited their grandparents for a couple of weeks. Now they would be separated for at least three weeks.

"The kids agreed they'd be better off on the ranch than the back seat of my Caddy." He grinned as he pushed away from the table and stood up. "I might be getting old, but I'm not crazy...yet."

Mac returned his grin as he, too, stood up. "I don't know about that, Avery. Two days at the Schlitterbann and two days at Six Flags with a couple of eleven-year-olds would try any man's sanity."

"So would my daughter, Mac," he warned as he extended his hand across the table. "But they're worth it, aren't they?"

"Damned right," Mac agreed, grasping the other man's hand with his, his clasp firm, his expression suddenly solemn, as if he were sealing a very special pact of friendship and understanding.

In a way he was, he realized, following Avery Chase out of the kitchen and up the staircase. And it should be scaring the spit out of him. Instead he was filled with a new and special sense of anticipation and a warm, inner glow of what could only be called happiness, the kind he'd never thought he'd experience again in his life. Pausing for a moment, he watched Maggie's father walk down the hallway and open the door to the bedroom next to Maggie's. Then, tucking his hands in the side pockets of his slacks, he started up the stairs. One night soon he wouldn't climb the stairs alone. One night soon Maggie would be by his side....

By Saturday morning Mac was beginning to wonder where he'd gone wrong. It had been almost two days since Avery and Deborah Chase had left with the children, and rather than being closer than ever to Maggie, he felt as if he'd been exiled to some very cold, very dark, very distant corner of the universe. And he didn't like it, not one damned bit, he thought, as he loosened the cinch and pulled the saddle off Bobby Dawson's gelding.

The horse was coming along as well as he had expected, but Mac had been too preoccupied with Maggie lately to take much pleasure in the success of his training. He tossed the saddle over a stall door, then reached for a brush and currycomb, welcoming the physical activity because it left his mind free to roam over the past few days.

Though he had expected a more volatile response from Maggie, she had surprised him Thursday morning when she'd agreed to her father's plans for the children without hesitation. Her voice had been cool and quiet, and there had been more than a hint of suspicion in her bright, blue eyes as her gaze had traveled between the two men. But she hadn't been angry. Of course, she hadn't seemed pleased by the prospect of being on her own with him, either. She hadn't given any indication that she shared his excitement or expectation at the thought of their being alone together at last.

At first he thought that she might be trying to hide her true feelings from her family, especially since she'd used every excuse she could find to avoid being anywhere near him until they drove away on Thursday afternoon. But Wednesday night she'd walked into his arms without hesitation, despite her parents' presence in the living room. And it was now Saturday morning. Her parents had been gone for almost two days, and her voice was still cool and quiet whenever she spoke to him, her eyes were still shadowed with suspicion on the rare occasions when she actually looked at him, and she continued to avoid him as if her life depended on it.

Certainly she'd had good excuses to slip upstairs early the past couple of nights, leaving him to chase guests out of the living room and the swimming pool at ten o'clock. And he'd chosen not to knock on her bedroom door on his way to the third floor because he'd figured she needed time. But damn it, anyway—

The gelding whickered and tossed his head as Mac applied the brush a little harder than usual on the horse's rump. "Sorry, boy," he muttered, his voice soothing, as he stroked the gelding's neck for a few moments. When the horse had settled down again, Mac crossed in front of him and started on his withers.

Had her father ignored his request and discussed their relationship with her? Mac didn't think so. The old fox was wise enough to know that his daughter wouldn't be pushed, and Avery Chase had known he was already pushing her when he offered to take the kids off their hands several days ahead of schedule. But what if Maggie had questioned her father about their late-night conference? She was too curious not to have mentioned it to one of them, and she certainly hadn't discussed it with *him*. And Mac didn't think Avery would lie to her.

With a muttered curse, he tossed the brush and currycomb onto a nearby bench, then led the gelding into a stall. Much as he wanted to blame Avery Chase, he couldn't do it. Because there was always the possibility that he'd only imagined that Maggie felt something more for him than friendship, that she'd stayed on at the Whispering Wind only to help him earn the money he'd allowed her to believe he needed.

But if she only thought of him as a friend, would she have responded to his kisses and caresses the way she had? Surely she'd known that what he was asking for, what he was offering was much more than companionship. He thought of the way she'd touched him with her hands and her mouth when he'd joined her in the swimming pool on Monday night. And he remembered the way she'd walked into his arms and rested her head on his shoulder when he'd returned from Dallas. And he knew without a doubt that she was drawn to him as strongly, as deeply as he was drawn to her.

So why was she avoiding him? He was back to square one and no closer to having an answer to his question than he'd been two days ago, much less two hours ago. Only Maggie knew why she was acting the way she was. And he was damned tired of waiting for her to let him in on the secret. He was going to find out what her problem was and solve it before he did anything else.

Turning on his heel, he headed down the long aisle separating the rows of stalls. If he wasn't mistaken, she'd said something about cleaning a couple of empty cabins as she'd flitted out the kitchen door shortly after lunch. It was a good bet she was still in one or the other of them. If she wasn't, he'd find her, wherever she was hiding. And then he'd... well, he'd think of *something* to get her out of her mood.

Maggie shoved the vacuum cleaner first one way, then the other over the cabin carpeting, and for the umpteenth time wondered *why* she'd been so determined to clean cabins today. Unless they had some drop-ins, they wouldn't need them until next week. She should have worked on the books or the grocery order. Then she would have been forced to think about something besides the embarrassing events of the past few days.

It was bad enough that her parents had come to the Whispering Wind to check on her, as if she were a child instead of a thirty-five-year-old woman. But then they'd insisted on staying until Mac returned to the ranch. And, of course, her father hadn't been satisfied with simply meeting Mac. He'd had to square off with him over a bottle of bourbon. She'd found the half-empty glasses on the kitchen table Thursday morning, and had been afraid to venture a guess at what had transpired between the two men the night before.

However, it hadn't been until her parents insisted on taking Christopher and Elizabeth with them that Maggie had wanted to crawl into a hole and pull a rock over her head. If it had been obvious to her, then surely it had been obvious to Mac that she was being foisted on him in a way he hadn't bargained for when he'd asked her to stay on the ranch. He'd gone along with her father's idea, but faced with the children's enthusiasm, he hadn't had much of a choice.

Considering the circumstances, she had decided that the least she could do was give him some space. Where she was concerned, she wanted him to have a choice. And she wanted to be ready to accept the fact that he might not choose to be with her, after all. He certainly hadn't come knocking at her door the past couple of nights, had he? Maybe a few kisses and caresses were all he'd needed to know that she wasn't what he want—

The vacuum died in mid-shove, the motor whining to a stop so suddenly that Maggie almost lost her balance when the suction let up and the machine rolled forward faster than she expected. "What the heck's the matter with you?" she muttered, punching the switch with her foot several times as she jiggled the handle.

"I was going to ask you the same thing." The unexpected reply, issued in a deep, low voice, came from somewhere behind her back.

"Mac!" Two seconds away from jumping out of her skin, Maggie whirled around and glared at him. He was leaning against the closed cabin door, twirling the vacuum cleaner cord in one hand, not even a hint of a smile on his dark, handsome face. "I wish you'd stop sneaking up on me. You scared me half to death . . . again."

"Sometimes sneaking up on you is the only way I can get your attention, Miz Connor."

"Oh, yeah?"

"Yeah." He started toward her, his eyes steady as he began to coil the cord. "You mad at me or something?"

"Why would I be mad at you?" She thought about moving behind the vacuum cleaner, but the look in his pale gray eyes held her still. Whatever he had in mind, no little piece of machinery was going to get in his way.

He stopped less than a foot away from her. He smelled of hay and horses, of sunlight and old leather. His jeans and shirt were worn and faded. Bits of straw and dust clung to his boots and his battered brown Stetson dipped low on his forehead. She could feel the heat radiating from his body as she tipped her head back to meet his gaze. His eyes holding hers, he reached around her and slipped the cord over the vacuum handle. Then he propped his hands on his hips.

"You're finished in here, aren't you?"

"Finished?" Momentarily confused by his closeness, not to mention his sudden change of subject, Maggie blinked her eyes and wet her lips. "Um, yes. I always vacuum last."

"And there are only four guests eating dinner at the ranch tonight?"

"Yes, the family in Cabin Five. The family in Cabin Four went to Sea World and won't be back until late. The couple in Cabin One are going into Bandera."

"I thought we'd do that, too."

"What?" She knew she wasn't stupid, but for some reason she was having a hard time following Mac's train of thought.

"I thought we'd go into Bandera for dinner. We can stop in at Blue Coot's Saloon and satisfy your curiosity, too." A barely perceptible smile softened the solemn expression on his face.

"But I really ought to help—"

"But me no buts, Maggie," he interrupted, resting his hands on her shoulders and giving her a gentle shake. "You've been working too damned hard around here lately.

You deserve a night off. And I need a night out." He traced the line of her jaw with one finger, his eyes full of the same yearning that tugged at her heart and soul. "Have dinner with me, Maggie. And let me spin you around the dance floor at Blue Coot's a few times. Please?" he asked, his voice suddenly soft and vulnerable.

She gazed at him for several seconds, her heart pounding in her chest. Was he asking for more than dinner and dancing? She wasn't sure. But she hoped so. Because she wanted more, so much more in the short time they had left together.

"What time do you want to leave?"

"About seven?"

"Sounds good to me." She glanced at her watch. It was almost five o'clock. If she headed back to the house now, she'd have time to wash her hair and do her nails. Turning away from Mac, she crossed the cabin and began filling her bucket with cleaning supplies. "See you at seven, then," she said as she lifted the bucket off the floor.

A moment later Mac took it from her, then reached for the vacuum cleaner. He waited quietly on the cabin porch while she closed and locked the door. Side by side they walked back to the house, neither of them saying a word. In the kitchen, Mac set the bucket on the counter and the vacuum on the floor. And then he caught her arm and turned her around to face him.

His kiss was hard and fast and full of promise. And it was over almost before it had begun. Maggie wanted to protest, but Mac placed a gentle finger on her lips.

"See you at seven, Miz Connor," he muttered. Then he was gone.

Chapter Ten

He paced the length of the living room for what had to be the tenth time in as many minutes. From the dining room he could hear the murmur of voices and the clink of cutlery as the family staying in Cabin Five finished their evening meal. Stopping in front of the wide empty fireplace, he glanced at his watch...again. It was exactly three minutes later than it had been the last time he'd checked, and he still had fifteen minutes to go until seven o'clock.

Bracing a forearm on the oak mantel, he bent his head and studied the toes of his brand new black boots. He had never been much good at waiting, and he felt as if he'd been waiting for tonight since the moment he'd first seen Maggie Connor standing in his living room, dripping all over the floor.

It had been only six weeks since she'd walked out of a storm and into his life. No time at all, really, but time enough to know that he didn't want her walking out again at the end of the summer. Yet he couldn't ask her to stay with him, not until he made a decision about the Whispering Wind. And when he made his decision he had to remember that she might not be willing to give up the life she'd made for herself and her son in San Antonio.

The trip to Dallas had left him more uncertain than ever about selling the ranch. But staying on without Maggie would be as bad as staying on without Jo. Though they were very different women, each one had given something special of herself to the Whispering Wind. And to him. Jo was gone now, and though he'd never forget her, thanks to Maggie, he had begun to accept her death and to finally stop blaming himself for it. And thanks to Maggie, he'd begun to believe that he might find happiness here once again. Now if only he could find a way to convince—

"Looks like I'm not the only one ready ahead of time."

At the sound of her light, teasing voice, Mac turned his head. She stood near the end of the old sofa, a soft smile curving her lips and brightening her eyes. He dropped his arm and took a step toward her, his eyes roving over her as he tried to control the urge to grab her, throw her over his shoulder and carry her back upstairs.

She was dressed in a pencil-slim denim miniskirt that was short without being too short, and sexy without being silly. She'd turned up the collar of her simple, sleeveless white shirt, her legs were bare, and she wore the flat, strappy white sandals she'd bought to replace the ones she'd ruined her first night on the ranch. She'd made no effort to tame her wild auburn curls and she'd replaced her small, modest gold hoop earrings with long silvery dangles hung with feathers.

Feathers...

By all means, carrying her back upstairs would be the wisest thing to do. If he took her to Blue Coot's, there was no telling how many lonely cowboys would make a pass at her. There was also no telling how long he'd keep from planting his fist in somebody's face.

"Is something wrong?" she asked, her voice full of uncertainty, her smile fading.

"Um, no." He paused a moment to clear his throat, then continued. "Nothing's wrong. You look..." He met her eyes and said what he thought. "You look wonderful, Maggie." Closing the distance between them, he caught her in his arms and spun her around. "Sure you can dance in that skinny little skirt?"

"Just try me," she challenged, her eyes flashing as she tipped her chin up.

"It'll be my pleasure," he murmured. Looping his arm around her shoulders, he led her through the now-empty dining room and out the side door.

"Want to take my car?"

"I'd rather watch you climb into the front seat of my truck."

"You're bad, Mackenzie Harrow."

"Why, thank you, Maggie Connor...ma'am...."

They had dinner at a small country café tucked away on a side street in downtown Bandera. Mac seemed to know everyone in the place. He stopped at one table after another as they followed the hostess through the dining room, and while she watched him trade greetings with friends, neighbors and business associates, Maggie began to realize just how well-liked he was in the community.

Though she had driven into Bandera quite often in the past weeks to buy supplies for the ranch, she'd almost always gone alone, and she'd been treated like the stranger she was. As Mac's guest, however, she was welcomed into the "family" with surprising enthusiasm. She had always assumed that small towns were insular by nature, and fitting in would be hard to do, but she couldn't remember feeling quite so at home anywhere as she did sharing a table with Mac at the Wagon Wheel Restaurant.

Of course she received more than a few speculative glances as she dug into her chicken-fried steak, but most were edged with kindness and an odd sort of encouragement. From the bits and pieces of conversation she overheard, she gathered that she was being touted as the one who might change Mackenzie Harrow's mind about selling the Whispering Wind. Maggie couldn't think of anything she'd rather do.

She also couldn't help but wonder how Mac felt about the rumors already flying around the room. He didn't seem to notice. Or if he noticed, he didn't seem to mind. He seemed content to talk about the guests staying at the ranch, the horses he was training, and just how crazy the kids might be driving her parents. And she wasn't about to push him, one way or another. Not on a night like tonight, a night so full of promise.

By the time they finally left the restaurant, it was dark. As they walked the short distance to Blue Coot's Saloon, moving down the sidewalk slowly, the evening breeze ruffling their hair, Mac caught her hand in his and threaded his fingers through hers.

"Was your dinner all right?"

"More than all right. It was wonderful, the best chicken-fried steak I've ever had. And there ought to be a law against the peach cobbler. It's sinful." Maggie smiled as she gazed up at him. "Thanks for taking me there. I really enjoyed it."

"Good, because you're going to be the talk of the town tomorrow." He returned her smile, his pale eyes full of mischief.

"In case you hadn't noticed, *we* were the talk of the town *tonight*." She ducked her head, focusing on the cracked concrete beneath their feet.

"Oh, I noticed," he replied, tugging on her hand, forcing her to stop and turn to face him. "Do you mind?"

Once again Maggie met his eyes. They were so warm, so full of quiet concern. "No, of course not." She hesitated for a moment, then continued, "Do *you* mind?"

"No, I don't mind, at all."

They stood in the center of the sidewalk, gazing at each other, grinning like a couple of naughty children up to no good. Then Mac tugged on her hand again, pulling her close. His smile fading, he buried his fingers in her hair, tilted her head up and kissed her full on the mouth for all of several seconds.

"Now they're *really* going to have something to talk about," she murmured when he finally released her. More than a few people had walked around them while she was in his embrace.

"Mind?" he asked, rubbing his thumb over her damp, swollen lips, seemingly oblivious to everything and everyone but her.

"Uh-uh." She shook her head, sending her long dangling earrings flying, and offered him another smile.

He held her gaze a moment longer, as if to reassure himself of the honesty of her answer. Then, releasing her hand, he slipped his arm around her shoulder and guided her across the street to the doorway of Blue Coot's.

Although it was still early by saloon standards, the place was hopping. A country-western band set up on a small stage in one corner of the wide room played old and new favorites just a few decibels under earsplitting, and several couples already whirled around the big dance floor.

Keeping her close beside him, Mac wove through the crowd, pausing occasionally to speak to more friends and neighbors until they arrived at the old oak bar that ran the length of one wall. As if she weighed nothing at all, he lifted her onto a bar stool, then waved to the bearded bartender who was filling frosted glass mugs with beer a few feet away.

"Thought we'd sit at the bar. It's a little quieter and we can visit with Blue," Mac said. He tucked a wisp of her wild, windblown hair behind her ear, then traced the curve of the feather on her earring with the tip of his finger, his touch gentle yet possessive.

"You said you grew up and went to school together, didn't you?"

"Well, I grew up. I'm not so sure about Blue. He's—"

"Hey, slandering my name again, buddy?" Blue Coot interrupted, as he braced his palms on the polished wood surface of the bar and leaned forward. Though his voice was gruff and his expression solemn, his dark eyes glittered with silent laughter and the corners of his mouth twitched upward for just an instant as he gazed at Maggie. "Don't pay any attention to him, ma'am. He ain't nothin' but a no-good, broken-down ole cowboy." Turning away from her, he extended his hand to Mac. "Good to see you again, pal."

"Good to see you, too." The two men shook hands, renewing the bond of their friendship with visible pleasure. "This is Maggie Connor. She's been helping out at the ranch this summer."

"Nice to meet you, Maggie Connor." He offered his hand and she took it without hesitation. "We close at one o'clock. Meet me at the side door and I'll—"

"Back off, Blue," Mac warned. "She's mine."

Though his voice was light and teasing, his eyes were so cold and steady that Maggie's laughter died in her throat. Her gaze swiveled between the two men as they stared at each other.

"Like that, is it?" Blue asked at last.

"Exactly like that," Mac affirmed.

"Well, it's about time."

To Maggie's surprise Blue offered Mac his hand again and Mac accepted, as both men grinned at each other in understanding.

"Hey, wait a minute," Maggie muttered, propping her hands on her hips and glaring at them. "I'm a person, not a piece of property."

"Now, darlin', don't get all riled up just because we're actin' like a couple of ruttin' bulls." Blue chucked her under the chin, his dark eyes full of the devil. "How about a beer?"

She raised her eyes to the ceiling and shook her head in exasperation. But when she met Blue's eyes again, she was smiling. "A beer would be wonderful."

"Comin' right up. You, too, Mac."

"Sure."

A moment later two foamy mugs appeared in front of them. "Say, you don't have any sisters, do you?" Blue asked, wagging his bushy eyebrows up and down.

"If she did, she wouldn't introduce them to you," Mac retorted.

"Oh, yeah?" Blue challenged as he moved away from them to serve another customer.

"Yeah."

Alone again, or as alone as it was possible to be in a noisy, crowded country-western saloon, Maggie and Mac sipped their beers and watched each other out of the corners of their eyes.

"I meant what I said." Maggie broke the silence stretching between them at last. "I don't appreciate being treated like a piece of property."

She didn't want to spoil the evening, especially since she didn't really mind his protective, possessive attitude all that much. In fact, it was rather nice to find out that he cared for her enough to let others know it. But she didn't *belong* to him, to *anyone* but herself. She was Maggie Connor, not Mackenzie Harrow's woman.

"I'm sorry. I had no right to say what I did." He smoothed his hand over her hair in gentle apology. "But when he started coming on to you..." He let his words trail away as he rested his elbows on the bar and rolled his beer mug in his hands. "I really blew it, didn't I?" he muttered.

"Oh, I wouldn't say that." She put her hand on his arm and rubbed her palm up and down, feeling his heat through the sleeve of his cotton shirt.

"You wouldn't?" He glanced at her over his shoulder, as if searching for more reassurance than offered by her words alone.

"Uh-uh." She leaned forward and kissed him on the cheek, breathing in his spicy scent. Then she slid off the bar stool and grabbed his hand. "Come on, they're playing our song."

"'Cotton-Eyed Joe' is our song?"

"Sure, why not?" She pulled him through the crowd and onto the dance floor, now packed with people.

"I don't know. I kind of thought maybe our song would be something slow, something...sexy...."

"Think again, Mr. Harrow," she teased, as they looped their arms around each other and fell into step with practiced ease.

They stayed on the dance floor quite a while, moving to the rhythm of one toe-tapping song after another, laughing as they spun around the dance floor, the Fred and Ginger of Blue Coot's Saloon. After a while Mac finally got his wish for something slow and sexy. Without hesitation, he drew her into his arms until their bodies molded together. Until they were as close as several layers of clothing would allow.

They swayed to the soft, gentle beat, their feet barely moving, her head pressed against his shoulder, his cheek resting lightly on her wild curls. He moved his hands to the small of her back, then down a little lower. She sighed, and turning slightly, brushed her lips against the base of his throat. He groaned as he bent his head and traced the curve of her ear with the tip of his tongue. She shivered delicately, twisting her fingers in the fabric of his shirt as every nerve ending in her body came to life.

"Maggie?" His voice was so low, so deep, so . . . ragged, his breath hot and damp against her skin.

"Yes?" She closed her eyes and rubbed her cheek against his chest.

"Let's go home."

She raised her head and gazed at him for one long moment, searching for all that he'd left unsaid and finding it in the depths of his pale gray eyes. "Yes . . ."

It seemed to take them forever to get through the crowd and out the door. They were halfway to the truck when Maggie remembered that they hadn't paid for their beers, but Mac assured her that Blue wouldn't mind.

"I think he'll understand," he said, an utterly masculine grin, full of pride and possession, lifting the corners of his mouth as he started the engine and pulled away from the curb. A moment later he reached across the seat and took her hand in his.

At his touch, Maggie turned to face him, a soft smile lighting her features as she studied his profile for several seconds. He was a handsome man, and though he often appeared to be cold and aloof, in the past few weeks Maggie had discovered just how warm and caring he could be.

She had watched him at work, as well as at play, with his daughter and her son, offering his time and attention to both children on an equal basis. And he had treated her parents with kindness and understanding, despite their unnecessary meddling. He was a good man, a very good man, and although it wasn't wise, she was afraid that she was falling in love with him.

They had no future together, not with Mac selling the ranch and moving to Dallas in a matter of weeks, and she with a life of her own, a job and a home in San Antonio. Nor did she have any real hope that *if* she loved him, her love would be returned. He might want her as a man wants a woman. He might even need her emotionally as well as physically. But she didn't think Mac was ready to risk loving again. And there was a good chance she wasn't, either. Yet she wanted to be with him in the most intimate way possible, tonight and for as many nights as possible until she left the Whispering Wind.

"Want to get the gate for me?"

"Oh, sure...." With a firm mental shake, she opened the door, slid to the ground and walked to the gate. As Mac drove past her, she tipped her head back and gazed at the stars sparkling in the sky. She loved it here, more than she'd ever loved any place she'd been. And wise or not, suddenly she knew that despite her mental game-playing, she loved Mackenzie Harrow, too.

A few minutes later they pulled up near the side door, and after dodging the puppies who seemed eager to play despite the late hour, they stepped inside the house. It was dark and cool and so quiet their footsteps echoed as they crossed the dining room and started up the staircase. On the second-floor landing Maggie hesitated, suddenly unsure what to say or what to do. Perhaps she should invite him to join her in her room. It would be easier for him there. But she couldn't seem to find the words—

"Something wrong, Maggie?"

Ever so gently he threaded his fingers through her hair and tilted her head back. In the near darkness she couldn't read his expression, but his eyes probed hers with unnerving intensity.

"I'm... I'm not sure... what to... do...."

"What do you want to do?"

"I want to...to make love with you, Mac," she replied, her voice whisper-soft as she traced the line of his jaw with her fingertips.

"And I want to make love with you...Maggie...."

He bent his head and kissed her so slowly, so deeply, so completely that she had no doubt he meant what he said. Resting her hands on his shoulders, she opened her mouth for him, curling her tongue around his in gentle welcome as she swayed into the cradle of his hips. Oh, yes, he wanted her. She sighed as she threaded her fingers through his hair and arched into him.

"Let's go...upstairs," he breathed against her moist, swollen lips, his hands moving over her back, her buttocks as he held her close.

"Are you...sure? Maybe we ought to use my...room...." She pressed her lips against the hollow at the base of his throat, the side of his neck, the edge of his jaw, nipping with her teeth, soothing with her tongue.

"Why?" He caught her head in his hands and tipped her face up, forcing her to meet his eyes.

"The third floor is your special, private place. I'm not sure I belong—"

He silenced her protests with a quick, hard kiss, taking her mouth with an almost painful urgency. Then he raised his head and scooped her into his arms. "*You* are special, Maggie. And in case you don't already know it, you belong with me."

As she clung to him, her arms locked around his neck, her face resting against his shoulder, he strode up the stairs, through the small sitting room and into his bedroom. Slowly he set her on her feet beside the big brass bed, then reached around her to turn on the small, lace-shaded lamp on the nightstand.

"All right?" he asked, his eyes holding hers as he smoothed a hand over her hair.

"All right," she agreed, a soft smile lifting the corners of her mouth. She traced the line of his jaw with her finger, then dropped her hand to his chest. Beneath her palm she could feel his heart beating almost as fast as hers.

"I want to take off all your clothes, Miz Maggie." He tipped his head down and released one button on her blouse, then another and another.

"I want to take off all your clothes, too." She worked on the buttons of his shirt, aware that her fingers were trembling just a little more than his.

"You know I won't hurt you. And I'll protect you," he vowed, dropping her blouse on the floor. A moment later, her bra followed. He paused for a moment, gazing at her small, firm breasts. "You're beautiful," he muttered. Bending his head, he kissed first one rosy peak, then the other, tugging at her gently with his lips, caressing her with the tip of his tongue. Then stepping back he reached for the zipper at the back of her skirt.

"You're beautiful, too," Maggie murmured. His shirt landed on top of her blouse. "And I trust you." She fumbled with his belt buckle as he slid her skirt and panties over her hips and down her legs.

An instant later, he hooked an arm under her knees, lifted her and settled her on the bed. Sitting down beside her, he unfastened the straps on her sandals and slid them off her feet, leaving her naked except for the silvery, feathered earrings.

"Hey, no fair," Maggie protested. "You're still half-dressed."

"Not for long." As good as his word, he pulled off his boots and socks, then shucked his jeans and underwear in one swift movement. "Come here, sweetheart. I want to hold you. I want to feel your body close to mine." Stretching out beside her, he gathered her into his arms.

She was as small and fragile and fiery as he'd imagined the first time he'd seen her, the first time he'd touched her. "Ah, Maggie, you feel so good, so good...." He eased away from her just enough so that he could touch her breasts and her belly, so he could thread his fingers through the damp, silky auburn curls at the juncture of her thighs. She moaned softly as his hand moved lower and he delved into her gently with one finger.

"Do you like that?" he asked, his voice dark and low as he nuzzled her earlobe, toying with the dangly earring hanging from it.

"Mmm, yes," she whispered, her breath hot against the bare skin of his chest, her palms moving down his stomach, rotating in smaller and smaller circles until she held him in her hands. "Yes..." she murmured again, savoring the hard length, the heavy, throbbing weight of his desire as she stroked him with infinite care.

Turning her head, she sought and found his mouth, and kissed him deeply as she arched into the rhythmic movement of his hand on her. She was burning up and she wasn't sure how much longer she could wait. "Mac, please... I want..." She moaned as he deepened his caress. An instant later his mouth closed over her breast. His teeth grazed her nipple, his tongue laved her soothingly, and she shuddered with the intensity of the pleasure he gave her.

Suddenly he couldn't wait any longer. He, too, wanted, and her hands on him were bringing him closer and closer to the edge. "Easy, Maggie, easy. Just give me a minute." He rolled away from her, ignoring her murmured protests, slid open the drawer of the nightstand and removed a foil packet. Seconds later, bracing himself on his forearms, he moved between her legs, his eyes steady as he met her gaze. "Let me love you, Maggie."

In answer, she wrapped her arms around his shoulders and lifted her hips, welcoming him as he thrust into her, burying himself deep inside her. She went very still, closing her eyes, arching back against the bed. And then she began to move beneath him, drawing him deeper as she locked her legs around his waist.

He had planned to go slowly, but he was hungry, so hungry, and only she could satisfy his need. Gripping her hips, he lifted her up, plunging into her faster and faster. "Look at me, Maggie. Look . . . at . . . me. . . ."

She met his gaze. She saw the dark, possessive glint in his pale gray eyes. And deep inside her she felt the same dark desire to have this man as her own. "Mine," she whispered as her body shuddered with a pleasure so intense that she felt herself spinning out of control.

"And mine," he growled, low in his throat, as he mated with her finally, completely and with utter abandon.

They lay together for a long time afterward, neither willing to break the bond between them with words or actions. Finally, as their breathing slowed and their sweat-slick bodies cooled, Mac rolled on to his side, eased out of her and pulled the blanket up around her before he slid from the bed and headed for the bathroom. When he returned a few minutes later, Maggie was sitting up, her back against a pile of pillows, the blanket covering her breasts. She had removed her dangly decadent earrings. And in her hands she held the framed photograph of Jo, Elizabeth and him that had been taken a couple of years before his wife had died. He had forgotten that it was on the nightstand.

"Elizabeth looks like her mother," she said, glancing up at him as he sat on the edge of the bed.

"Yes, she does," he agreed, taking it from her. "I'm sorry, Maggie. I should have put it away."

"Why?" She gazed at him, her bright blue eyes questioning. "She was your wife and Elizabeth's mother. She was a very important part of your life for a long time. You loved her. How could you just . . . put her away?"

He set the picture back on the nightstand, not trusting himself to speak. He had told her she was special earlier in the evening, but he hadn't realized just how special she was until now. How could he be so lucky, not once, but twice in a lifetime? He reached out, switched off the lamp. For several long moments, he sat in the dark. Then the bed shifted under him as Maggie scooted to the other side.

"Come to bed, Mac," she invited, holding back the blanket for him. "It's late and if we don't get some sleep we'll never be able to get up in the morning."

He settled in beside her without a word and lay on his back, staring into the darkness for the space of several heartbeats, blinking back the moisture that blurred his vision. Then he turned toward her, reaching for her, wanting her with an intensity as emotional as it was physical. She came to him without hesitation, nestling against him, sighing deeply, contentedly, as if she'd finally come to the end of a very long journey, a journey home.

"Ah, Maggie...love...are you sure you want to sleep?" He kissed her forehead, her cheek, her chin, and felt her smile as she rubbed her face against his chest.

"Only if that's what you want," she assured him, her hand moving down his body. "But I think you want something else, don't you?"

"I want you." He rolled her onto her back, taking her hands in his and pulling them up over her head. "You..." He trailed kisses down her neck and along her shoulder. "Only...you...."

She had been afraid it would be awkward waking up with him in the morning, but it wasn't. In fact, it was as if they'd been doing this for years instead of for the first time. They shared a hot shower, and only the realization that several hungry guests would be expecting a hearty breakfast at eight o'clock kept them from tumbling back into bed afterward.

Mac had bundled her into an old robe, slipped on a pair of jeans, and like the gentleman he was, he had escorted her back to her room sometime around six-thirty, leaving only after several long, slow kisses.

The rest of the day they saw little of each other, the work of running the ranch keeping them as busy as usual. But late that night, after the last guests had vacated the living room and they'd closed the pool and turned off the lights, Mac wrapped his arm around her waist and guided her toward the stairs. They didn't pause at the second-floor landing as they had the night before. Instead they continued up to Mac's bedroom without a word. Because no words were needed when he touched her . . . when she touched him. . . .

"Hey, I've been looking all over for you," Mac growled, his low voice edged with more than a hint of concern as he walked out on the side porch and pulled the door closed.

It was past ten-thirty, the house and grounds quiet in the moon-shadowed darkness. She was sitting on the top step, her back against the wooden railing, her arms loosely wrapped around her knees, Bonnie and Clyde lying close beside her. She tilted her chin and smiled up at him as the puppies snuffled at his boots. Then she turned her head away, staring out into the star-speckled night.

For nearly two weeks they'd shared a nightly routine that had ended in his bed. Sometimes they had been too tired to do anything except sleep in each other's arms, but they'd slept together and they'd awakened together. Yet tonight he hadn't been able to find her anywhere in the house or the barn, out by the pool or near the cabins. And foolish as it seemed now, he'd begun to panic, as he imagined her sick or hurt and unable to find *him*.

"What are you doing out here? Hiding?" he asked, as he scooted the puppies out of his way and sat down on the step beside her. There was something distant about her that he didn't like, especially after the closeness they'd shared, a closeness he wasn't ready to relinquish.

"Not exactly."

She shrugged, not looking at him. And when he put his arm around her to draw her near, he felt her stiffen for just an instant before she leaned against him, resting her head on his shoulder. Warning bells rang in his head as he brushed his lips against her soft, curly hair. She sighed deeply, as if from the bottom of her soul, and rested one small, pale hand on his thigh.

"What's wrong, Maggie?"

Again she shrugged, then shook her head, not saying a word. Easing away from her, Mac threaded his fingers through her hair and tipped her face up, forcing her to meet his gaze. In the moonlight, her eyes shimmered with sadness and uncertainty as she stared at him.

"Ah, sweetheart, tell me what's bothering you." He kissed her cheek, nuzzled her earlobe, nipped at her neck. "Please tell me," he muttered as she relaxed in his embrace and wrapped her arms around his waist.

"I'm...I'm feeling...guilty," she murmured, rubbing her cheek against his chest.

"Guilty?" Grasping her upper arms in his hands, he set her away from him, his eyes probing hers.

Certainly they hadn't done anything wrong in the past two weeks. They were a couple of consenting adults who... who...cared for each other physically as well as emotionally. In fact, it had been a long time since Mac had felt that anything was as right as he and Maggie were together. And he'd assumed that she felt the same way. So why, all of a sudden, was she talking about guilt, as if a sin had been committed?

"Guilty about *what?*" he demanded, his voice harsh, when she didn't respond as quickly as he expected her to.

"Not about *that,*" she assured him, seeming to read his mind. "Oh, Mac, never that." A rueful smile tugging at the corners of her mouth, she reached up and rested her palm against the side of his face, tracing the outline of his cheekbone with her thumb. "I'm feeling guilty because although I've been missing our children more and more every day, I wish...I wish they weren't coming home for another week...or two, or—"

Relief flooding through him, he pulled her into his arms, hugging her as hard as he could without squeezing the life out of her. "I know what you mean," he agreed. "We're not going to be able to—"

"Be together," she finished for him, rubbing her forehead against his shoulder.

The past couple of weeks had been like a honeymoon, but tomorrow they'd be picking up Christopher and Elizabeth at the airport in San Antonio. For all intents and purposes their honeymoon would be over, because Maggie could no longer share his bed once the children had returned. Not unless he married—

Now where the hell had *that* thought come from? He wasn't ready for marriage. He wasn't prepared to utter vows of love. Not when he knew what he did about happily-ever-afters. And neither was she, he assured himself. In fact, they hadn't said anything about love yet. And their time together on the Whispering Wind would end in August when he sold the ranch and she went back to San Antonio. Wouldn't it? Shouldn't it? Yes...*No*...

"Of course we can be together, Maggie. If you want..."

"Oh, I want, Mac. But..." She tipped her face up and pressed her lips against the hollow at the base of his throat.

But it won't be the same....

Her unspoken words hung between them for the space of several heartbeats. Then Maggie drew away from him and took his hand in hers.

"Let's go upstairs. All right?"

"All right."

He stood up and helped her to her feet. Slipping his arm around her shoulders, he opened the door. Halfway across the dining room, he stopped and scooped her into his arms, then lengthened his stride. He had no intention of letting tonight be their last night together, yet he couldn't deny the quiet desperation that drove him with unfamiliar urgency.

He set her on the bed and watched as she pulled off her clothing as quickly as he. And then he was beside her, taking her with his hands and mouth as she took him, demanding even as he met her demands until he could wait no longer. Thrusting into her, he cried out her name as she arched her back and convulsed around him. He didn't want it to end...didn't...want it...to end. Again he cried out her name, as he lifted her hips and plunged into her, shudders racking his body as he took all that she had to give and gave all of himself in return.

Chapter Eleven

Settling onto a chaise lounge in a shady spot near the swimming pool, Maggie stretched her legs out in front of her, tucked her hands behind her head and willed herself to relax. Although the sun was early August hot, the breeze that drifted over her was several degrees cooler and carried a hint of rain. Turning her head, she saw the clouds beginning to build on the western horizon. The storm that had been forecast for tonight was well on its way. Maybe that was why she was so restless. Heaven help her, she had never been as restless as she'd been since she arrived on the Whispering Wind.

Over a week had passed since Christopher and Elizabeth had returned from visiting with their respective grandparents, and for most of that time Maggie had been too busy to enjoy any real private time. But today, with all of their guests either riding at the Triple Z Ranch or off on excursions to one destination or another, and with Mac and the kids on their way to Bandera to buy feed and supplies, the house and grounds were deserted. She was on her own, with nothing to do but relax. Only she couldn't. Though she'd finally forced her body to be still, her mind refused to stop whirling a mile a minute, thoughts of the past, present and future crowding together in a jumbled mess.

Unfortunately, thinking any further into the future than the next few hours did nothing but give her a headache. And thinking about the past two months did nothing but make her heart ache. As for thinking about the present... Against her better judgment, she'd allowed herself to be drawn into life on the Whispering Wind, a life she'd grown to love as deeply and completely as she'd grown to love Mac and his daughter. Despite her vows of independence and self-sufficiency, she knew that if he asked her to stay, and if Christopher agreed, she would. She'd give up her job and her home for him without hesitation and without regret.

But he wasn't going to ask her to stay. As far as she knew, he hadn't changed his mind about selling the ranch. Nor had he indicated in any way that he wanted their relationship to continue after the end of the summer. He might enjoy making love with her, but *loving* her was something else altogether. It entailed the kind of commitment, a *permanent* commitment, he wasn't ready to make. She had known it from the beginning, and had tried to accept it. But it was getting harder and harder to do with every day that passed, with every day that brought her closer and closer to their final parting.

If she had any sense at all, she'd stop torturing herself with impossibilities and enjoy the few weeks they had left together. In three weeks she'd have to return to San Antonio and begin preparations for the coming school year. Teacher in-service days had already been scheduled for the last week of August, and Christopher needed new clothes and school supplies.

Actually she didn't have to return to San Antonio then. The forty-five-mile drive wasn't an impossible commute. Many of Mac's friends did it on a daily basis, something he'd mentioned a few days ago. But no, she'd only be delaying the inevitable, making the final break that much harder to bear. It had been a wonderful summer, but the summer wouldn't last forever. And there was no use wearing out her welcome. Far better to leave of her own accord, than to wait for him to ask her to go.

In fact, maybe she'd be wise to consider leaving at the end of next week. There were only two families of four, and a couple, scheduled to stay at the ranch the third week of August, and no one at all scheduled for the fourth and final week of the summer season. Surely with Rosa's help Mac could handle a few guests on his own for a week. He might even appreciate the extra time to settle his business affairs without having her behind his back. He had to decide between the job offers he'd received, and he had to arrange the move to Dallas, two things he hadn't done yet.

In the near distance she noticed a small cloud of dust and a moment later heard the crunch of tires on the dirt-and-gravel road. She hadn't expected anyone to be back until close to dinnertime and according to her watch it was only four o'clock. Swinging her legs over the side of the chaise, she picked up her shorts and T-shirt and slipped into them. Whoever was coming, she didn't want to greet him in her bathing suit.

As she finished snapping her shorts and slipped her feet into her sandals, a big black Lincoln came into view. Following close behind was a double-cab pickup truck similar to Mac's, with a logo bearing the name Associated Surveyors of San Antonio on the door panel. Both vehicles turned onto the drive leading to the side door of the house, then stopped.

A big, heavyset man wearing a summer suit climbed out of the car and was joined by one of the four men in the truck. The other three were removing various pieces of what Maggie assumed was surveying equipment from the truck bed. No one had bothered to knock on the door or in any other way announce their presence. It was as if *they* owned the Whispering Wind, not Mac. No, not *they,* the man in the Lincoln, standing with his hands on his broad hips, gazing at the house and the barn with a proprietary air that set Maggie's teeth on edge.

"Well, we'll just see about that," she muttered, starting up the path toward them as one of the surveyors began to set up a tripod. "Can I help you?" she called, her voice louder but no less angry than when she'd been talking to herself.

The heavyset man took his time turning to face her. He also took his time looking her up and down as something closer to a sneer than a smile twisted the corners of his wide mouth. "Yeah, you can pack your bags and trot your cute little behind back to San Antonio... ma'am," he drawled, shoving his hands into the side pockets of his suit pants and rocking back on his heels. Behind him the surveying crew snickered.

"I beg your pardon?" Maggie felt her face flush a crimson shade of red as a tremor of rage shook her body. Of all the offensive—

"You heard me, little lady. Go back to San Antonio. Let Mac finish his business here. If you two still want to play house, you can do it in Dallas...." He allowed his words to trail away suggestively as he opened his car door and pulled out a roll of blueprints. Then he turned to the chief surveyor. "The house comes down and so does the barn. The hotel will go there and the tennis courts—"

"And just who the hell are *you?*" Maggie demanded, her voice incredibly cold and steady considering the anger shaking her to her very soul.

"Why, darlin', I'm Dale Sherman. The soon-to-be owner of the Whispering Wind *Resort*." He smiled the smarmiest smile Maggie had ever seen, obviously entertained by her impotence.

"Over...my...dead...body." She ground out the words as she wanted to grind his face in the gravel. If only she were bigger, stronger. But she wasn't as impotent as he thought she was, either.

Ignoring his disgusting snort of laughter, she walked around him, giving him the same wide berth she'd give anything nasty, climbed the steps and entered the house. With single-minded determination she climbed the stairs to the third floor, opened Mac's closet and pulled out his rifle. She knew that it was loaded, and thanks to her father, she knew exactly how to use it. After assuring herself that the safety was on, she tucked the stock under one arm, and barrel pointing toward the floor, headed back downstairs.

By the time she stepped out onto the side porch most of her anger had evaporated, yet she was no less determined to get rid of Dale Sherman. Releasing the safety, she raised the stock to her shoulder, lifted the barrel skyward and fired. One shot was all she needed to get the men's attention.

"Now, see hear, little lady—"

"Call me little lady again, Mr. Sherman, and I'm going to get really, really angry." She clicked on the safety and lowered the rifle, then continued. "In fact, if you don't pack up your people and get off the Whispering Wind immediately, I'll be so angry there's no telling what I might do." She held his gaze, her eyes unwavering.

"There's no need to get all riled up. I was just havin' some fun with you, ma'am." He held up his hands in mock surrender as he attempted what only he could assume was a genial smile.

"Have your fun somewhere else." Maggie raised the rifle again, sighting down the long barrel. "And do it now."

She could see the indecision in his eyes, as the surveyors muttered and shuffled around behind him. With a very small smile, she clicked off the safety and wrapped her finger around the trigger.

"Damn it, you're not going to get away with this, you little—"

"Watch it, Mr. Sherman. Foul language makes my fingers itch."

He glared at her for one long moment. Then, his voice harsh, he ordered the crew to pack up their equipment. Turning toward her one last time, he raised his fist and shook it at her. "Mackenzie Harrow is going to hear about this," he declared, as he climbed into his car. Several seconds later, he floored the accelerator, sending dust and gravel flying as he drove away, once again followed closely by the pickup truck.

When they'd finally disappeared from sight, Maggie lowered the rifle. She was shaking so hard she could barely open the door or climb the steps. But somehow she made it to Mac's bedroom and stowed the rifle in his closet. It would have to be cleaned, but she'd do it later. Right now she knew she wasn't up to it. In fact, she wasn't up to anything except...except...

She gazed at the big brass bed and remembered all the nights full of love and laughter. And she thought of Dale Sherman's plans. As if drawn by a magnet, she crossed the room, sat on the bed. She picked up the photograph of Mac, Jo and Elizabeth and stared at it for several seconds. Then holding it to her chest, she curled up on her side and began to cry...for all that had been, and for all that would never be.

Mac cradled the telephone receiver and sat back in his desk chair. He should be mad as hell at Maggie for the stunt she'd pulled that afternoon, even angrier because she hadn't told him about it herself. Finding out that she'd gone after Dale Sherman with a rifle from Sherman himself wasn't exactly what he needed to make his evening complete. But for some odd reason, the thought of her running Dale off the ranch made him smile.

She was really something else, he thought, his heart swelling with admiration and . . . love. Any doubts he might have had about her feelings for the Whispering Wind had vanished. She cared about the ranch as much as he. Surely she must also care about him and his daughter. Though she'd never said it in so many words, he'd seen it in her eyes and felt it in her touch. Hadn't he? Memories of the long nights they'd spent together filled him with hope and desire.

He had to think of a way to convince her to stay, and he had to do it soon. He wouldn't mind if she kept her house in San Antonio. And although he didn't like the idea of her commuting, if she wanted to continue teaching at her school, he'd learn to live with it. It would be better if she transferred to a school closer to the ranch, but the final decision would be hers to make, and he would support her, whatever she chose to do.

He wanted her to know that being his wife didn't mean that she'd have his foot on her neck. He loved her independent spirit, her self-sufficiency and her take-charge attitude too much to do anything to hold her down. Of course, he really ought to talk to her about pulling a gun on one of the county's wealthiest and most well-respected citizens. Knowing Dale Sherman as well as he did, Mac had no doubt that he'd said something to provoke Maggie. The man could be a real son of a bitch, and Mac wasn't particularly fond of him. But he didn't want to alienate the man, either.

Sherman had offered him a way out when that was what he thought he'd wanted and needed most. Now, selling the ranch was the last thing he wanted to do. Thank heavens he hadn't signed the papers yet. Dale wouldn't be pleased when Mac advised him that the sale was off, but his displeasure would be relatively short-lived. There were several other similar properties for sale in the area. None was as nice as the Whispering Wind, at least as far as Mac was concerned. However, the old boy would have other possible places to build his dream resort.

But enough about Dale Sherman, Mac thought as he stood up and headed for his office door. He wanted to see Maggie, and if only for a few moments, he wanted to hold her in his arms and kiss her and assure her that everything would be all right. She had been so quiet when he'd returned from Bandera, and there'd been a bruised look about her eyes. Now that he'd finally found out why she'd seemed so hurt and unhappy, he intended to do something about it.

She had become a part of his life, a part of his very heart and soul, and he didn't want to let her go. Now if only he could muster the courage to tell her. Maybe not tonight, but sometime soon when they had more than a few moments alone together. He realized what he was risking, as well as the vow he was breaking by loving her. But knowing her as he did, how could he do anything else?

As he walked toward the house in the deepening twilight, lightning lit the sky on the western horizon and a short gust of wind rustled through the branches of the oak trees. The storm that had been building since late afternoon was drawing closer and closer. From the height and breadth of the thunderheads rolling toward the east, Mac judged that they'd be in for a rough night. With luck, however, the storm should blow through by morning, leaving behind nothing but some much-needed rain.

The kitchen and dining room were dark and empty, but the living room was brightly lit and full of people. Mac paused in the arched doorway, hands on his hips, scanning the noisy crowd. Several adults sat on the old sofa, watching a baseball game. Elizabeth, Christopher and two younger children were scrunched together on the player-piano bench singing "The Yellow Rose of Texas" at the tops of their little lungs, while three teenagers circled the pool table setting up shots as solemnly as Minnesota Fats. Maggie, however, wasn't there.

He glanced at his watch. It was almost nine o'clock. Crossing the room, he stopped by the player piano and flicked the switch, turning the machine off.

"Hi, Daddy. Are we making too much noise?" Elizabeth gazed at him, her eyes full of mischief and not a hint of apology.

"You *could* tone it down a little. And you might try singing on key," he teased, tweaking her braid.

"Oh, Daddy..."

"Oh, Lizzie Beth..." he mimicked. Then, his voice a shade more serious as his gaze shifted to Christopher, he continued. "Where's your mom?"

"She went up to our room right after we finished cleaning up the kitchen. She said she was gonna take a bath and read for a while. I think she's kinda tired."

"She's not sick, is she?" Mac tried to mask his sudden concern, not wanting to alarm the boy. She had been working hard all summer. Had she been working too hard, worrying more about the ranch than about herself and ignoring her health? A chill crept up his spine as he remembered Jo doing just that a couple of years ago.

Christopher shrugged and shook his head. "I don't think so. She's not sneezing or coughing or anything. I think she just needed some private time."

"I can understand that," Mac admitted, smiling once again. "I think I'm going to go upstairs for a while, too. I'll be down around ten or ten-thirty to close up for the night. Think you can handle everything until then?"

"Of course, Daddy."

"Sure, Mr. Harrow."

"See you later, then."

He took the stairs two at a time and turned down the second-floor hallway without hesitation. They'd have more time alone together than he'd anticipated, he thought, still smiling as he knocked on the door to Number Five.

"Who . . . who is it?"

"It's me, Mac."

"Um, Mac . . . I'm, um, I'm not . . . dressed."

Mac stared at the closed door, his smile fading. Through the thick wood her voice sounded strange. And she hadn't thrown open the door and stepped into his arms as he'd hoped she would.

"Maggie, darlin', I've seen you without any clothes on," he teased, lowering his voice suggestively. He didn't want to barge into her room, but if she didn't—

"Just . . . just a minute, okay?"

"Okay."

He heard her moving around the room, her footsteps quick and light, then a moment later she opened the door. She had put on her long, white sleeveless robe, the one with the lace around the high neck and the tiny, pearl buttons down the front. It had taken him forever to unfasten them, he thought, his smile returning as he took a step toward her, then fading again when she took a step back.

"Is . . . is something wrong?" she asked, her eyes wide as she gazed up at him.

"I was about to ask you the same thing." From what he could see of her face in the dimly lit hallway, it looked as if she'd been crying.

"I'm fine. Just a little tired. Thought I'd make it an early night." Her eyes wavered as she lowered her lashes.

"Chasing Dale Sherman off the Whispering Wind with a loaded rifle *can* take it out of a person, can't it?" he drawled, tucking a finger under her chin and gently lifting her face.

She stared at him for several seconds as her face turned a pale shade of red. "He called you?"

Mac nodded, his eyes steady as he held her gaze.

"I, um, I'm sorry. I shouldn't have done it," she murmured at last, her voice whisper-soft. "Are you . . . are you mad at me?"

"What happened?" he asked, ignoring her question about the events of the afternoon. He had gotten an earful from Dale about the events of the afternoon. Now he wanted to hear Maggie's side of the story before he let her off the hook.

"He came here with a surveying crew while you were gone. When I asked him what he was doing, he . . . he told me to mind my own business and go back to San Antonio." She hesitated for a long moment, then continued. "He's not a very nice man. And he's going to tear down the house and the barn. He's going to turn the ranch into a *resort*. I can't believe you're going to sell it to him."

For just an instant, Mac was tempted to tell her he'd changed his mind about selling the ranch to Dale Sherman or to anyone. But there was so much more he wanted to say, and one very important question he wanted to ask, and somehow he just didn't think the time was right. He was sure that she'd glossed over her exchange with Sherman. She'd been angry enough to use a rifle to get rid of him, and she was obviously still upset, not only with Dale but with him. And he wasn't as pleased with her as he should be, either.

"Why didn't you tell me what happened when I got back this afternoon? You had to know I'd find out one way or another," he said, shoving his hands into the back pockets of his jeans. "I would have rather heard about it from you than from him."

She turned her head away, no longer meeting his eyes. "I was going to tell you. Tomorrow..."

When she glanced at him, the sadness and uncertainty in her normally bright eyes cut into him. It was all he could do to keep from pulling her into his arms. He had to remind himself that not only did he disapprove of what she'd done, he didn't like the way he'd found out about it.

"You could have been hurt, Maggie." He spoke his thoughts aloud, willing her to look at him.

"I know how to use a rifle," she bristled, glaring at him.

"I'm not saying you don't. But if anything ever happened to you..."

"I can take care of myself." She tipped her chin up at a dangerous angle, challenging him to deny it.

If Mac knew anything, it was when to hold and when to fold. And it was definitely time to fold. If he didn't get away from her, he'd end up doing something he might regret. Like backing her into the room, locking the door, tumbling her onto the bed and kissing her senseless. Then again, maybe he wouldn't regret it, he thought, taking a step toward her, then another. He couldn't think of a better way to shut her up and once she stopped talking—

"Hi, Mom. Hi, Mr. Harrow. Whatcha doing?"

"Talking to your mother," he growled from between clenched teeth. Pasting a smile on his face, he turned to look at Christopher, hovering in the doorway, a curious expression on his young face.

"Ready for your bath, kiddo?" Maggie asked, her voice so full of relief that Mac caught himself smiling in earnest. "Mr. Harrow was just leaving. Weren't you?" She gazed at him with wide, innocent eyes, daring him to contradict her.

"Yeah, I was just leaving," he agreed, his eyes holding hers. "We can always talk more in the morning." He rubbed a thumb over her lips, savoring their softness against his work-roughened skin. Then he dropped his hand and turned on his heel. "And we will," he added, a moment before he pulled the door closed behind him.

Long after Mac had left the room and her son had fallen asleep, Maggie stood by the window and stared out into the darkness, watching the storm approach. The wind had picked up considerably in the past hour, bending and twisting the branches of the oak trees surrounding the house. Lightning streaked across the sky, the arcs and flashes brilliant, almost blinding, and followed more and more closely by the crash of thunder.

Although it hadn't begun to rain yet, it reminded her of the storm that had kept her awake her second night at the ranch. As she had then, Maggie knew that she wouldn't sleep until the bulk of the bad weather had passed. Unlike that night, however, she wasn't going to wait it out in the living room. She was going to stay in her bedroom where she had no chance of running into Mac, literally or figuratively. It had been hard enough dealing with him earlier without falling apart. And if she fell apart, she'd say or do something she would more than likely regret.

She had cried for a very long time after Dale Sherman had gone, and her tears had left her empty and aching and much too upset to talk about what the man had said and what she'd done in a rational manner. That was why she hadn't said anything about his visit when Mac returned from Bandera. Of course, she had known that Sherman would call, but she had hoped that he'd wait until the following day. He hadn't, and as a result Mac was angry with her...again. Not only had she failed to mind her own business, the one thing guaranteed to set him off, she had also failed to be honest and up-front about what she'd done.

When would she learn that she had no right interfering in his life? When would she finally realize that he, and he alone, had to make the final decision about selling the ranch? He hadn't indicated in any way that he wanted or needed her on a permanent basis. And why should he when she was so darned determined to let him know she could take care of herself?

She couldn't deny that he'd been concerned about her facing off with Dale Sherman, and not only because of how her actions might affect the sale of the ranch. He had been concerned about *her*. And what had she done? She'd told him in no uncertain terms that she didn't want or need his concern when, in fact, she wanted and needed it more than anything else. If she wasn't so frightened of her feelings, she'd tell him. Then she'd beg him not to sell the ranch, and she'd ask him to marry her. She would, if she wasn't so scared that he'd laugh in her face, pat her on the head and send her back to San Antonio.

Of course, maybe he was scared that *she'd* laugh in his face if he asked her—

Beyond the window a bolt of lightning tore through the sky, illuminating the yard, the pool, the cabins and the barn for an instant in its bright glow. Maggie blinked, seeing stars as if a camera flash had gone off in her face, then jumped as an explosive crash rattled the windows and rocked the house.

"Mom? *Mom,* what happened?" Christopher cried, his voice high and frightened.

"Just lightning and thunder," she reassured him, as she stared out the window. It had been close, very close. She wondered if the house had been hit, or perhaps—

"Oh, God," she whispered, as another flash of lightning lit the sky. "One of the cabins is on fire." She whirled away from the window. It hadn't begun to rain yet, the cedar-shingled roofs were dry from weeks of baking in the hot summer sun, and with the gusts of wind— "Stay here, Christopher. Do not, I repeat, do *not* go outside. I have to get Mac."

She pulled open the bedroom door and ran down the hallway. Calling his name, she took the stairs to the third floor two at a time.

"Maggie, what's wrong?" He was sitting up in bed, the sheet folded down around his waist, revealing his bare chest. He ran his fingers through his hair and shook his head, as if to chase away the fuzziness in his brain.

"One of the cabins is on fire. The one nearest the barn. It's empty, but Mac, we have to warn the other guests and get the horses out." Her words tumbled over each other, all but defying her attempts at coherency. He was half-asleep and moving slowly. She wanted to grab him and shake him, but there wasn't time. "Call the fire department and Juan. I'm going out." She spun around, gathered the hem of her long gown in one hand and raced out of the room.

"Maggie, *no,*" he shouted. "Don't go out there."

She ignored him, as she ignored the gut-clenching fear that threatened to immobilize her, moving down the staircase and across the dining room as quickly as possible. She had to go. She had no choice. Mac wasn't dressed and she was. Mac knew the number for the fire department and she didn't. And Mac could start the pump in the shed near the pool, attach the long, thick hose he kept on hand for just such an emergency, and maybe, just maybe, using the water in the pool, he could put out the fire before it spread. And if he couldn't, she had to be sure that their guests and his horses were safe.

She wrenched open the side door, hanging on to it with both hands as the wind grabbed it and tried to tear it from her grasp. The puppies, whimpering with fear, crowded around her ankles, almost tripping her in their hurry to get in the house. Allowing herself to be swallowed up by the storm, she stumbled down the steps, the wind beating against her, the lightning flashing over her head, the thunder crashing all around her.

In the few minutes it had taken her to wake Mac, the fire had spread across the roof of the cabin, sparking and snapping with a terrifying life of its own. The stench of wood smoke and the acrid odor of burning wires filled her nostrils while the thick, heavy vapors hampered her view of the other cabins. She couldn't tell if the guests were up and out or not. And her cries of warning would never reach them from such a distance.

Ducking her head, she folded her arms across her chest and began to run, barely mindful of the gravel cutting into the soles of her bare feet as she offered a silent prayer for the rain that surely must be hanging in the clouds. She stopped at the cabin closest to the one on fire and pounded on the thick wooden door.

"Wake up. Please, wake up," she cried. The door swung open and the couple staying there stared at her silently with sleepy eyes. How could they have slept through the storm? "You have to get out now. *Hurry,*" she added. "The cabin next door is on fire."

The word *fire* set them in motion immediately, freeing Maggie to go on to the next cabin. As she raised her fist to beat on the door, it opened and the family of four tumbled out.

"Go up to the house," she instructed as she turned away.

Only one family remained and they were staying in the farthest cabin. Glancing over her shoulder, she saw the fire creeping across the roof of the burning cabin, the wind blowing sparks and cinders toward the barn. Muttering another prayer, she started down the path. She had taken only a few steps when she was met by the family, huddled together as they hurried toward the house, obviously aware of the danger.

Without a word, she changed direction, her eyes on the barn, her heart pounding with exertion. Her knees had begun to tremble, but she refused to stop. Tiny pinpricks of heat bit into her scalp, her face and her arms as she passed the burning cabin. In the distance she could hear the whine and throb of an engine and masculine voices shouting, and from farther away the trill of a siren drawing closer. And then, as if in answer to her prayers, a sudden sting of icy raindrops sent tiny shivers racing through her body.

"Yes, *yes*," she cried, tipping her face up in welcome as she reached for the handle of the barn door.

"No," Mac shouted, wrapping his arm around her waist like a steel band and dragging her back. "No, Maggie. You're not going in there. You're going back to the house."

She sagged against him, drawing on his strength, but only for an instant. "Let me help you," she pleaded, twisting around to face him as the rain began in earnest, drenching them both in less than a minute. Beyond the door she could hear the horses stamping and kicking and whinnying with fear. "We can get them out a lot faster if we work together."

She was right, and she knew that he knew it. Yet he hesitated, his arms tightening around her as he held her against his bare chest. "If anything happens to you . . ."

"I'm used to the horses and they're used to me. How many are in the barn?"

"Windstorm, Bobby's gelding and a couple of mares. The mares are on the right." He stepped away from her, grabbed her shoulders and bent his head until his eyes were level with hers. "They've got halters on. The leads are on the posts. Take one mare at a time out to the field behind the barn. I'll take care of the others. All right?"

"All right." She nodded her head as Mac pulled open the barn door and switched on the lights.

Quickly, yet calmly, they moved down the aisle separating the stalls, thankful that the storm hadn't knocked out the electricity. At least they could see what they were doing, and that made doing it that much easier. In a matter of minutes, the four horses were racing across the open field, safe from any threat of fire.

They left the barn together, arms around each other, and headed toward the cluster of men aiming hoses at the now-smoldering roof of the nearby cabin. The rain beat down on them, plastering their hair and clothing to their bodies, but nobody seemed to mind as they watched the last of the flames sputter and die. Two fire trucks screamed up the drive and slid to a stop, and the firemen took over for Juan and the male guests who had pitched in to help.

Maggie stood in the circle of Mac's arms, shaking with delayed reaction and a bone-deep chill from the icy rain, refusing to return to the house until she was sure the fire was out. Then she slogged through the mud, clinging to Mac, exhaustion seeping into every part of her body. Somehow she managed to climb the steps to the side porch, where Mac left her to rejoin the other men. But once inside, she sagged onto a dining-room chair, folded her arms on a tabletop and rested her cheek against them. From the living room she could hear the chatter of their guests and the aroma of hot coffee drifting toward her from the kitchen. She ought to talk to them, and a cup of coffee would be wonderful. She was freezing cold and dripping wet. And she was so tired....

"Is the fire out, Mom?"

"Is my dad okay?"

Maggie raised her head and smiled reassuringly at Christopher and Elizabeth. "The fire's out and your dad's okay. How about you two?"

"We're helping Rosa serve coffee and cinnamon rolls in the living room. Want some?" Elizabeth asked, her dark eyes full of concern.

"Some coffee would be wonderful. And I sure could use a towel." She scraped her wet hair off her face as another shiver raced up her spine.

"I'll get the towels." Christopher spun around and headed toward the laundry room, Elizabeth close on his heels.

"And I'll get the coffee," she called over her shoulder as they slipped through the swinging doors.

Several minutes later, a little warmer and a little drier, Maggie sent the children back to bed. Then she walked into the living room and mingled with the guests, apologizing for the inconvenience, thanking them for their cooperation and assuring herself that everyone was all right. Though she was all but weaving with exhaustion by the time the fire chief allowed them to return to the cabins, she stayed until the last guest had filtered out of the house. Then, still cold and wet, she curled up on the old sofa to wait for Mac.

She was almost asleep when he scooped her into his arms. Cursing under his breath, he carried her up the stairs and into her bedroom and set her on her bed. A moment later he had the shower running in her bathroom.

"Come on, Maggie, you're cold as ice." He pulled her to her feet and led her to the bathroom doorway. "Get under the shower and stay there until you're warm. Okay?"

She gazed at him and nodded her head. "Okay, Mac." She reached up and touched his face with her hand. "You're all smoky."

"So are you." He turned her to face the mirror, and smiled when she gasped at her image.

"I'm a...m-m-mess," she stuttered, her teeth chattering.

"And you're going to end up with pneumonia if you don't get warmed up."

"You, t-t-too. Go upstairs. I'll b-b-be all right n-now."

"Sure?"

"S-s-sure." She smiled as she touched his face again.

"Maggie...I..." Grabbing her shoulders, he pulled her into his arms and held her as if he never intended to let her go. Then he took a step back, bent his head and kissed her hard. "Thank you," he whispered as he released her.

"You're welcome," she replied, her voice soft. "Now get out of h-here."

"Yes, ma'am." He grinned at her for one long moment, then turned on his heel and padded out of her room, closing the door with a quiet click.

Several seconds later, Maggie stepped under the hot spray, willing its warmth to drive away the chill. Unfortunately she was still shaking when she finally crawled into bed sometime near dawn.

Chapter Twelve

Three days had passed since the night of the fire and Maggie had been feeling progressively worse each day. Just tired, she'd told herself as she'd dragged her body out of bed a couple of hours later than usual the morning after. Thank goodness everyone else had slept late, too. And no one had complained when she'd combined breakfast and lunch into a simple, yet hearty buffet brunch.

Since all of the buildings on the ranch were insured, Mac had contacted the local agency and reported the fire as soon as possible. Only a portion of the roof had been destroyed by the flames, but smoke and water had done minor damage to the interior of the cabin. Several of the guests had pitched in to help them salvage the furniture and bedding that had survived the blaze.

An adjustor had arrived in mid-afternoon, evaluated the situation, then advised Mac that he would have the money to make repairs within a week or ten days. Mac had nodded his head as the two men sat down at the kitchen table to complete the paperwork. Maggie couldn't imagine why Mac would bother to rebuild the cabin only to have Dale Sherman tear it down. Maybe he'd finally decided not to sell the ranch after all. Unfortunately she'd been too busy to ask him, and by the following day she'd had other things on her mind.

A touch of flu, she had told herself the next morning, as she gulped aspirin to ease her throbbing head and burning, itchy eyes, then swallowed a spoonful of cough medicine to relieve the hacking that started whenever she took a deep breath. Though she wanted to stay in bed, she couldn't. Not with Mac on his way to Alpine to return Bobby Dawson's gelding.

There had been guests checking in and checking out, towels and bedding to launder, cabins to be cleaned and meals to be prepared. Juan, Rosa and the kids had been as helpful as ever, but she had felt as if she was moving in slow motion, weighted down by an invisible ball and chain that made even the simplest tasks almost impossible to do. She finally stumbled into bed after eleven and slept like a dead person until her alarm rang at six o'clock the next morning.

By early that evening, as she loaded the last of the dinner dishes into the dishwater, Maggie knew that whatever was wrong with her, it was more than a touch of the flu. Added to her other symptoms, she was increasingly short of breath, an odd, aching sensation had settled in her chest, and according to the thermometer, she was running a low-grade fever.

She should have driven into Bandera and gone to the clinic, but it was Juan and Rosa's day to visit their daughter and brand-new baby grandson. She hadn't had the heart to ask them to change their plans. And since Mac was still in Alpine, it had been up to her to keep things under control at the ranch, something she couldn't do very well from a doctor's office.

But tomorrow, first thing in the morning, she would find out what was ailing her, she promised herself, as she reached for a towel and dried her hands. She eyed the half dozen pots and pans soaking in the double sink and shook her head. She couldn't leave them there all night. Neither could she muster the strength to scrub them just yet.

She crossed the kitchen and sat down at the table. Propping her elbows on the smooth, wooden surface, she closed her eyes and massaged her forehead. She couldn't remember ever feeling quite as bad as she did tonight. If only Mac were here. She opened her eyes and glanced at the clock. He should be home any time now. Once he arrived, she'd go up to bed. But for now... She folded her arms on the tabletop and put her head down. For now she'd just close her eyes a little while, and maybe she'd feel better.

As he guided the truck up the gravel drive past the cabins and the swimming pool, the empty trailer rattling along behind, Mac remembered how angry he'd been over two months ago when he'd returned from another trip to Alpine to find strangers on his property. Now the lights in the cabins, the cars parked nearby, and the people in the pool, including Christopher and Elizabeth, made him smile. He was home at last, and more determined than ever to talk to Maggie about the future, *their* future on the Whispering Wind.

He had used the fire and its aftermath, then the trip to Alpine to put it off, but after two days away, he didn't want to wait any longer. The hours he had spent on the road had given him more than enough time to think about what he wanted and what he needed to make his life complete. He wanted Maggie with him now and always, he wanted her son and his daughter to grow up together, and if she was willing, he wanted another child.

Lights were on in the living room, dining room and kitchen. Switching off the ignition, he looked at his watch. She was probably still in the kitchen. He glanced over his shoulder, checking on the children. They were getting out of the pool. If he hurried, he'd have time to talk to her before they returned to the house. He climbed out of the truck and started toward the kitchen door, the puppies scampering along beside him.

"Maggie." He called her name as he swung open the door and stepped across the threshold, a smile lifting the corners of his mouth. "Maggie, darlin', where are—"

He saw her sitting at the table, head down, face flushed, her eyes closed. She was as still as death, not stirring at all at the sound of his voice. He grabbed the door frame to steady himself as memories of another night and another woman slumped at the same table hit him with the force of a brutal blow, stealing his breath away. His heart began to pound. Fear clutched at his gut. Despair settled deep in his soul.

Not Maggie... Please, God, not her, too, he prayed as he strode across the distance separating them and hunkered down beside her.

"Maggie, sweetheart, wake up," he whispered, threading his shaking fingers through her curls, feeling the dry heat of her skin against his palm. She was burning up with fever and her breathing was too light, too shallow. "Maggie, *please...*"

She opened her eyes and tried to smile as she raised her head. "Hi, Mac." She took a deep breath and began to cough as she rubbed her hand against her chest. "Sorry about the mess in the sink, but I'm not feeling too good." As if she'd used the last of her strength, she closed her eyes and rested her cheek on her forearm again.

"Daddy, you're ho—"

Mac stood up and spun around to face the children. "How long has she been sick?" he demanded, his voice harsh and full of anger as he glared at them. "And where is Rosa?"

They stared at him, wide-eyed, clutching their towels in their arms, neither one daring to speak for several seconds.

"What's wrong with my mom?" Christopher asked at last, his face pale, his voice trembling with fear and uncertainty.

"She was coughing a little bit yesterday," Elizabeth said, slipping an arm around Christopher's shoulders. "But she didn't say anything about feeling sick, did she?"

"No." The boy shook his head as he moved away from Elizabeth. Brushing by Mac, he stopped beside Maggie and rested a hand on her cheek. "Mom...*Mom*...wake up," he begged, his voice suddenly thick with tears.

Again Maggie opened her eyes and tried to smile. "I'm fine...just a little...tired. Don't worry about me. And Juan and Rosa are visiting her daughter, remember? They'll be back later tonight," she murmured. Then she closed her eyes again.

"Go upstairs and get dressed *now*," Mac ordered. "We're taking her to the hospital in San Antonio." It was happening again, as it had two years ago. He was going to lose her, just as he'd lost Jo to the Whispering Wind, just when he'd been so sure that everything, *everything*, would be all right.

As Christopher and Elizabeth ran out of the kitchen, he crossed to the sink and soaked a small towel in cool water. With infinite care, he eased Maggie out of the chair and onto his lap, then pressed the damp cloth to her face, her neck and the top of her chest, trying to draw the heat out of her body. She curled against him without a word, and as he held her he was reminded of just how small and fragile she was.

"We're ready." Both children stood before him. Elizabeth held a pillow and blanket in her arms, while Christopher carried his mother's purse.

"Let's go, then," he said, offering a nod of approval for their quick thinking. He stood up, Maggie cradled in his arms, and started toward the door. "We'll take her car. It'll be faster." His long strides eating up the ground, he headed toward the garage, the children loping along behind him.

He tried to control the panic welling up inside him as he sped toward San Antonio, mentally cursing the miles separating them from the nearest hospital, miles he covered more quickly than he'd ever done before. At least the emergency room wasn't crowded. And one look at Maggie was all the nurse in charge needed to convince her she'd be better off lying on a bed in a treatment room than sitting on a chair in the waiting area.

She had dozed most of the way to the hospital and though she'd been awake when they had arrived, she hadn't protested when Mac lifted her into his arms and carried her inside. She had gone just as quietly with the nurse, leaving him to complete the necessary paperwork, giving him a good idea of just how sick she was.

Very sick, he thought, as he settled down on a vinyl couch to wait, a frightened child tucked under each arm. But how could she have become so ill overnight? Surely she'd been feeling fine the day after the fire. A little tired, maybe, but they'd all been tired. And yesterday morning she'd been up as usual. She'd even had a thermos of fresh coffee and a bag of warm sweet rolls for him to enjoy on his way to Alpine. He would have noticed if she wasn't feeling well. Wouldn't he?

Apparently not. He'd been too busy, and he'd had too many other things, ranch-business things, on his mind to pay close attention to Maggie. And so here he sat once again, in a hospital emergency room, his guts tied into knots, his heart pounding with fear, while some doctor poked and prodded the woman he loved, trying to find out what was wrong with her.

He wanted to believe it wasn't the same as it had been with Jo, but he couldn't. And he couldn't stop blaming himself for allowing Maggie to get so sick. Once again he had been too damned preoccupied with the ranch to worry about—

"Is my mom going to be okay?" Christopher asked, his soft voice full of fear.

"I don't know, son."

Elizabeth buried her face against his chest and began to cry. He tightened his hold on both children, trying to offer the reassurance he couldn't put into words without risking a lie.

"Maybe . . . maybe we ought to call my grandpa," Christopher suggested as he, too, began to cry.

Blinking back the tears blurring his own eyes, Mac shook his head. "Let's wait until we hear what the doctor has to say. She's been in there over an hour. We should know something soon."

In fact it was almost another hour before the doctor joined them in the waiting room. By then Mac and the children were the only ones remaining on what was a blessedly slow night, and the children were sound asleep. Sitting on the coffee table across from Mac, the doctor smiled, his tired eyes warm and sympathetic and oddly encouraging.

"She's going to be just fine," he began, obviously eager to quell Mac's growing fear and trepidation. "She's got pneumonia, but we caught it early. The nurse is giving her an injection of antibiotics. I'm going to let you take her home tonight. Not back to the ranch, but to her house here in San Antonio. Then I want you to bring her back tomorrow morning at ten for another injection. And in the meantime, I want you to give her one of these every four hours." He handed Mac a small bottle of pills. "She's going to have to take it easy for several days, but she'll be good as new in no time, Mr. Harrow.''

"Pneumonia?'' Mac stared at the doctor, then ran a hand over his face, trying to wipe off the stupid look he knew he was wearing. *Pneumonia?*

"She said something about getting caught in the rain and catching a chill.''

"Yeah, she did.''

"Well, don't worry, Mr. Harrow. She's going to be all right.'' As the doctor stood up, a nurse wheeled Maggie into the waiting room and helped her out of the wheelchair.

"Maybe she should stay here overnight,'' Mac suggested, his eyes on the doctor.

"No way,'' Maggie said. "No offense, doc, but I hate hospitals. And my house is just a couple of miles away.'' Bending over, she smoothed a hand over Christopher's hair, then gently shook his shoulder. "Come on, kiddo, wake up. I'm ready to get out of here.''

"Are you okay, Mom?''

"Except for a little touch of pneumonia, I'm fine.''

"Bring her back in the morning,'' the doctor said, as Mac and Elizabeth got to their feet. Maggie and Christopher were already on their way to the door.

"I will,'' Mac muttered, his arm around his daughter as they turned to follow them out the door.

They made the drive to her house without saying much. Maggie's bravado faded quickly once she was out of the hospital and in the car. Aside from giving Mac directions to her house, she said nothing. And since Mac had no idea what to say to her, he was quiet, too.

Her house was neither large nor small, the white stucco walls, arched windows and red-tiled roof accentuating its one-story Spanish-style architecture. It was set back from the street, surrounded by a large, neatly manicured lawn and well-lit with carefully spaced security lights. Probably compliments of Avery Chase, Mac thought, as he pulled into the driveway. The old man would throttle him when he found out he'd allowed Maggie to end up with pneumonia.

The house was as pleasing to the senses inside as it was outside. Saltillo tile floors, white walls, brightly colored fabrics and warm wooden furniture filled the rooms. And though the house had been closed up for over two months, the stale, musty air dissipated quickly after Maggie turned on the air-conditioning.

Leaving her in her bedroom, Mac followed the children down the hallway and helped them get settled on the twin beds in Christopher's room. Then he stopped in the kitchen to call Juan and Rosa to tell them what had happened and to ask them to look after the guests until he returned.

By the time he got back to Maggie she was in bed, too. She had pulled the sheet and a lightweight cotton blanket up around her shoulders, and her eyes were closed. In the pale glow of the lamp on the nightstand, Mac could see the dark shadows beneath them.

He wanted to stretch out beside her and hold her in his arms, but he no longer felt that he had the right. Because of him and his obsession with the Whispering Wind, she'd ended up in a hospital emergency room, too sick to stand. Luckily they'd caught the pneumonia before it became truly life-threatening, but what would have happened to her if he'd stayed away another day or two? What would have happened to her if he'd allowed her to work like a dog for another day or two before he *finally* noticed she wasn't feeling well? Though he didn't want to think about it, he knew that it was past time he did. He had lost Jo because of the ranch. He wasn't going to lose Maggie, too. At least not that way.

"Come to bed, Mac." She opened her eyes and smiled at him as she extended her hand to him.

He sat beside her and wove his fingers through hers. "In a little while," he murmured, brushing his lips against her pale cheek. Her skin was much cooler than it had been earlier. The medication she'd received at the hospital must be kicking in. "You sleep now, all right?"

"All right," she agreed, closing her eyes again.

He stayed with her until her grip on his hand relaxed. Then he tucked her arm under the blanket, turned off the lamp and walked out of her room. He wandered through the rest of the house, checking doors and windows. He found a beer in her almost empty refrigerator and carried it with him into the living room where he sprawled on the shades-of-green-and-purple patterned sofa. Maggie's colors, he thought, smoothing a hand across the nubby cotton fabric as he stretched his legs out on the hunter green rug.

Maggie's colors in Maggie's house, where she'd had a life of her own, on her own, for the past three years—the kind of life she had chosen to live until he and his daughter had interfered. The kind of life she deserved to have....

How could he have ever considered asking her to stay on the ranch with him? He must have been crazy. But he wasn't crazy anymore. He'd gotten a fresh dose of good, old-fashioned common sense while he was at the hospital, the kind of common sense he'd had in February.

Setting his empty beer can on the coffee table, he stood up and headed back to her bedroom. It wasn't time for her pill yet, but it was time for him to be with her, at least for a little while, for the little time they had left. He pulled off his boots and his clothes, and slid under the blankets. Careful not to wake her, he curved his body around hers and settled an arm across her waist. She sighed and turned into him, her hair soft against his arm, her face pressed against his chest.

"Ah, Maggie, what am I going to do without you?" he muttered, staring into the darkness, willing away the tears in his eyes.

*   *   *

Something was wrong. Something was very, very wrong and Maggie wasn't sure how to make it right. Over the past ten days she'd recovered from her bout of pneumonia and gone back to her normal routine at the ranch. But with each day that passed, as she steadily regained her strength, it seemed that Mac drew away from her a little more, avoiding her physically, whenever possible; blocking her out emotionally, whenever it wasn't.

At first she'd assumed that he was too busy doing double duty to spend more than a few minutes with her while she was confined to bed. But she'd been up and around for a week, and though she'd moved a little slower than usual for a few days, she'd managed to carry her share of the load. And still it seemed as if he had no time for her, no time to share a few words, a smile, a quick hug and kiss when they were alone.

"And when was the last time you were alone together for more than sixty seconds?" she asked herself, as she paced the length of the living room. "Not once in the past week."

But there was no reason why they couldn't be alone together now. The last of their guests had checked out that afternoon. Juan and Rosa had returned to their cabin after dinner. Christopher and Elizabeth were enjoying an early evening swim in the pool. And since he wasn't in the house, Mac must be out in the barn. Hiding. But why? What had happened to the warm and caring man she'd grown to love over the long summer months? She had to find out. And she had to find out if he wanted her to go or stay.

He hadn't said anything about . . . *anything*. She had the feeling that she'd been cut loose and allowed to drift. And she couldn't afford to drift any longer. Surely he'd been thinking of asking her to stay on the ranch...before she got sick.

Before she got sick ... The operative words, she thought, stopping by the window and gazing out across the lawn. It seemed as if everything had changed since the night he'd taken her to the hospital. Was it her imagination or not? She could think of only one way to find out. She had to confront him and ask him. Because if he wanted her to go, then she'd better start packing their bags so they could leave in the morning.

Ignoring the sliver of uncertainty that sliced through her heart, she turned away from the window and headed for the side door. He *wouldn't* tell her to go. He would pull her into his arms and kiss her and tell her that he loved her as much as she loved him. He'd ask her to stay with him on the Whispering Wind, to be his wife ...

He was in the barn, just as she'd suspected. He was grooming Windstorm, dragging the brush along the stallion's back and down his rump. As the horse turned his massive head to acknowledge her presence, Mac glanced at her for a moment. Then he turned back to the task at hand without saying a word.

"Hi. I thought I'd find you in here," Maggie said, stopping a few feet away.

"Something wrong?" His voice was gruff and low and lacking any hint of warmth or welcome.

"I don't know, Mac. *Is* something wrong?" All right, so he wasn't going to pull her into his arms and kiss her. She folded her arms across her chest and ducked her head. "Are you ... are you mad at me?"

"Of course not."

"I—I've been getting the feeling that you've been avoiding me lately, and I was wondering why." She hated the awful stammer in her voice almost as much as she hated the gnawing pain that blossomed deep inside of her.

"Just busy getting things wrapped up around here. Dale Sherman's coming out to finalize the sale sometime next week." He moved around the horse as he spoke, putting the animal between them. He glanced at her again, his expression unreadable in the dimly lit barn. "I want to thank you for all your help this summer, Maggie. It meant a lot to...Elizabeth, having you here."

He couldn't have hurt her more if he'd hit her. She closed her eyes and leaned against the stall door. "Oh, Mac...you can't—"

"I can and I will," he cut in, his voice harsh and unrelenting. "Elizabeth and I will be better off in Dallas. And you and your son will be better off in San Antonio. That's where you belong. Not...not here." He paused for a moment, then continued in a softer tone of voice. "Go home, Maggie."

She dropped her arms to her sides and took a step toward him. If she could touch him, if she could force him to look at her and *listen*... "I feel like I'm home now, Mac. I feel like the Whispering Wind *is* my home."

He didn't speak for several seconds. He worked on Windstorm, his arm rhythmically stroking down the animal's neck and chest. Finally he paused, raised his head and nailed her with his cold, pale eyes. "Well, darlin', in that case why don't you have your daddy call me. I'm sure he can afford to buy this place for you, if you want to keep on playing dude ranch. But I'm not going to stick around and watch," he drawled.

If it hadn't been for the horse in the way, she would have crossed the distance separating them and slapped him senseless. There wasn't anything he could have said that would have cut her more deeply, and he knew it. She stared at him for one long moment, her face growing hot, her fingers clenching and unclenching. Then she turned on her heel and started toward the door.

"We'll be gone first thing in the morning," she vowed, tossing the words over her shoulder without a backward glance.

He watched her walk away, biting back the words that would stop her, words of apology, words of wanting and needing and loving. He couldn't say them aloud, not now. Maybe one day when he and Elizabeth were settled...but for now, he had to let her go. Otherwise she'd talk him out of selling the ranch. She'd convince him with her certainty that they belonged together on the Whispering Wind, working side by side until...until Maggie or her son or his daughter ended up sick or hurt or worse?

He propped his forearm on Windstorm's back and rested his forehead against it. He couldn't risk it. He was too afraid of losing one of them or all of them as he'd lost Jo. Even if it meant he'd never see her again, he had to get her off the ranch. He had to force her to go back to her safe, secure life in San Antonio.

The stallion shifted, stamping his foot and tossing his head. Stepping back, Mac rubbed a hand over his face and shook his head. He had made the right decision. Maybe one day he'd actually learn to live with it.

"Maybe when cows fly," he muttered, smoothing the brush over the horse's gleaming coat. "Then again, maybe not...."

"What are you doing, Mom?" Christopher walked into their room, allowing the door to slam shut as he moved around the bed.

"Packing our suitcases. We're leaving in the morning." Maggie met his gaze, mentally willing him not to argue even though she knew she was wishing for the moon.

"But, Mom, we can't. Elizabeth said—"

"Mr. Harrow is going to sell the ranch. He's meeting with Dale Sherman next week to finalize the deal. Then he and

Elizabeth are moving to Dallas." She tried to state the facts calmly, but she heard the quiver in her voice. And when she saw the look of devastation on her son's face, a look that mirrored what she was feeling deep in her heart and soul, it was all she could do to keep from crying. "We had a wonderful summer, didn't we, buddy? But now it's time for us to go home."

"No." He shook his head as he backed away from her. "I don't want to go back to San Antonio. And Elizabeth doesn't want us to go." He turned and started toward the door. "I've got to talk to her."

Maggie caught him as his hand closed around the doorknob. "Uh-uh, Christopher. Not tonight." She pulled him into her arms and ran her fingers through his hair, still damp from the swimming pool. She had no idea when Mac planned to talk to his daughter, but she had a good idea it wouldn't be until the last possible moment. He wouldn't want a scene. And neither did Maggie. "You can say goodbye in the morning."

"But, Mom—"

She put her hands on her son's shoulders and held him away from her. She could feel the tears she'd refused to shed sliding down her cheeks. "Please, son, don't argue with me. I don't want to go, either. Don't make it any harder..."

He gazed at her for several seconds. Then finally, as if he understood at last, he nodded his head. "I'm sorry, Mom." He put his arms around her, buried his face against her chest and held on to her as she held on to him.

"I'm sorry, too, Christopher."

Several times during the long night, Maggie wished that she hadn't decided to wait until morning to leave. However, by the time she'd finished packing, it had been late, Christopher had fallen asleep, and she'd been too physically and emotionally drained to face even a relatively short drive in the middle of the night.

She wasn't feeling much better when her alarm woke her at six-thirty. She couldn't remember when she'd finally fallen asleep. She only knew that she wasn't ready to get up. And she would never be ready to go. Yet she had no choice, and the sooner they were on their way to San Antonio, the better.

She dressed quickly, then woke Christopher and packed the last of their things while he pulled on a pair of shorts and a T-shirt. Leaving him to disconnect his computer and pack it in a cardboard box, she picked up a couple of suitcases and carried them down the stairs as quickly and quietly as possible, barely glancing at the closed door to the third floor. Apparently they were still sleeping, which was just as well.

She set the bags on the side porch, shushing Bonnie and Clyde when they yapped at her, then walked around to the garage to retrieve her car. By the time she returned with it, Christopher had the computer box and other suitcase on the porch. As she opened the trunk he walked through the door, carrying her overnight bag and purse.

"We can take Clyde with us, can't we?" Christopher asked.

He set the bag and purse on the steps and sat down, welcoming the puppies onto his lap.

"Of course. He's your dog." Maggie loaded the suitcases into the trunk and closed it. "Why don't you sit in the back with him, and I'll put your computer on the front seat?"

"Okay," he agreed.

Maggie wanted to grab him and hug him. He was trying so hard not to let his unhappiness show. "Well, that's everything," she said instead, as she tossed the overnight bag and her purse beside the computer. "Guess we'd better—"

"Maggie . . . *Maggie!*"

The side door flew open and Elizabeth, still dressed in her nightgown, stepped onto the porch. Anger and hurt shadowed her dark eyes as she glared at Maggie and Christopher.

"What are you doing? Where are you going?" she cried.

"Your dad said we had to leave." Christopher stood up and faced her, holding Clyde in his arms.

"Oh, no, he wouldn't. He...wouldn't." She brushed past Christopher and hurled herself into Maggie's arms. "Maggie, don't go. Please, *please* don't go."

"I..." Maggie hesitated, mentally cursing Mac for not speaking to his daughter, for not telling her about his decision. "Elizabeth, honey, we have to leave. The summer's over. And...and I have to...to get ready for school."

"Say goodbye, Elizabeth."

At the sound of his voice Maggie raised her head. He was standing on the porch, wearing nothing but a pair of jeans, his hair hanging in his face, his eyes bleak and weary. The girl turned in her arms and faced him.

"Daddy, please..." she begged, her young voice ringing high and wild in the early morning stillness.

"We'll see you again," Maggie murmured. "We can write, and if you want, you can come and spend next summer with—"

"*Daddy!*"

"Just...say...goodbye," he ordered, grinding out the words as he averted his eyes from the scene before him.

Maggie felt the girl tremble in her arms and feared she might say something or do something she'd regret for the rest of her life. Bending quickly, she turned Elizabeth around to face her, cupped her chin in her hand and forced her to meet her gaze.

"Goodbye, Lizzie Beth. I'll miss you. And I'll think about you every day." Blinking back the tears in her eyes, she leaned forward and kissed her on the cheek.

"I'll miss you, too, Maggie," Elizabeth murmured, wrapping her arms around her neck and holding on tight for just a moment. "I love you."

"I love you, too." Maggie closed her eyes and hugged the girl, then released her and stood up. "Come on, Christopher. Get in the car." She opened the door for him as Elizabeth moved away from her.

"Bye, Elizabeth. Take care of Bonnie."

"I will. And you take care of Clyde."

They gazed at each other for several seconds, then Elizabeth climbed the porch steps, picked up her puppy, brushed by her father and walked into the house. Holding Clyde in his arms, Christopher slid into the car and pulled the door closed, leaving the two adults alone.

She ought to just go, Maggie thought. He wasn't even looking at her. But she had something to say to him, and she intended to say it, face to face, eye to eye. She moved away from the car, stopping at the foot of the porch steps as he finally met her gaze.

"Maggie—"

"Don't *Maggie* me," she warned, her voice low as she stared at him. "Just shut up and listen. Jo died because she had a very deadly form of cancer, not because you were preoccupied with the ranch. I caught pneumonia because I stood around in a cold, wet nightgown, playing Lady Bountiful after the fire, instead of taking a hot shower and changing into something dry right away. *Not* because you were *preoccupied* with the ranch. "You're not to blame for what happened to Jo or to me.

"The only thing we know for certain, as long as we're alive, is that we're going to die. And everyone we love is going to die someday, too. But life wouldn't be worth living if we didn't risk loving because we're so afraid of losing.''

She hesitated for a moment, waiting for him to say something, *anything*, but he turned his head away without speaking. "Fine, have it your way, then," she muttered, spinning on her heel. In less than a minute, she was in the driver's seat, turning the key in the ignition. And then, without a backward glance, she pressed down on the accelerator, sending dust and gravel flying as she guided the car down the drive.

"Maggie! Maggie, wait . . ." he called, running down the steps and onto the drive as he realized, finally and completely, exactly what he was losing. But it was too late, much too late. If she saw him or heard him, she didn't stop. And after all he'd said and done, he really couldn't blame her at all.

Chapter Thirteen

"What a way to spend a Friday night," Maggie muttered, the Saltillo tile floor cool against her bare feet as she wandered from one room of her house to another, hands tucked in the pockets of her long pale blue terry-cloth robe.

For the first time in the three weeks since she'd left the ranch she was alone, and feeling very, very lonely. Her warm, cozy house had never felt quite so big or so empty and her single, independent life-style had never seemed quite so unappealing. Of course, there was no rule that said she had to stay home, alone, while her son spent the night at a friend's house. But if she couldn't be with Mac, she didn't want to be with anyone.

"And I'm not exactly alone," she murmured, sitting down on the living-room sofa next to Clyde. "I've got you to keep me company, even if you're not supposed to be up here," she chided as she allowed him to crawl into her lap.

Welcoming his cuddly warmth, she smoothed a hand over his head and scratched his ears, smiling at his sigh of contentment. He had adjusted to life in a suburban neighborhood quite easily. Christopher, too, had made the transition successfully, rejoining his small circle of special friends and falling into the back-to-school routine without any obvious problems. He mentioned the ranch less and less frequently, obviously accepting what couldn't be and moving on in a way Maggie had to admire.

If only she could do the same. Unfortunately it was almost impossible. No matter how hard she tried, she couldn't put thoughts of Mac and Elizabeth out of her mind. They stole up on her at odd moments during the day and interfered with her ability to sleep at night. Maybe she could have stopped him from selling the ranch if she hadn't let him drive her away. Perhaps if she had fought for what she wanted with a little more determination, she would have been able to convince him as well.

Maybe she could have convinced him that they belonged together on the Whispering Wind. But then, she would have spent the rest of her life wondering if she'd backed him into a corner, if she'd coerced him into making a commitment he didn't really want to make. He needed *someone* to help him run the ranch, but that someone didn't have to be her. Forcing him to think of her as part of a package deal would have been wrong, and she would have regretted it in the end.

And where was it written that they had to be on the ranch to be together? If he cared for her as much as she cared for him, if he really wanted her and needed her, they could be together in Dallas or San Antonio or anywhere else, in the whole, wide world. If he loved her...

A big *if,* one she was finding more and more difficult to contemplate. Because *if* he loved her, surely he would have contacted her by now. Three weeks, three long weeks without a telephone call or a letter had been almost more than she could bear.

Which of the job offers had he taken? Were he and Elizabeth staying with Jo's parents until he found a suitable house of his own? Had Dale Sherman begun to tear down the house and the barn yet? She wasn't sure she wanted to know. Just thinking about it added to the aching emptiness she felt each time she considered the possibility that she'd never see Mac and his daughter again.

She had promised Elizabeth she'd keep in touch, and she had Jo's parents' Dallas address. But she had forced herself to wait. The move would be hard enough on the girl. Better to let her memories of their summer fade a bit. Mac might be trying hard to forget the ranch and everything, as well as *everybody* connected with his last summer there, so he could get on with his new life. If so, he probably wanted Elizabeth to do the same, and he wouldn't thank her for interfering. In fact, there were probably a lot of things about her for which Mackenzie Harrow was anything but thank—

With a sudden growl of warning, Clyde jumped off her lap and raced across the living room. As he reached the foyer, he skidded to a halt and began to bark. When Maggie joined him, he snuffled at the door and whined, his tail wagging, then scampered over to her and sat down, his head cocked to one side. A moment later, the doorbell rang, and he scampered back to the door, scratching at the wood with one paw and whining again.

Obviously it was someone the animal knew, but who could it be? Maybe a stranger who'd befriended the pup, with just such a late-night prowl in mind. Not taking any chances, Maggie stood on the balls of her feet and peered out the peephole. A moment later, she rocked back on her heels, one hand pressed to her chest, her eyes closed.

"Mac..." she whispered, almost afraid to say his name aloud. She risked another look out of the peephole. He was standing on her front porch facing the door, hands shoved into the side pockets of his jeans, his head tipped down. It was impossible to read his expression in the pale glow of the porch light, but Maggie didn't care. All that mattered was that he was there. "Mac," she said his name again, her voice stronger as she unlocked the door and swung it open.

"Hi." His voice was low and rough as he raised his head, his pale eyes full of uncertainty. Then he ducked his head again as Clyde jumped up against his legs to greet him.

"Clyde, no," Maggie admonished, grabbing the dog's collar and pulling him down. *"No."* She shook her finger at him and frowned as he freed himself and leaped at Mac again. "I'm sorry—"

"It's okay—"

As Mac bent to scratch the dog's ears and Maggie reached for his collar again, his head bumped against hers.

"Sorry."

They said the word in unison, stepping apart as if they'd been burned.

"I'll put him in the backyard." Maggie moved away from the door, her fingers looped in Clyde's collar. "I'll be right back."

She dragged the reluctant puppy down the hallway and through the kitchen as Mac stepped into the foyer and closed the door. He was still standing there when she returned a few moments later, turning his Stetson around and around in his hands.

"You should have gone in the living—"

She stopped short as he met her gaze. In the brighter light of the foyer, she could see the shadows under his eyes, the day's growth of beard darkening his face. For the first time she realized he was wearing ranch clothes, faded jeans, a plaid shirt, scuffed boots.

"Oh, Mac, what's wrong?" She closed the distance separating them and placed a hand on his arm. "Is it Elizabeth? Has she been hurt?"

"Elizabeth is fine. She wanted to come with me, but I convinced her to stay at the ranch with Juan and Rosa." He lowered his eyes for one long moment, then met her gaze once again.

"She's at the ranch?" Maggie stared at him, trying to understand what he was saying. "You didn't sell the Whispering Wind?"

"Elizabeth never would have forgiven me if I had. And I never would have forgiven myself," he admitted. "I finally realized that neither one of us would be happy anywhere else, and we deserve to be happy."

"You will be," Maggie said, moving her hand from his arm and taking a step back. And I'll be happy for you, she thought, forcing herself to smile as she took another step back. I *am* happy for you. "But you didn't have to drive to San Antonio to tell me," she added, trying to keep her voice light and teasing. "You could have called—"

"I have something else to say to you. Something I want to say face-to-face." He moved toward her, not allowing her to put any distance between them, and threaded his fingers through her hair.

"I acted like a damned fool three weeks ago. And I'm sorry, Maggie. Sorry I said what I did to you, sorry that I chased you away when all I really wanted was to ask you to stay. But I was afraid. And I'm still afraid of...of losing you. Because I love you." He paused for a moment, rubbing his thumb along her cheek, his eyes searching hers. "And we'll only be truly happy on the Whispering Wind. *I'll* only be truly happy, if you're there with me. A few weeks ago you said you felt as if the ranch *was* your home. I hope you haven't changed your mind. Because I want you there with me, now and always, as my wife and my partner. You don't have to give up your job or your house. And you don't have to decide—"

"Mac," she cut in, reaching up to cover his lips with her fingertips. "Will you just hush a minute?"

When he nodded, she moved her hand, cupping his whisker-rough cheek in her palm for a moment. "I think you're going to have to shave," she said, a soft smile lifting the corners of her mouth. Then she turned and started down the hallway.

"Maggie, what the hell—"

"On second thought, what's a little whisker burn when two people love each other as much as—"

He caught her arm, stopping her just inside her bedroom doorway. "What about..." He let his words trail away as he tipped his head toward Christopher's room.

"He's spending the night at a friend's house." She took his hat from his hands and tossed it on the rocking chair in the corner. Then she began to unbutton his shirt. "I hope you plan to do the same."

"Spend the night with a *friend?*" He caught her hands in his and held them still, his eyes probing hers. "I'd rather spend it with the woman I love, with my future wife, with you, Miz Maggie Connor."

"Sounds good to me, Mr. Harrow. As long as I don't have to promise to obey," she teased.

"I'll settle for love and honor, as long as it's for the rest of our lives." He bent his head and kissed her, his mouth gentle yet possessive as his hands fumbled with the belt on her robe. "I love you, Maggie."

"And I love you...."

"I wish I could have taken you on a real honeymoon," Mac murmured, as he slipped his arm around his wife's shoulders.

They stood together on the side porch of the ranch house, enjoying the last rays of October sunshine as they watched her parents, Jo's parents and their children drive away in Avery Chase's Cadillac. The wedding had been just the way they'd wanted it, small and personal, with only a few close friends and relatives present. Then Maggie's parents had hosted a luncheon at the Wagon Wheel following the ceremony at the church.

Now her parents were on their way back to Houston, taking Jo's parents and the two children with them, and leaving Mac and Maggie to enjoy the long weekend alone. Mac had wanted to take Maggie somewhere special, but she had insisted on staying at the ranch rather than wasting any of their precious time together traveling. Monday was a school holiday, giving them an extra day before Maggie had to go back to work. She had put her house up for sale but she had kept her teaching job, determined to fulfill her contract with the school district despite the long commute. She would find a job closer to home next year.

"Maybe we can go somewhere another time," Maggie suggested, wrapping her arms around her husband's waist and nuzzling against his chest.

"When?"

"Mmm, I don't know."

He wanted to give her so much. It was still hard to believe that all she really wanted was to be with him on the Whispering Wind. And she wanted another child, his child, their child, to bond them together in a very special way.

"Maybe after the baby?" He turned her toward the door and guided her inside, his hand moving down her back, toying with the tiny pearl buttons that fastened her cream silk dress.

"What baby?" she teased, her voice low, as she kicked off one high-heeled cream satin pump and then the other. "Do you know something I don't?" As Mac released the last of the buttons, the dress fell down around her ankles. She stepped out of it and turned to face him, wearing nothing but a lacy bra, matching panties, a garter belt and sheer silk stockings.

"I know that I love you, Mrs. Harrow. And I can't wait to see my child growing inside you," he said, his voice suddenly softly and oddly tentative as he scooped her into his arms and carried her up the stairs. "As long as you're sure..."

"I've never been more sure of anything in my life," she whispered, wrapping her arms around his neck and reaching up to kiss his cheek. "As long as *you're* sure you're going to change diapers and warm bottles at three in the morning. You *did* say we were partners, didn't you?"

"Oh, yes, ma'am," he agreed, grinning like the wolf who'd been waiting in the woods, as he dumped her in the middle of his bed. He stripped off his dark gray morning coat and tossed it onto the floor. "We're partners all right." His fancy shirt, his elegant tie and his tailored pants landed in a heap atop the coat. "Partners for life," he growled, stretching out beside her and pulling her into his arms.

"And you're not going to get bossy and start telling me what to do, right?" She trailed tiny kisses along his jaw, then nibbled at his ear as he fiddled with her garters.

"Yeah, right. Except sometimes, like now," he muttered. "Get those damn things undone, Maggie. They're driving me crazy." He slipped his hands under the narrow lacy ribbons, his palms rough and warm against her skin.

"Mmm, good," she murmured, rubbing one silky leg against his bare thigh. "That was the idea...."

*   *   *   *   *

Silhouette Special Edition

Ahoy, Readers!

Debbie Macomber is back at the helm with

NAVY BRAT

Navy brat Erin McNamara planned to pass adulthood joyfully embracing the landlubber's life—even if it meant steering clear of Lt. Commander Brandon Davis, the navy man who set her heart racing at twenty knots per minute! But Brandon was equally determined not to give up his *seafaring* ways. And although the outlook was stormy, he simply had to navigate irrepressible Erin into becoming his navy bride!

This April, drop anchor with NAVY BRAT (Special Edition #662), Debbie Macomber's follow-up to NAVY WIFE (Special Edition #494) and NAVY BLUES (Special Edition #518)—and set your sights on future navy stories—only in *Silhouette Special Edition!*

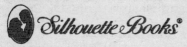

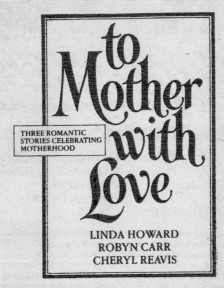
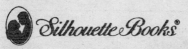